M[illegible]
To my favor[illegible]
Hope you enjoy it!
All the best
[illegible] Hunter

Runaway Girl

a novel by

LEO HUNTER

Pittsburgh, PA

ISBN 1-56315-275-4

Paperback Fiction

First Printing — 2002
Library of Congress #2001098571

Request for information should be addressed to:

SterlingHouse Publisher, Inc.
7436 Washington Avenue
Suite 200
Pittsburgh, PA 15218
www.sterlinghousepublisher.com

Book Designer: Beth Buckholtz
Cover Design: Jeffrey S. Butler — SterlingHouse Publisher, Inc.

Printed in the United States of America

Chapter 1

October 1999

Jesse Waller, a good-looking high school football star, was at the checkout counter of the local Kroger supermarket. For the third time in as many minutes, the cashier asked him if he would like to meet her for a cup of coffee when she got off work. She was slim, redheaded, and too attractive to ignore, but she was so much older than he was, practically an older lady pushing thirty, at least in his nineteen-year-old mind. She could almost be his mother. He thought of his own mother who had died two years before. He looked at her wedding ring and ignored the moves of the sexy "older" woman. She paused and smiled at him, running her tongue provocatively over her full lips before handing him his change.

"Come on, lady," Jesse said impatiently, looking around to see if anyone else was near them. "I have to get this stuff home to my dad." He held his hand out, wiggling his fingers for his change.

She cradled his hand in hers and slowly counted out the change, pressing each bill and coin into his palm. Her eyes were searching his for some encouragement. An irritated sigh escaped his lips, but he let her play her game. The change counted, she continued to hold his hand hostage.

"So, how 'bout it, cowboy?" she asked. "Just a cup of coffee. It'll be fun."

"No. I gotta go," he said and tried to pull his hand free. She tightened her grip and locked eyes with him.

"I get off at nine o'clock," she added. "Be here for me. You won't regret it. That's a promise!"

"Aw, lady," he said. "Give it a rest, will you? I told you — I gotta go," he said, wrenching his hand from the woman's grip. He stuffed the money in his pocket and snatched up the small plastic bag of groceries. He knew she was an easy chance to score, but that's not the way he wanted to make his first time with a woman. In his haste to leave, he collided with a shopping cart pushed by Connie Mathers, a rather plain lady who looked to be in her early forties. The noise ricocheted off the white walls of the market and attracted the attention of everyone in the adjacent aisles.

"Oh, gosh, I'm really sorry," Jesse offered, totally embarrassed. He could feel the flush on his face as he tried to find the right words to say. He glanced at the cashier and saw she was giggling at him, which only made things worse. As he was apologizing, Connie's seventeen-year-old daughter, Karyn, scoped out the young man's good looks and polite manner as he spoke to her mother. Karyn was immediately attracted to him and found herself uncharacteristically shy. She tried to avoid eye contact with him, but failed. Jesse noticed Karyn, but he was too embarrassed to say anything. He felt like a dork.

"That's all right," Connie replied. "No harm done." She eyed the young man. He was nearly as tall as her husband, Drake, and just as handsome. He had a certain confidence about him as he stood before Connie. Karyn also gave him a careful once-over, noticing the firmness of his body along with his even features.

"I guess I need to watch where I'm going," he said to Connie after taking a quick glance at Karyn. "It's a good thing I don't drive like I walk," he added.

Connie laughed and smiled at him, then pushed her cart toward the exit. Karyn walked silently beside her mother, glancing back at the embarrassed Jesse. Jesse's eyes followed Karyn for several seconds. He tried not to stare, but Karyn, at five-feet six-inches with shoulder-length blonde hair, was so exquisitely pretty he couldn't take his eyes off her.

Jesse left the store several paces behind Connie and Karyn. He knew who Karyn was from school. While Jesse was a senior, and Karyn only a junior, it was hard to miss someone like Karyn as she strolled down the halls wildly chattering with her girl friends. She was also one of the contestants for Homecoming Queen. In fact, although he'd never actually met her, he had voted for her that very morning, just because she was so pretty.

Jesse had caught Karyn's eye in school, too, but this was the closest she had ever been to him because they had shared no classes. Jesse wasn't like most of the other jocks. He played football well enough to be the star of the team and there was even talk that he might get All State this year, but he didn't flaunt his status with others. In fact, he was rather shy and quiet. She had also heard that Jesse had spent the last year in jail. She knew he was a year older than most of the other seniors, so she believed the rumors. Karyn wondered if he was as dumb as the other jocks she had dated.

There was a home football game at the high school on Friday. As usual, Jesse had played very well, receiving a couple of touchdown passes followed by a spectacular sixty-yard race to the goal for a third touchdown in the first half of the game. The fans had gone wild. Then, on the next play, he was taken down with a hard hit to his left elbow. For the rest of the game he was on the bench, nursing a sore arm. Karyn sat in the fifth row of the stands and desperately wanted Jesse to notice her in front of all her friends so she cajoled the team water boy to get Jesse's attention. The seventeen-year-old water boy was so infatuated with Karyn that he raced over to Jesse, slapped him on the shoulder, and motioned up to Karyn.

Jesse turned to see Karyn wave and smile at him from the stands. He stared as she mouthed the words, "Meet me after the game." He hesitated, but Karyn was so persistent and he finally nodded. The coach yelled at Jesse to pay attention to the game and leave the dollies for later. After the game, the icing of his sore elbow took so long that when he finally left the locker room, she was gone. He was more disappointed than he wanted to be.

The next Monday, Jesse was at his locker when he saw the slim, leggy Karyn go by, wearing rather tight designer jeans and a matching blouse, chatting noisily with several of her friends. He thought about stopping her and asking her for a date, but that's not the sort of thing a shy guy did in front of a bunch of girls. He was watching her when she glanced over and their eyes momentarily met. Karyn noticed a subtle reaction in him and winked. Jesse desperately wanted to meet her alone, but how? Everyone knew her father was Drake Mathers, Vice President of Cox Chemical Corporation, a Fortune 500 company. Karyn's family was rich by almost anybody's standards, and she seemed so far beyond his reach. Jesse stood by his locker and thought about how vastly different their backgrounds were.

That evening, Jesse was at the kitchen table trying to do his homework but thinking more about Karyn Mathers than the homework. The kitchen door slammed behind him as his father came in. As usual, he had been drinking heavily.

"Whaz' fer dinner, Sport?" Willie Bob slurred as he weaved his way into the kitchen.

"Uh, nothing," Jesse replied. "I ate already. I can fix you a BLT sandwich," he said, not looking up from his books. Willie eyed his son, poring over his homework at the kitchen table.

"Aw, thass okay," Willie replied. "I kin git somethin' m'self." Willie kept an eye on Jesse as he went to the refrigerator. He didn't mind fixing himself a sandwich. In fact, Willie and Jesse often traded off making meals in the evening.

Jesse lived with his father, Willie Bob Waller, in the poorest section of town. Willie Bob was straight out of the hills of West "by God" Virginia and still retained most of his Appalachian ways. Their home was seedy at best, with several trashed cars parked around the yard. Jesse never had anyone come to his house because he was ashamed of it. His father didn't ever come to any of Jesse's football games, which suited Jesse just fine. He didn't want his father at the football games because he never knew if he'd show up sober or dead drunk.

"Whatcha workin' on?" Willie asked while he spread some peanut butter on a slice of bread.

"Econ," Jesse replied. "Economics." Willie Bob's brow knit.

"Jess, you're nineteen years old, now. You oughta have a job," Willie said with a bite of sticky peanut butter sandwich in his mouth.

"Aw, Dad, don't start up with me," Jesse replied, still not looking up from his books.

"Now, all I'm sayin' is —"

"Dad!" Jesse interrupted. "I know what you're saying. You're saying I'm not a man unless I have a job."

"Well, ain't that true?" Willie shot back. "A man's worth is in how hard he works!"

"Yeah, and how much he can drink, and how well he can fight!" Jesse countered. "I know your philosophy of life, Dad."

"Well, it got me where *I am*," Willie Bob retorted.

"Yeah, and just where are you?" Jesse said, trying to restrain the resentment mounting inside him. Every time they had this discussion, it was the same. His dad would tell him he should get a job, and that a man's work was what made him a man. Then Jesse would tell his dad that he did want a job, but not one in a foundry or a mine. It wasn't that Jesse felt such work was beneath him; he simply wasn't interested in that kind of work. He wanted to do something more with his life.

"I done all right fer m'self," Willie said indignantly. "Why, when me an' your mom came to Michigan —"

"I know, Dad," Jesse interrupted again. "You didn't have a 'pot to piss in,' as you always put it, 'nor a window to throw it out of'."

"Well, we didn't, but we made a damn good life here. Better'n we'd had if'n we stayed in West Virginia!"

"I don't doubt that, Dad, and I think you *have* done well for yourself, but I want to do well for myself, too."

"You kin have ever'thing we got — jus' take that job at the foundry, dammit!" As soon as Willie began cussing, Jesse knew the discussion had ended and the argument had begun. It would only go downhill from there.

"I don't want a job in a foundry! I want to go to college!"

"Why? So's you kin play football all the time? You'd be better off at home learnin' t' fight and take care o' yourself."

"Dad, let's not argue about this," Jesse said, trying vainly to avoid the coming confrontation, but it was too late. Willie Bob rounded the corner of the kitchen counter, slamming his plate with the half-eaten sandwich onto the counter.

"Lookit," Willie growled. "You ain't a man 'til you kin make your own way, and make the way fer your kin. *You* ain't a man! *You* ain't even got a job — not a real one, leastways!"

Jesse stood to meet his father face to face. He knew what was coming. It was always the same. Two or three times each week, Willie would come home drunk and they would have the same argument. Then Willie would try to slap some sense into him.

"I have a job," Jesse said, ready to block the blow that was sure to come. "You know I work weekends at the auto shop." Jesse had been working part time at a local auto repair facility for the last two years and he'd become a fairly good mechanic. It didn't pay much; just enough for him to refurbish a 1994 Camaro and keep gas in the tank, but he did learn one helluva lot about cars.

"That ain't a real job 'cause you cain't keep yourself. You cain't live on your own!" Willie was only three feet from Jesse.

"Dad, let's not argue," Jesse said.

"Who's arguin'?" Willie shouted. Jesse could smell the familiar odor of alcohol on his breath.

"It's *you* that's always arguin'!" Willie continued. "It's *you* that don't wanta git a job an' be a man!"

"Dad, I don't want to live like this," Jesse replied, trying to let his father know that he wanted a better life for himself and whatever family he may have in the future.

"How do you know what you want?" Willie bellowed. "You're just a kid! Nineteen years old! You're still wet behind the ears! You don't know *nothin'!*"

"I know what I *don't* want, and I don't want to live like *this!*" Jesse's muscles were tightening.

Willie Bob glared at Jesse. He was still chewing the last bite of his sandwich, but very slowly. Jesse had learned over the years which signs to watch for. When Willie stopped chewing, Jesse had to block the blow that would immediately follow. He watched as Willie Bob chewed slower and slower.

Willie's eyes narrowed and he stopped chewing. Jesse's hand shot up just in time to block the roundhouse swing his father made. Jesse's other hand rose instinctively to block the follow-up blow from Willie's other hand. Willie Bob made two more attempts to slap some sense into his son, but without connecting. Jesse had developed the reflexes of a professional boxer over the years with his father. For a drunken Willie to hit Jesse would take a small miracle. Willie glared at his son, breathing hard, drowning Jesse in whiskey fumes.

"I jus' cain't seem to make you understand," he growled. "I jus' cain't seem t' make ya see that they's lotsa good jobs out there, jus' waitin' fer you to go an' git 'em!" Willie had expended some of his pent-up wrath by now and turned away from Jesse. The fight didn't last very long this time.

"I know you want the best thing for me, Dad," Jesse said. "But I know what I want, too."

"I jus' want you to be a man, is all," Willie replied. He looked at Jesse. In Jesse's face he could see some of his late wife's features. He missed Rachel terribly. There wasn't a day gone by that he didn't think about her. "I need another drink," Willie said suddenly, heading toward the cabinet over the chipped white enamel double sink.

Jesse wished his father didn't drink so much. Willie had always been a drinker, but it hadn't been this bad until after Rachel died. He watched his father carry the bourbon bottle toward his bedroom. After the door slammed, Jesse returned to his homework. Homework always got his mind off things and gave him some relief.

Chapter 2

The next day in school, Jesse sat in the lunchroom, looking over his Econ notes before his test the following hour. As he often did, he sat alone. Even though he was a varsity football player, he didn't hang out with the other jocks. In fact, Jesse was what most people would call a loner. Although he was friendly with everybody, he had no close friends in school. Karyn watched him from several tables away. Her friends were talking around her, but she wasn't listening to them. She was studying Jesse's face, his hands, and his movements. She noticed the Ace bandage wrapped around his elbow from the injury last Friday. She had never seen any of the jocks crack a book, let alone pore over one like Jesse was doing. She wondered if he had to put in extra time just to keep his grade point high enough to continue playing football. While Jesse sat there, Mrs. Teal, the English Lit teacher came to Jesse's side.

"Jesse?" she said over the din of lunchroom chatter.

"Oh, Mrs. Teal," he said, rising to greet her.

"Jesse, I have some good news for you," she said. He immediately hoped it was something about the scholarships.

"Yes, Ma'am?"

"You've been chosen to be on the Homecoming Court," she said with a wide smile. "Congratulations!" She held out her hand. He took it without much enthusiasm.

"Homecoming Court?" he asked hesitantly.

"Yes. You were chosen because of your combined scholastic standing and your athletic abilities."

"I thought the Court was all chosen weeks ago," he said.

"One of the boys ran into a bit of trouble and has been disqualified," she explained. "There isn't time to do another student vote, so the teachers did their own little vote and you won hands down. You'll be on the Court. Who knows? You might even get elected King!" Mrs. Teal was excited for Jesse. Jesse was a year older than most of the students, and that year gave him an edge in maturity. He had little interest in being on the Homecoming Court, or even in going to the Homecoming festivities. He had never attended a Homecoming dance in his four years of high school. All he wanted to do was play in the Friday night football game and then go home so he could rest before going to work on Saturday. Work was important because he needed the money to buy a new set of tires for his Camaro. If he had to do this Homecoming thing, he was afraid he wouldn't be able to afford the new tires.

"Does this mean I have to find a date?" he asked.

"Not necessarily," Mrs. Teal smiled. "You will be matched up with one of the girls on the Court. They're all very pretty. After the parade and ceremony, you can meet with your date if you have one, or even go home if you wish, but you'll miss a lot of fun." She knew Jesse paid little attention to girls. In fact, he hadn't dated since he was a sophomore, almost three years ago. During his sophomore year, his mother became very sick, and the house was never neat enough for him to feel comfortable to invite anyone over. However, Mom had always pushed Jesse to do well in school so he would be the first in their family to get a college education. He was trying hard to make her dream come true.

Jesse studied Mrs. Teal's eyes for a moment and said, "Okay. What do I need to do? I've never done this before."

* * * *

"Karyn!" one of her friends insisted. "Karyn, I've been talking to you," Amanda Jennings said as she tugged on Karyn's arm to get her attention.

"Oh, what?" Karyn replied, coming out of her reverie.

"What is wrong with you, girl?" another said. "You are, like, so *gone*! You're in another world!"

"No, I'm here, I was just thinking." Karyn replied.

"So what's to think about?" the girl asked. "It's a fact that you'll be the Homecoming Queen, for sure!" Of the six girls at the table, three were in the running for Homecoming Queen, although everyone knew that with Karyn's wholesome beauty and popularity, the only real contest was for who came in as the second Princess. It was a matter of fact and they all accepted it. They wanted to be seen with Karyn because she was so *in*. She was *the* person to be seen with. If Karyn liked you, you were definitely part of the inner circle. Karyn set the standard for popularity throughout the school. Although she was a junior, she was the school's *de facto* trendsetter. She had dated more popular boys than anyone else, been more places and had more money to spend than the rest of them. Karyn used boys only for what she could get out of them, like having a date for going to concerts or movies, then dumping them. Karyn was a tease and she enjoyed it.

"So who are you going to Homecoming with?" someone asked. "Have you decided yet?"

Karyn had received seven invitations to the Homecoming dance, but hadn't chosen her date yet. No one really turned her on. Boys were just a game to her, and after leading them on, she never even allowed most of them to kiss her. She glanced back at Jesse again as he looked over his Econ notes. There was something about him that appealed to her. Perhaps it was his attitude, his confidence. She wasn't sure.

That evening, Jesse called his best friend and stepbrother, Mike.

"Mike, I've been tagged to be on the Homecoming Court," Jesse said.

"Hey, that's great," Mike replied. "That's quite an honor."

"I don't know what to do," Jesse said. "They said I didn't have to have a date, but what do I wear? Should I wear a tuxedo? How much does it cost? What's the deal?"

"When I went to that school, if you were on the court, it didn't cost anything," Mike told him. "And you don't really have to wear a tux if you don't want to, but you probably should. But I get the feeling it's not the cost you're really worried about." Mike could read Jesse like an open book.

"Yeah, you're right," Jesse replied. "Mike, I don't know anybody — any girls, anyway. I should have a date, but I don't know any girls I'd want to go with. Besides, I don't have a tuxedo."

"Jesse, you don't know any girls, period," Mike corrected.

"Yeah, well, you know what I mean."

"Jesse, if you want a date, all you have to do is go up and ask someone. The worst they can do is say 'no'. And as for the tux, you can rent one for about ninety bucks."

"Mike, it's not that." Jesse went on.

"I know what it is," Mike replied. "My guess is that you're not sure you even want to do this. I'd guess you're pretty uncomfortable with all the hoopla, aren'tcha?"

"I guess that's it," Jesse confessed. "I don't want to take a girl out for just one gig and then never see her again. It seems to me that I'd be using her and that's not right."

"Well, they said you didn't have to have a date," Mike offered.

"Yeah, but I'd be the only guy there without a girl."

"So who cares?" Mike said. "You can do what you want, talk to whomever you want, and then leave when you want." Jesse listened in silence. "Jesse," Mike went on, "this is an honor and you shouldn't turn it down unless it violates your personal code." Mike had been a Marine and was thinking like one. "An honor should be accepted with humility and respect."

"You're right. I guess I needed to hear that," Jesse said. "I guess I'll go. I may even find a date." Mike knew Jesse would go, but figured he wouldn't find a date.

* * * *

"Mom, do you believe in love at first sight?" Karyn asked her mother that same evening.

"Well, I don't know if it was love, but I knew I liked your father the moment I set eyes on him," Connie said. She studied her daughter. "Is there something more I should know?"

"Well, no," Karyn replied. "I was just wondering." Karyn had been thinking about Jesse off and on all day. She couldn't get the image of him sitting alone in the lunchroom out of her mind. She didn't know what love was, but she knew there was a special feeling when she thought of him.

"Have you decided which young man you're going to Homecoming with?" Connie asked.

"No. Another guy asked me today. That makes eight." Karyn was dawdling with the straw in a can of Pepsi. Connie was proud that her daughter was so popular, because in high school and college, even though she was moderately attractive, she wasn't like her daughter. Karyn had received the best genes from both of her parents.

"Why haven't you decided?" Connie asked. "It takes time to prepare for such a big dance. You should give the young man more time to get everything together." Karyn was still playing with the straw. She couldn't care less about making anything easier for someone else.

"I'm thinking of going with Jason. You know, the guy from Daddy's Detroit Athletic Club." She looked up to her mother to see the reaction. Jason was a large, ungainly lad, not known for intellect or social skills, but he came from one of the best families in town.

"Well, if that's the one you want to go with, you'd best let him know soon." Connie couldn't imagine her daughter going with Jason. They were a total mismatch.

"No, I'm just teasing," Karyn said with a smile. "But I don't know who to go with."

"Whom," her mother corrected. "Pick someone. It's only a dance, not a marriage. Pick someone you like to be with and who knows how to have a good time. The idea is to have fun." She looked at her daughter, sitting curled up in a chair in front of her and knew something was going on inside that head of hers, but wasn't sure what it was.

* * * *

The next day in school it was announced that Jesse would be the replacement for Dave Lewis, the senior disqualified for the Homecoming Court because of poor grades. A few of the students had questioned it, but for the most part, everyone knew Jesse and approved the choice.

During class change before the last period of the day, Harold Peoples, an overweight bespectacled boy, caught up to Karyn and her friends.

"Karyn?" he called, out of breath from his effort to catch up to the girls. They turned to see Harold lumbering up to them like a small hippo.

"Karyn?" he repeated, "Uh, I gotta ask you something." He looked between Karyn and the four other girls with her.

"Yeah," Karyn replied. "What is it?" Her tone was sharp. She had known Harold since second grade. Like Karyn, he was also a junior, and his father worked for her father in the same office at Cox Chemical.

"Uh, Karyn — will you go to Homecoming with me?" he blurted. Karyn's eyes went wide with amazement as her friends began to giggle. Harold's face went red as he wondered if he had said something wrong. Karyn glanced at her friends with a wry smile.

"Why, yes, Harold," she replied. "I'd *love* to go to Homecoming with you!" Her friends shrieked with laughter.

"Thank you, Karyn," Harold replied, a little smile curling at the corners of his mouth.

"You don't think she's serious, do you?" Amanda Jennings asked Harold, wide-eyed. Harold's face fell as he looked first at Amanda and then Karyn, waiting for an answer.

"Of course I'm serious," Karyn replied with a half grin. "I'm going to Homecoming with Harold," she said emphatically.

"You're *not* going to Homecoming with this nerd!" Jessica Blake retorted. "Not with *him!* He has a face like a *pizza!* " she groaned, totally disregarding Harold and his feelings.

"I'm going with Harold. He's an old friend and we've gone to school together for years. His dad and mine are good friends." Karyn was miffed with Jessica for publicly challenging her decision. Harold waddled away, so pleased with himself that he forgot to make any arrangements for the evening. The girls watched him go, then stared at Karyn in total disbelief.

"Why are you going with *him?*" Jessica moaned. "Justin Nevers asked you and he's a *hunk!*"

"Look," Karyn said. "Every guy in school wants to go with me, and I don't know who I want to go with. I don't want to piss off Justin by going with Jason, or Chad, or any of the cool guys. This way I get to go, I'll hang out with everyone, and I won't hurt anybody's feelings." It didn't matter to Karyn that the only feelings she would hurt would be Harold's by using him so she could be a social butterfly at the Homecoming. Her friends, then understanding her motives, applauded her decision.

* * * *

It was the week before the Homecoming game. Karyn sat in the stands, huddled with her friends and a large cup of hot chocolate. As she watched Jesse play, she couldn't help but notice his butt in those tight football pants and felt that slow yearning return. Starting to feel dreamy, she leaned over to Jessica and talked to her just loud enough to be heard over the din in the stands.

"What do you know about Jesse Waller?" she asked.

"He's a hunk and he's really built," she replied. "And he never talks to girls. And he's got great buns!"

"Why doesn't he talk to girls?" Karyn asked, ignoring the rest of Jessica's remarks.

"You're really interested in him, aren't you?" she grinned.

"Should I be?" Karyn countered, a little surprised by the boldness of the question.

"Gawd! Not him!" Jessica replied, shaking her head. "He's been in *jail!*"

"Who?" Amanda interrupted suddenly, entering the conversation and temporarily forgetting about the game.

"Jesse Waller," Jessica said. "Karyn was asking about Jesse."

"Oh, him," Amanda sneered. "Good looks, great bod, but trouble in River City," she frowned. "I heard he spent a year in jail." A roar went up around them as Jesse picked a long pass out of the night sky and ran forty-one yards for a touchdown. The girls looked at the scoreboard to see Northville High now had 38 points, and Jefferson only 12. Jesse was having another great night.

"Why was he in jail?" Karyn asked.

"Don't know, but he was gone all last year," Amanda said. "Whatever it was, it was bad. Probably selling drugs or something." The band was playing

Hail to Northville like they always did when the team scored a touchdown. Karyn looked down to see Jesse flop down on the bench while the defensive team trotted onto the field.

"Besides, he's dumb as a wooden post," Amanda added. "He's always on the honor roll, but I think they just give him the grades so he can play football. He never says anything."

"That figures," Jessica agreed. "That description sure seems to fit most of the jocks *I've* ever dated!" They all laughed, but Karyn's eyes were drawn back to Jesse as he sat wrapped in a blanket on the team's bench. She knew under all that padding was a very strong, very masculine body. The strange feelings inside her grew more prominent each time she saw him.

"So, are you ready for the dance next week?" Jessica asked Karyn.

"Yeah. Harold's got someone to pick me up." Karyn didn't remove her eyes from Jesse's back as she talked. She watched his every move and once again, felt that strange giddiness.

"He's not picking you up himself?" Amanda probed.

"He doesn't know how to drive," Karyn replied.

"I *still* can't believe you're going with *Harold*," Jessica moaned.

"I can't either," Karyn admitted. "It seemed like the thing to do at the time." She knew the whole school was talking about her choice in Homecoming dates. It had been like a whirling tornado when the rumors went around. No one could believe the soon-to-be Homecoming Queen, Karyn Mathers, was actually going to the dance with the class nerd, Harold Peoples.

"It's not too late to back out," Amanda said. "Just tell him you changed your mind."

"No, I said I'd go with him and I will," Karyn said. "Harold *has* been a friend since almost kindergarten." Jessica and Amanda rolled their eyes. Amanda stuck her finger in her mouth and made retching noises. They all giggled.

Chapter 3

On Saturday of the next week, Karyn was getting dressed for the big event with her mother's help. They had shown off the contestants in a parade during the football game the night before, and the dance was that evening. The gown she wore cost nearly five hundred dollars, but it made her look like Audrey Hepburn as she glided down the staircase in *My Fair Lady*.

"You look lovely," Connie purred in a motherly way.

"You sure do," her father, Drake Mathers, added as he walked into her room.

"Dad! Get out of my room! I'm not dressed yet!" Karyn cried out, grabbing one of her many pillows in an attempt to cover herself.

"You're dressed," he countered. "There's nothing showing. Besides, I used to change your diapers," he added for good measure.

"How does she look?" Connie said to Drake, pleased with their daughter's appearance.

"She looks okay," Drake said. "But have you seen her report card?"

Karyn paled. The report cards had come out the week before, but Karyn had intercepted hers. It was always a battle with her father when the grades came out. He wanted nothing less than perfection, which translated into straight As. Karyn was intellectually capable of that, but had no interest in a four-point grade average. She was far more interested in the social activities that her high school offered.

"No. Is it time for the grade reports already?" Connie asked, turning to Karyn.

"Um, maybe," she replied, her worried eyes on her father.

"Oh, yes it is, and I got hers already. I got it last Tuesday."

"How did you get my grades?" Karyn asked, her heart pounding.

"I called the school and sent someone to pick them up," he replied, his voice barely hiding the anger. "They were very cooperative."

Karyn knew what would happen next. There would be an argument about how smart she was, what kind of grades Drake expected, how she was disappointing him by getting anything less. Connie knew it, too.

"Drake —" Connie began.

"You stay out of this," he interrupted. Connie instinctively took a step backward from Drake.

"Please, this is a special night for Karyn," Connie said. She wanted to add, "Please don't ruin it," but she knew that would only make him angrier.

"Oh, I know all about it," Drake growled. "She's going to the Homecoming with Harold Peoples, George's son. He's bragged about it all over the office!"

"Harold's a nice boy," Connie said. "We've known him for years, ever since he was little."

"Harold's a sniveling, fat wimp and I can't stand him!" Drake hissed angrily, "Just like his father! It's made me the laughing stock of the entire office!" Drake pointed a menacing finger at Karyn. "And it's all your fault!"

"Daddy," Karyn began, "I didn't mean —"

"No back talk from you!" Drake bellowed. "First you lie about your grades, then you do something like this to me! You just love to make me look bad, don't you?"

"Daddy!" Karyn pleaded, her tears filling her eyes.

"Don't!" Drake commanded. "Just don't! Haven't I done enough for you? Didn't I provide a good enough life? Wasn't your allowance big enough?" Karyn received fifty dollars per week as her allowance. She spent every penny of it on clothes, music, and social activities. Additionally, she always charged the big-ticket items to his Platinum Visa. Drake glared at her. Karyn stepped back.

"Didn't I tell you to improve those grades? A C-plus average for someone with your brains is an insult!" Drake glanced away from Karyn for an instant. "Haven't we gone through this before?" Karyn took another step backward. Drake looked at his daughter with disdain.

"Daddy —" Karyn began but was cut short by the crack of Drake's hand on her face. Karyn shrieked in pain. Connie kept to the side while tears streamed down her face.

"It's not just the grades this time," Drake said between clenched teeth. "You got what you wanted. You embarrassed me at the office. Well, you took it too far this time, young lady! You're grounded for six weeks this time! I want you in your room every night by nine so you can think about what you did to our family!"

Karyn held her hand on her red cheek while Drake stormed out of her room. Connie waited until she heard the door slam then went to Karyn and held her close.

"Mom, I didn't mean to get Daddy in trouble at the office," Karyn sobbed. "I just didn't know who to go with! Does this mean I can't go to the dance?"

"Your daddy didn't say you couldn't go, so I think it's all right," Connie said. "Let's get you dressed and ready for the dance. Harold will be so proud of you."

Karyn didn't care one whit if Harold was proud or not. She didn't care one whit about Harold in general. She had used Harold only so she wouldn't make any of the cool guys upset with her.

An hour later Karyn and her mother were talking quietly when a car pulled up in front of the Mathers' house. The redness from Drake's slap had faded almost completely away.

"I think Harold's here," Connie said as she peered out the window. "It looks like he's gone all out for you." Karyn joined her at the window. A black stretch limousine sat in front of the house. The gray-uniformed driver stood holding the door open as Harold waddled up the steps to the front door.

"This may not be so bad after all," Karyn said out loud to her mother.

"Of course not, dear," Connie replied, pressing the window curtain back into place. "Harold is a fine boy and has a good head on his shoulders."

The doorbell rang and Connie went to answer it while Karyn stole another glance at the limo through the curtains. She was pleased that Harold had done that. She intended to rub it in to her friends, of course, by telling them that Harold knew how to do things in a first-class way — that is, in contrast to the other boys in school.

On the way to the dance, Harold tried to make small talk, but while he could talk for hours about the newest Pentium computer chips, he didn't have a clue who Hootie and the Blowfish were. Karyn ignored most of his prattle.

At the Homecoming Dance, Harold did his best to be the perfect date, but most of the time Karyn ignored him. The time finally arrived to hear the results of the election for Homecoming Queen and her court. The emcee called for silence and then the names were called, starting with the fourth-place winners.

Jesse stood quietly to the side, wearing a rented tux, but no date on his arm. The emcee was a professional. After playing the crowd for several minutes, he finally got to second-place. Karyn stood next to Harold, but wouldn't allow him to touch her.

"And the second-place Princess is..." then the emcee paused again and with a mischievous grin he looked directly at Amanda and Karyn.

"And the second-place Princess is... *Amanda Jennings!*"

Shrieks and applause went up from the crowd. Everyone then knew Karyn was the Homecoming Queen. Karyn's friends mobbed her, tears streaming from their cheeks, all giggles and smiles. Harold was literally pushed out of the way and forgotten.

The crowd quieted down as the emcee announced the second-place Prince. Jesse was half hoping it would be him because he didn't want to have to deal with being the Homecoming King. But he also half hoped it *would* be him because it was apparent that Karyn was the Homecoming Queen. The emcee stared at Jesse and Paul Wright.

"The second-place Prince is... *Paul Wright!*" Cheers erupted as the throng of students knew that Jesse was the Homecoming King. Jesse was mobbed and buffeted about. Several of the guys from the football team hoisted him up above the crowd for a minute, proud that their pal had won. The emcee announced Karyn and Jesse purely as a formality.

Jesse walked slowly to the platform amid slaps on the back and congratulations. He approached the mob around Karyn. She was surrounded by her friends and didn't see him.

After what seemed like a long time to Jesse, the crowd parted and Karyn saw Jesse waiting for her. She looked up at him, her eyes wide open, and something happened inside her. For the briefest of moments, they were the only two people in the room. The band played the theme to Miss America as they walked to the podium to receive their crowns.

"I've never been this close to you before," she whispered to him as she held her hand out for him. Jesse didn't know he was supposed to take her hand and lead her to the podium.

"Well, I guess you're right," he replied. She smiled up at him and looked radiantly into his eyes. He didn't smile back.

A few minutes later they were crowned. Karyn looked as though she was born to wear a tiara of diamonds, but Jesse felt like a fool in the silly little gold-plated crown they had placed on his head. The emcee reminded the crowd that the Homecoming Dance couldn't officially begin until the Queen and King had the first dance. The music started and Jesse stared at Karyn in shock.

"We're supposed to dance?" he asked incredulously. "Nobody told me I was supposed to dance!"

"Of course, we're supposed to dance. This *is* a dance, after all," she said.

"I don't know how to dance," Jesse replied nervously.

"Sure you do," Karyn said. "*Everybody* knows how to dance. It's easy. Just follow me and I'll do most of the work." Jesse stared at her. She saw the concern in his eyes and whispered, "Let me help you." Then she gently took his hands and guided them to the proper positions.

She started to slowly move to the music. Jesse stumbled and the crowd giggled. He had always been a jock and had never learned to dance. He felt awkward and had difficulty picking up the beat, but then started to move with Karyn. He was nervous and beads of sweat formed on his forehead. He had the musky smell of a man... the aroma of masculinity mixed with Old Spice aftershave. Karyn drew in large doses of the heady scent and began to feel things she'd never felt before. She pulled him close to her body and laid her cheek against his shoulder.

When Karyn pulled Jesse close, he felt a woman's body against his for the first time in his life. He could smell Karyn's perfume.

"What perfume are you wearing?" he asked, trying to find something to talk about.

"It's called Opus 1," she replied, not lifting her head from his shoulder. Opus 1 instantly became his favorite. Her elegantly styled hair tickled his chin as she slid her arm tightly around his neck, pulling him even closer to her. He felt her warm body against his and was self-conscious. As she moved against him, he felt stirrings inside him he'd never known before. His heart started to thump and he felt lightheaded.

After an eternity the emcee invited the other members of the Homecoming Court to dance, then soon after that, the rest of the crowd. Karyn and Jesse were congratulated until the song ended. Then Jesse tugged at Karyn to leave the floor.

"Where we going?" Karyn asked. The dance had elevated her hormones to heights she'd never known before and she wanted more.

"I need some punch," Jesse replied. What he really needed was to get off the dance floor.

"Okay," Karyn said. "Let's go get some punch." Jesse wanted to abandon the crowd and go home. He was out of his element and knew it. On the way to the punch bowl, he saw Harold and almost dragged Karyn over to him.

"Harold, I want to thank you for allowing me to dance with your date," Jesse said as he passed Karyn's hand to Harold in a chivalrous gesture. Harold looked up to Jesse with surprise while Karyn snatched her hand away from him and stared at Jesse.

"Thank you for the dance, Karyn," Jesse said to her, his voice nervous. "It was really nice."

"Where are you going?" Karyn demanded. "I thought you wanted some punch. Are you leaving?" Jesse glanced around the room then back to Karyn.

"Well, yeah. I have to be at work early tomorrow."

"It's not even nine-thirty! It's still early," Karyn complained. Some of her friends were already cloistered around her.

"Well, it's not early for me," Jesse replied. He was afraid someone would tell him he had to dance some more. He wasn't sure what to do with the feelings he had from dancing with Karyn, and felt like he had to escape.

"You have to stay," Karyn demanded softly. "You're the Homecoming King!"

"Mrs. Teal said all I had to do was be here for the Coronation," he said. "She said I could leave after that."

"But —" Karyn began to protest. She didn't want Jesse to leave and she was prepared to make him stay at any cost. Jesse took her hand and placed it in Harold's hand again.

"Harold," he said. "You're a good man. You have the prettiest date in this room!" Harold grinned up at Jesse, his pale face looking even worse under the colored lights. Karyn jerked her hand away from Harold again. Jesse walked away from Karyn and dropped the silly little crown on the podium, then disappeared behind the curtains of the stage.

She was really pissed at him. She felt like he was walking out on her, not just the dance. She was really, really pissed at him.

* * * *

It was almost one o'clock in the morning when Harold delivered Karyn back to her house in the black limousine. He helped Karyn out of the long, black car and escorted her to the front door. Karyn curtly said goodnight and entered her home, without so much as a thank you to him, closing the big front door in his face. However, Harold's image had been greatly enhanced by having had a date with Karyn Mathers. Everyone now knew that Harold Peoples definitely knew how to treat a lady and he was a happy guy. Even though he had only two dances with Karyn the whole evening, he didn't care.

Jesse was in his room, lying on his bed staring at the dark ceiling, thinking about Karyn. He couldn't get his mind off the slim, sexy blonde with the perfect figure. She evoked strange feelings in him the whole time they were together. His mind replayed the events over and over as he savored the sensations, the feeling of her body touching his, and the scent of her perfume. He wondered if he should ask Karyn out on a real date.

Chapter 4

Monday dawned gray with a cold drizzle filtering through the overcast sky. Karyn's mood was as gray as the dreary skies. Drake had grounded Karyn until almost Thanksgiving. She was rummaging in her locker while a crowd of her friends stood around her, chattering loudly about the dance. Suddenly, the girls became quiet. One of Karyn's friends poked her arm to get her attention. She turned to see Jesse standing there, his awkwardness showing in his face.

"Could we talk for a minute?" he asked, his face beginning to blush.

"About what?" she asked, looking up at him like she didn't care. She wanted to be angry at him for leaving her at the dance, but she had that strange feeling again that caused goose bumps all over her.

"It's personal," he said, glancing at the other girls. They had closed in around them and were giggling and rolling their eyes while making banal comments.

"Sure," she said. She turned to the others and said, "Hey, you guys. Get lost! I'll catch up with you later." They scattered like leaves in the wind.

"What do you want?" She looked at him as they started to walk down the hallway toward her next class. Her mood was noticeably improved and more relaxed.

"Would you like to go out with me?" he asked her with a little boy's shyness.

"Any time," she said without hesitation. "Absolutely."

"That's great! When are you free?" They had stopped by the door of her next classroom.

"I said any time," she replied.

"How 'bout Friday?" he asked. Karyn remembered she was grounded and her father would certainly find out if they were to go out on the weekend, but she wasn't about to let this opportunity pass her by.

"How 'bout tomorrow?" Karyn fluttered her eyes innocently.

"Tomorrow?" Jesse asked. That would be great, plus if they went out Tuesday, then he hoped he might be able to see her again on Friday as well.

"Yes, tomorrow. Meet me after school. We can find something fun to do." Karyn knew her father wouldn't get home until at least seven or later. She could easily come up with an excuse to keep Mom happy.

"I'll meet you at your locker right after sixth period," he said, his heart pounding.

"Deal!" She smiled and gave him a little wink as she walked into the classroom. Karyn had been playing games with boys since she was five, and knew how to play Jesse, but there was something different about this game. This one was more serious.

When class ended the next hour, Karyn's friends mobbed her to find out what had happened. She told them only what they needed to know. Being extremely private, Jesse, on the other hand, told no one. Other than the guys on the football team, he didn't know anyone who would be interested, and he didn't want to face the ribbing he'd take from them.

Jesse's only real friend was his older stepbrother, Mike. That evening, Jesse called Mike to tell him about his upcoming date with Karyn after school.

"That's great!" Mike said. "And you say she's really a fox?" he added.

"Aw, Mike, you gotta see this girl!" Jesse told his bother. "She's like an angel! She's slim and has this long, blonde hair, and has these big blue eyes you could get lost in... just like Mom's favorite actress, Doris Day!"

"Sounds like you've already got lost in them," Mike replied. "So when do I get to meet this special lady?"

"Don't know," Jesse said. "Maybe this weekend. We'll see." Just then he heard the kitchen door slam. Jesse knew Willie Bob was home.

"Mike, I gotta go," Jesse said impatiently. "Dad's home."

"Yeah. Okay," Mike said. Mike knew the odds were about even that Willie would be drunk and Jesse would have to face off with him. "Tell Dad I said 'Hi'."

Jesse's dad entered the room in time to see Jesse hang up.

"Who was that?" Willie asked casually. He wasn't drunk.

"It was just Mike," Jesse said, relieved that his father was sober. "He says 'hi'."

"Hi right back to him, too," Willie replied. "Didja check on that job at the foundry?"

"Not yet, Dad," Jesse answered.

"Well, you oughtta. It pays pretty good, maybe more'n five hunnert dollars a week, " Willie said as he rummaged in the kitchen cabinet for the bottle of Jack Daniels he'd bought a few days ago. "They might fill up soon and you'll miss a good opportunity."

"Thanks, Dad," Jesse said. "But I have to graduate high school first. They don't take anybody without a high school diploma."

"That's bull," Willie Bob replied. "When they need help, they'll take anybody." Jesse knew that to argue with his father would be futile, so he kept his mouth shut. Willie gave up looking for the Jack Daniels and found the sour mash moonshine whiskey he always kept there. He proceeded to pour himself a stiff drink. Jesse knew Willie was preparing to get roaring drunk that evening and decided to take off and avoid the inevitable conflict that would follow.

* * * *

Tuesday was bright and clear, the warmest day in several weeks. Jesse met Karyn after school as planned.

"So where do you want to go?" Jesse asked. Karyn was used to being courted with extravagant gifts and special places. She was about to suggest going to a rather expensive coffee shop known for the best *cafe au lait* outside of Paris. "I was thinking about going to Kensington Park," he offered, "Or maybe to Bower's for a chocolate shake." He didn't have a lot of money and was hoping to find something cheap to do.

"*Kensington Park?*" she asked incredulously. "*No*body goes to the park!"

"Yeah. I know," he replied with a grin. "The park's good, maybe better than Bower's. I go there all the time. Nobody will bother us there." Karyn eyed him suspiciously but then she figured the park might be okay, and besides, it got her out for a few hours.

"Okay. Let's go to the park," she said, a little miffed. She really wanted to be courted and wooed by this hunk. Jesse led her out to his car, a 1994 Camaro. It sat shining and pristine in the sun. Karyn was not at all interested in cars, but she noticed how clean and perfect the Camaro was.

"Is this a new car?" she asked, thinking perhaps Jesse came from a wealthy family that could afford to buy him a new car.

"Nope, this is a '94. I bought it wrecked and restored it myself." Karyn didn't understand that Jesse had taken every nut and bolt off the car and repaired, refinished, or replaced every part on the car. It had been a labor of love, one of the few things he and his father, Willie Bob, had done together. It had taken him two and a half years, but the result was a perfect Camaro that was better than when it rolled off the assembly line.

The afternoon at Kensington Park went surprisingly well. They walked the paths in the autumn sunshine, talking about all sorts of things. They discussed people they knew, their classes, their likes and dislikes. Jesse was knowledgeable of everything from cars to international affairs. Karyn knew nothing about anything except school gossip, rock and roll, and the art of flirting. He told her about certain national political events, and why he had the opinions he had. Karyn's opinions were limited to the newest fashions in New York. They bought cokes and Fritos at a refreshment stand near an exit, then wandered over the leaf-strewn paths until almost six o'clock. Every step of the way, Karyn was becoming more impressed with him. She took his hand and wouldn't let go.

At a little after six, Jesse dropped Karyn off at her house. He knew she was from a wealthy background, but was unprepared for the magnificence of her home. He walked her to the huge front door. At the door, he considered trying to kiss her, but instead, simply held her hand for a moment and gazed into her ocean blue eyes.

"I hope we can do this again," he said. "I hope we can do it soon."

"How about tomorrow?" she blurted out, more aggressively with him than any other boy she'd ever met. "I'll see you at my locker, same time, okay?"

He smiled and left. She stood at the big door in the late-day sun watching his car until it was out of sight. She could hardly wait for tomorrow.

* * * *

In the next three weeks, barely a weekday went by that Karyn and Jesse didn't meet. Karyn was still grounded, but the after school meetings seemed an easy way to get around that. She felt like a giddy fourteen-year-old having her first huge crush. However, within a week, Connie knew something was going on. She watched for Karyn at the front window, but said nothing to her. One day, she saw Jesse drop Karyn off and remembering Jesse from the incident in the grocery store, she felt he was a decent lad based on the way he handled himself there. Connie decided not to say anything to either Karyn or Drake.

On their dates, Karyn and Jesse would talk about all kinds of things, many of them regarding school. One day Karyn started asking more personal questions.

"Do you like school?" she asked.

"You asked that a few days ago," Jesse replied. "I told you it was okay."

"But do you really like it?" she asked.

"Oh, there's a lot of things I'd rather do than sit in class," he said with a smile. "Why?"

"I was just thinking," she said. "I was just thinking that when I first met you, I thought you might be the typical dumb jock that everyone hears so much about, but you're a lot smarter than most of the other guys I know. "

"So what's your point?"

"My point is, you could get really good grades if you wanted to," she answered. She intended to inspire Jesse to get better grades. She was sure he didn't apply himself to his fullest potential.

"Like how good?" he asked innocently.

"I don't know," she said. "You could probably get all As and Bs."

"How about all As?" he asked. "Is that good enough?" Karyn stared at him, flabbergasted.

"You don't get all As! Only nerds like Harold get all As!"

"No, I don't get all As," Jesse replied. "I got a few Bs my freshman and sophomore years." He glanced away sheepishly.

"But you've had all As since then?" Karyn couldn't believe her ears. "What's your grade point?"

"Three-point-eight-seven," he said quietly. Karyn studied his face for signs he was teasing her. She could tell from his eyes that he wasn't.

"I've got a two-point-five," she said at last, "But I have to admit I don't work very hard at it. And I thought I was going to teach *you* something."

Jesse smiled and nodded. "Let's talk about something else, okay?" he said quite deliberately. She was relieved to change the subject anyway.

"So what are your plans for life?" he asked her.

"Plans for life? It's a little early for making plans for life, isn't it?"

"Never too early." Jesse looked at her seriously. "I have plans."

"Like what?" she asked, growing more interested by the minute.

In the next half hour Karyn learned that Jesse maintained his excellent grade point in the hope that he would get a sports or academic scholarship to college. He wanted to get an education and make a better life for himself than the one his father had made. Jesse wanted to be the first of the Waller family to get a college education.

Then Karyn moved closer to Jesse and asked him where he lived. It was hard for her to miss the embarrassed look on his face.

"I live on Hawthorne Street," he said, hoping she wouldn't press the issue.

"Where on Hawthorne? That's a long street. It goes clear across town."

"Um, on the east side. Would you like some ice cream?" he asked, trying to move the conversation in another direction.

"No. Where on Hawthorne?" she continued.

"The twenty-one-hundred block," he said.

"That's not a very good neighborhood," Karyn noted. "You live in the slums?"

"It's not that bad," Jesse said defensively, "Although it's not what you'd call the high rent district, either."

"Not that bad?" Karyn groaned. "That place is a — a —"

"Never mind," Jesse said. "It's where I live, so let's just drop it." Jesse looked away. Karyn could see it was a sensitive subject for him and, for the first time in her life, considered another person's feelings and let it go.

Karyn and Jesse continued to see each other nearly every day after school. Their dates consisted of walks, hanging out in the local coffee shop, and often studying at the city library, which Jesse took very seriously. The feelings within each of them grew, but Jesse was both too polite and too disciplined to take advantage of Karyn, not that they had much opportunity to do anything except kiss and hug a lot. Weeks blended into months and Karyn's girlfriends were constantly trying to get the details of Karyn's relationship with Jesse. Up to that time, Karyn had always told her friends all about her dates, but it was different with Jesse. She was uncharacteristically mum about what was going on between them. She wanted their dates to be her own personal business.

Connie still hadn't told Drake about Jesse. As they saw more of each other, Karyn became careless about keeping it hidden. Drake was almost never home before seven in the evening, and Karyn took advantage of that. She began to stay out later, spending more time with Jesse, holding him close and sharing warm, lingering kisses.

Jesse was not like any boy she'd ever met. He never tried to take advantage of her. He had a head on his shoulders and a plan for his life. He was single-minded in getting good grades and a college scholarship. Jesse helped Karyn with her studies and her grades had improved considerably. Although Karyn wasn't interested in school for anything more than social activities, she was very interested in Jesse and enjoyed anything they did together, even if it was studying. She dreamt about him many nights, something that had never happened before. She was falling in love, and so was Jesse.

Karyn was seeing Jesse almost every weeknight, but never on the weekends, because Drake was home. Jesse noticed Karyn was never available on weekends, but he didn't press the issue because he had to work all day Saturday and Sunday anyway, and most Fridays. One Friday afternoon, Karyn suggested they go see a movie. A new Tom Cruise blockbuster hit was out and Karyn wanted to see it with Jesse. *Top Gun* had been one of Jesse's favorite movies so he liked almost anything Tom Cruise was in.

After the movie, Jesse brought Karyn home. As Jesse stopped the Camaro in front of the Mathers' home, the front door opened and there stood Drake, glaring at the Camaro. Karyn's heart missed a beat when she saw her father. She didn't know it, but two weeks earlier, he had found out that Karyn was seeing Jesse and had checked him out.

"Busted," she said.

"What?" Jesse asked.

"Busted. I've been busted." Jesse looked at Karyn and followed her eyes to see Drake framed in the big doorway. The rage was apparent in Drake's face.

"What's going on?" he asked, mystified by what he was seeing.

"I've been grounded," Karyn admitted reluctantly. Jesse could see the fear in Karyn's face.

"When? For how long?" Jesse asked.

"Since the night of the Homecoming."

"You gotta be kidding!" Jesse just looked at her. Drake stomped down the porch steps and jerked the car door open.

"What the hell do you think you're doing?!" Drake demanded as he reached into the Camaro and grabbed Jesse's shirt. Jesse pushed Drake away with a forceful shove. Connie stood on the front porch, her hands nervously clutching a handkerchief.

"Get out of that car!" Drake bellowed as he grabbed at Jesse again.

"Hey! Let go!" Jesse yelled. He jumped out of the car to face Drake. Karyn scrambled out of the car and ran around to get between Jesse and her father.

"Daddy! Please!" Karyn pleaded. "He doesn't know!"

"Doesn't know what?" Drake growled as he tried to reach past Karyn to grab Jesse. Jesse knocked Drake's hand away again.

"He doesn't know I'm supposed to be grounded," she said. "It's not his fault."

"You just go inside," Drake snorted. "I'll take care of you later!"

"Daddy, *no!*" Karyn protested. Karyn knew her father and she didn't dare leave him to deal with Jesse on his own terms.

"*Karyn!*" Drake lowered his voice in a menacing way. Jesse was becoming angry at the way Drake was talking to her.

"Daddy, he didn't do anything wrong! I did! Not him!"

"Karyn, I'm not telling you again!" Drake had now turned his complete attention to Karyn.

"Or what?" she screamed. "Or you'll ground me again? So what? I'm already grounded and it didn't do any good. I'm *sick* of being grounded!

I'm *always* grounded! What else can you take away from me?" Drake started after Karyn and she ran into the house with Drake hot on her heels. On the porch steps, he turned and pointed a finger at Jesse.

"You stay away from my daughter, you hillbilly shit!" Jesse stared at Drake, but said nothing. "This is all your fault and I'll get you for it!" Drake stomped into the house and was out of sight before Jesse had a chance to reply. Jesse then looked at Connie's hopeless expression.

"I think you'd better go now," Connie said nervously, and followed Drake into the house.

Jesse stood in the driveway watching the house for several moments. He heard a muffled scream from inside and started for the front door. Connie tapped on the window and motioned for him to leave. Jesse trod back to the Camaro and climbed in but didn't leave right away. Connie peered through the curtain at Jesse in the car, thinking that if anyone ever heard Drake, when angry, cuss at home, they would never believe he was the smooth, sophisticated, perfect gentleman they knew in the office or at social functions. She was surprised Drake had exploded at Jesse, since he would normally have let Karyn come inside so he could confront her without witnesses. Jesse continued to sit in the car for a few minutes and then left.

It seemed like forever until Monday came. He was waiting for Karyn at her locker when she came strolling into school, noisily chatting with Amanda and Jennifer.

"Are you all right?" he asked anxiously, barely nodding at the other girls.

"Oh yeah, sure," she said breezily, as though Friday night hadn't happened.

"What's the deal with your dad?" he asked.

"No problem. Sometimes he gets like that," she laughed. "He's probably going through male menopause or something. Anyway, he blows up then it's all over in a few minutes." Jesse studied her for a moment, waiting for her to tell him more.

"Did he hit you?" Jesse asked. Karyn shot him a dirty look. Amanda's eyes widened in surprise.

"Well, did he?"

"Oh, give me a break!" Karyn said, "Daddy wouldn't hit me. He was just mad 'cause I didn't stay grounded." She rolled her eyes at Amanda and Jennifer and heaved an exasperated sigh.

"So what happened?" Jesse persisted.

"I'm not grounded any more," Karyn said with a smile. "I can go where I want and see whom I want," she said with a smile. "It's all taken care of." She touched his cheek and gave him a warm smile. Jesse didn't completely believe her.

"No, it's okay. Really," she went on. "We had a good talk and it's all over."

In fact, Drake had slapped Karyn several times, and he had extended her grounding to the end of the school year, but Karyn had no intention of either obeying her father or telling anyone about their fight. He simply didn't like the fact that Jesse was from the wrong side of the tracks. Even though her grades had improved by studying with Jesse, that wasn't good enough to please Drake. Karyn continued to see Jesse every day after school just as she had for the past three months.

Chapter 5

The hardest time came during the Christmas holidays. Karyn's family always took a Caribbean cruise during the Christmas holidays. Jesse worked every day he could, saving money for college. However, he bought Karyn an expensive tennis bracelet for Christmas. When the cruise ship was in Nassau, Karyn got away one night and called Jesse from a pay telephone.

"Hi, sweetheart," she said, her voice conveying the feelings inside her.

"You've never called me 'sweetheart' before," Jesse commented.

"Yes, I have," she protested. "Lots of times!"

"Never," he corrected. "I would have noticed it." Karyn thought for a moment.

"Maybe I haven't," she finally conceded. "But that doesn't mean you aren't my sweetheart and besides, you've never called me 'sweetheart,' either."

"And that doesn't mean you aren't *my* sweetheart, either," he countered. The conversation was short, but very important to both of them. It was the first time that they really spoke about their feelings for each other. Their crush was fast becoming real love, although neither realized it yet.

"I really miss you, Jesse," Karyn said with a lump in her throat.

"I really miss you, too, baby," Jesse replied. "It was once said, that 'absence is to love what wind is to a fire. It extinguishes the small and enkindles the great.' "

"That's really nice," she finally said after a period of silence. "Are you telling me you love me?" Jesse hesitated. It seemed like such a big step — to say he loved her. Those words seemed like a huge commitment and it was sort of scary. Now it was Jesse's turn to hesitate. Karyn listened to the hollow sound of Jesse's breathing for what seemed like an eternity, then spoke.

"I love you, Jesse Waller," she said softly, her heart pounding, but full of wonderful feelings.

"I love you, too, Karyn Mathers," Jesse replied slowly. They were important words to Jesse and he felt wonderful saying them out loud. Karyn was his girl and there was no doubt about it.

Several more seconds of silence ensued, then Karyn said, "I gotta go. I'll see you after the holidays. I can't wait!"

"I can't either," Jesse replied. "I'll count the minutes."

"I'll count the seconds," she said. "Good-bye, sweetheart," she said, emphasizing the word "sweetheart." Her heart was flying to heights she had never known before. She was in love, in love, in love.

"Good-bye," Jesse replied. He, too, was in love.

Karyn carefully hung up the telephone and turned to see her mother standing there.

"Oh, Mom!" she cried with a start. "I didn't know you were there!" Karyn wondered just how much her mother had heard.

"I saw you on the phone and just came over. That was Jesse, I presume?"

"Yeah," Karyn said sheepishly.

"He's quite the young man," Connie said softly. "It seems he's won your heart." She took Karyn by the hand and guided her gently out into the warm tropical night. "Are you sure he's the right choice?" she asked as they walked toward the starlit beach.

"He's really special, Mom," Karyn said.

"I can see that, but what do you know about him?" Connie asked.

"I know a lot about him. I've been seeing him for a long time."

"I know. Every day after school." Connie patted her daughter's hand.

"You *knew?*" Karyn asked.

"Since the first week," Connie replied.

"How did you know?" Karyn asked. "I mean, I was so careful not to..."

"I'm your mother, dear," Connie replied.

"Does Daddy know?" Karyn asked.

"I haven't told him that you're still seeing him," Connie said. "But, to be honest, I think he should know." Connie had intended to tell Drake that Karyn was still seeing Jesse, but Connie didn't want Drake to slap Karyn again. The longer Connie waited to tell Drake, the more difficult it became to tell him because she was afraid of his temper.

"Thanks, Mom," Karyn said, and gave her mother a big hug. "Jesse really is a nice guy. There's something so special about him."

"I understand," Connie said. "I remember when I had those same feelings about your father."

"You make it sound like you don't have those feelings any more," Karyn said.

"Oh, feelings change as you get older. Situations change as you grow with another person. Sometimes it's good and sometimes it's not, but if the foundation is solid, then you stick it out. As they say, 'for better or worse'." Connie was remembering the giddy highs she had with Drake when they first started to date. She also remembered their wonderful lovemaking in the early years of their marriage before Drake had become so important at Cox Chemical. She longed for the old days, but knew they were gone forever. Sometimes she wished Drake had never received that first promotion. She would have happily stayed in their first little house and had more children, living on their meager income. She would have been totally happy for the rest of her life, if only she could have maintained those early feelings. She wondered if her happiness was the price of Drake's success. Now, twenty-four years later, it was probably too late to even think about it.

"You know he was in jail last year, don't you?" Connie asked Karyn as she continued their talk. Drake had checked Jesse out and heard the story about his jail time.

"Yeah, I heard. Everybody at school seems to know about it, except nobody has any details." Karyn looked across the water.

"Does he ever talk about it?"

"Nope. He's never said a word."

Connie studied her daughter then said, "Honey, I know I'm repeating myself, but are you sure he's the right one for you?"

"Mom, I can't explain it. There's something so special about him and I just know that whatever he did, he won't do it again. He's a really good guy. I mean, you know, he's not like the other guys. He doesn't try to touch me the wrong way, and he talks about things I've never, ever thought about before. He's... he's..."

"I understand," Connie said, again remembering the early years of her marriage to Drake. "I admit he's quite a handsome boy."

"Mom, he's a *hunk!*" Karyn said, "But that's not why I like him. I can date any hunk in school I want, but Jesse's the one I always want to be with." She looked in her mother's eyes. "And Mom," she said. "Thanks for covering for me with Dad."

Connie nodded although she wondered if she was doing the right thing.

* * * *

Jesse came home from work on New Year's Eve. The shop had closed early to let the guys prepare for their annual wild night of partying. At five-fifteen he walked into the house to see his father in the kitchen, already drunk.

"Hey, Sport, whatcha doin' tonight?" Willie Bob asked. The smell of his alcohol-laden breath filled the room.

"Nothing," Jesse replied. "I was just going to hang out. Maybe rent a movie."

"C'mon with me and the guys. We're gonna party 'til the cows come home!"

"No thanks, Dad" Jesse said. "I've got some stuff to do."

"Aw, c'mon!" Willie cajoled. "C'mon and hang out with the *men!* We got some serious drinkin' t' do."

"No, Dad. Really, I don't want to," Jesse replied. Willie's face froze and he stood up from the table, knocking the worn out chair onto its back.

"You know what your problem is? You're afraid to stand up an' be a *man!*" Willie took a step toward Jesse, a menacing look in his eye. Jesse tried to ignore him by opening the refrigerator and looking over the contents, searching for something to eat, but nothing appealed to him.

"Didja hear me?" Willie bellowed. "I said you weren't a *man!*"

"Yeah, I heard you, Dad," Jesse replied softly, his head still in the refrigerator. Willie stumbled to Jesse and slapped him hard on the shoulder.

"*Didja hear me?!*" Willie bellowed again, louder. Jesse stood up from the refrigerator, let the door swing shut, and faced his drunken father.

"Dad, if you want to go out with the guys, go ahead. It sounds like fun, but I'm tired and not in the mood."

"'Not in the *mood*,' you say? You sound like a woman. You sound like an ol' pussy woman who don' wanna do it! Thass what they say when they don' wanna fuck!" Willie glared at Jesse, hoping for a reaction.

"Whatever you say, Dad," Jesse said and turned to leave the kitchen. Willie threw a hard punch into Jesse's back, knocking Jesse against the wall. Although Willie was nearly fifty, he was still tough and wiry, with power in his lean frame. Jesse spun around to face his father.

"Dad, let's not fight tonight. It's a holiday and you should be out celebrating with your buddies, not home fighting with me."

"I cain't go out with my friends," Willie said, his voice low and slurred. "I'm too ashamed."

"Of what?" Jesse asked.

"Of my son. He ain't a *man!*"

"Aw, Dad, knock it off," Jesse said and left the kitchen. He dug in his pocket for the keys to the Camaro.

"You ain't a man!" Willie repeated, following Jesse into the living room. "Hell, *Mike's* a better man than you, an' he ain't even my own *blood!* He makes me more proud than you do. He's a *Marine!!*"

"Yeah, Dad," Jesse replied, heading for the door with the keys in his hand. "I know Mike's a Marine. You tell me about it every week or so. I'm proud of Mike, too." He was turning the doorknob.

"You jus' gonna walk away from a fight?" Willie challenged.

"Yeah, Dad. I'm going to walk away. That's what Mom would've wanted."

Willie Bob glared at Jesse, then turned his eyes to the picture with the gold frame on the television. The framed picture was clean and stood on a lace doily, quite noticeable in contrast to the rest of the house.

"She was a good woman," Willie Bob muttered. "She was a real good woman." A tear filled the corner of Willie's eye, which he immediately wiped away with the back of his hand. Willie Bob enjoyed the reputation of being a hard-working, hard-drinking man. What no one knew was that Willie was a real softie inside, and that his heavy drinking was to shield himself from the pain of his wife's death. Willie loved his wife very much and couldn't understand why she was taken away from him. He also loved Jesse and his stepson, Mike, with all his heart. Unfortunately, his "West Virginny" upbringing didn't allow him to show any emotion because it wasn't manly.

"Yeah, she was," Jesse confirmed, looking toward the same photo. He saw the familiar face, ringed in reddish-brown curly hair. Her nose was straight and fine, her lips full and inviting. Her clear, blue eyes looked at him from the portrait. He studied the gentle curve of her perfect face, the warm smile, and felt her love all over again.

Willie studied the picture, too. She was a beautiful woman, sought by many of the local men in the hills of West Virginia, but it was Willie who won her heart. He remembered his first date with her. He took her and her four-year-old son, Mike, into Parkersburg for ice cream. No other man had ever wanted to include her son in any way, and with that simple gesture, Willie had won the heart of the prettiest girl in the county. They were married a year later. They hadn't been apart a single night for nearly seventeen years until she had to go into the hospital for her cancer treatments. The end came quickly and Willie had felt empty ever since. Willie Bob couldn't understand why someone as sweet and beautiful as Rachel had to die. He missed her terribly and had even stopped going to church. The ache in his heart diminished only when he was drunk, so he spent a lot of time drinking.

"I shore do love that woman," Willie muttered in slurred words. Looking at Rachel's picture always softened Willie's temper.

"Me too, Dad," Jesse said.

"Aw, go on an' find some friends to see in the New Year with," Willie said.

"You know where to find me." Jesse knew exactly where Willie Bob would be. There were three bars where he hung out. He would always wind up in the one just two blocks from the house so he wouldn't have to drive home. Jesse knew he would be there the rest of the night.

Jesse rented a movie and watched it until midnight. At midnight he stepped outside into the cold Michigan winter night to listen to the car horns and firecrackers at the stroke of midnight. He remembered happier days when his mother and father, putting on some crazy hats and blowing lots of horns, would always hustle him and Mike out to listen to the revelers bringing in the New Year. He thought one day, if he ever got married, he would do that with his kids. The picture in his mind was that of him and Karyn bundling up two kids to take them into the cold New Year's Eve night. He thought of Karyn and wondered what sort of wife she would make. He was very lonely that night.

Chapter 6

It was January, school had started and Karyn continued to see Jesse almost every day after school. Neither of them knew Drake had enlisted the principal to watch Karyn. The principal noticed them studying together in the library one day and called Drake immediately. Drake left work early and was waiting for Karyn. He was watching from the window when Jesse dropped Karyn off half a block from her house. As Karyn entered the house, Drake confronted her in the foyer.

"I thought I told you to stop seeing that damned hillbilly!" Drake shouted. Karyn stood mute. "Why don't you listen to me?" Drake continued. "Don't I do enough for you? Haven't I given you everything you ever wanted?" Karyn said nothing, her heart beating a staccato in her breast. Connie stood off to the side, as she always did, worried for her daughter.

"What am I going to do with you?" Drake shouted. "You're already grounded and that doesn't seem to make any difference."

"I've stayed grounded for the last year," Karyn answered softly. Drake glared at her.

"No, you haven't," Drake countered. "Because you're still seeing *him!*"

"Daddy, you said I was grounded," Karyn replied, more strength in her voice. "And you wanted me to improve my grades. I did both."

"Bullshit!" Drake shouted, moving closer to his daughter.

"Daddy, I've been home every night. You told me to be in my room by nine and I have been. I haven't even gone to the ball games. I don't go to parties, and I don't even attend club meetings. Now my grades are almost all As, like you wanted, because Jesse studies with me. What more do you want?"

"I want you to listen to me!" Drake stepped within striking distance. Both Connie and Karyn knew what was coming next.

"I don't want to stop seeing him!" Karyn suddenly shouted back. "I want to be with him all the time!" Karyn was used to getting her own way, and was willing to fight for it. She would stand up to anybody, including her father, to get what she wanted.

The crack of Drake's slap echoed off the walls of the foyer. Karyn went down on the floor. It was the hardest Drake had ever hit her. Connie rushed to Karyn's side, but Drake pulled her back and slammed her against the wall.

"You stay out of this," Drake growled at Connie. "This is between her and me, and I don't need you sticking up for her like you always do!" Karyn stood up and faced her father.

"Hit me all you want — I won't stop seeing him!" she screamed. There was another crack and Karyn went down again. Drake stood over her for several seconds while she rubbed the side of her face. He spun around and stormed from the foyer. Karyn pushed herself up from the floor and fell into her mother's arms.

"Jesse would never hit his daughter," Karyn said softly. Tears were streaming down both their faces.

That incident only made Karyn more resolute. She became obsessive about seeing Jesse. Connie tried to talk her out of seeing Jesse, but Karyn would have none of it. She saw him every chance she got, and openly. It was two weeks before school was to let out for the summer when Drake received another call from the principal that Karyn was still meeting Jesse after school. Drake left the office early and waited for Karyn to come home. At about six-thirty, Karyn walked into the house.

"Where have you been?" Drake demanded.

"At school," Karyn replied, somewhat mystified that her father was home before seven.

"Who were you with?"

"What does it matter?" Karyn replied as she tried to walk past her father in the foyer. He grabbed her arm. "Ow! Let go! You're hurting me!"

"You've only begun to hurt, young lady," Drake said. "The principal told me you're still seeing that goddamned hillbilly. Don't you know he's not good enough for you?"

"Oh, he's good enough for me," Karyn snapped. "*I* may not be good enough for *him!*"

"I told you to stop seeing him months ago! Why do you always have to challenge me?"

"This is what I want and I'm not going to stop seeing him just because you don't like hillbillies!" she retorted.

"But that damned hillbilly isn't good enough for you!" Drake repeated, louder. "In fact, no boy in that whole school is really good enough for you!"

"If they aren't good enough for me, who is?" Karyn demanded. "And why don't I get any say-so in this? It's *my* life!"

Drake stepped closer to Karyn with a menacing look on his face.

"So now what?" Karyn roared. "You gonna hit me again, Daddy?

Go ahead! Who cares?" Drake glowered at her and began to raise his hand.

"Go ahead, Daddy!" Karyn challenged. "Hit me! You always do. Hit me again and again but it won't make any difference! I'll never stop seeing Jesse!"

Drake had always slapped Karyn so he wouldn't leave incriminating marks. However this time, totally losing control of himself, he punched her in the face.

Tiny droplets of blood from her nose splattered on the wall. Karyn didn't remember hitting the floor. She lay there dazed for a few seconds as her nose bled over her blouse. Connie screamed and dashed between Karyn and Drake. She used her body to shield Karyn, but he literally threw Connie out of the way, then pulled the stunned Karyn upright onto her wobbly legs.

"You will do exactly as I say or I'll make you sorry you were ever born," he growled through clenched teeth.

"Go to hell," Karyn muttered through her swelling face.

Drake held her firmly with one hand as he drew back with the other and hit her in the face again. This time Karyn fell to the floor like a rag. Connie broke past Drake again and gathered her unconscious daughter into her arms. Drake hovered over both of them, waiting for another smart-assed remark from his daughter.

"Get away!" Connie screamed. "Get out!"

"I'm not done with her!" Drake bellowed.

"Haven't you done enough for one day?" Connie sobbed, holding her daughter. Karyn's head hung limply as the blood ran from her nose and mouth. "Just get away!" Drake stood over them for several more seconds.

"How can I raise a daughter if you interfere every time I try to teach her a lesson?" he yelled as he stormed into his study, slamming the door behind him.

Karyn blinked her eyes as the fuzzy image of her mother came into focus. She moved her swollen lips and winced with the pain.

"Oh, Karyn dear, we must get you to the hospital," Connie said.

"No, Mom. I'm all right," Karyn said feebly. "I just need to rest for a few minutes." Karyn wrapped her arms awkwardly around her mother. Drake opened the door of his study and glared at the two of them.

"You're grounded until you graduate, young lady," he said with an air of authority, and went up the circular staircase. When Drake was out of sight Karyn struggled to her feet.

"Mom, I gotta get out of here," Karyn said softly. "If I stay here, he's gonna kill me." Connie said nothing, but, in her heart, she knew Karyn was right. "He can go to hell if he thinks he can treat me this way," Karyn said.

"But dear, where will you go?" Connie asked.

"I'm going to see Jesse," Karyn replied, "Then I don't know where I'll go."

"I don't think that's wise," Connie said, fearing Drake's wrath when he found out that they were together.

"Mom, I don't give a shit what you think! You stand there and let Daddy do whatever he wants and it's okay with you. Some day, you've gotta grow some balls and stand up to that asshole! Otherwise, he's gonna turn on you and do the same thing!" Drake had never hit Connie and she honestly didn't believe he ever would. Still, she lived each moment of her life afraid that at any minute he could completely lose his temper.

"But dear —"

"Don't 'but dear' me!" Karyn said angrily. "You haven't helped much. Oh, you're always there to make excuses for him, but I've had it! I'm outta here!"

* * * *

Karyn wasn't sure just where Jesse lived, but she knew it was on Hawthorne, in the twenty one hundred block. She began walking but she knew it would take quite a while to get there so she stuck out her thumb. In seconds, a car stopped next to her. It was Amanda's mother.

"Good Lord, girl! What happened to you?" she said, looking at Karyn's face as she slid into the car.

"I don't want to talk about it," Karyn said. Mrs. Jennings knew something terrible had happened in the Mathers' household, but didn't want to believe it.

"Can I take you to the hospital? Are you going there?" she asked.

"No. No hospital. Just take me to the twenty-one-hundred block of Hawthorne," Karyn said.

"But that's the other side of town," Mrs. Jennings said.

"It's okay. I know what I'm doing."

Mrs. Jennings hesitated, wondering if someone from the slums had done the damage to Karyn's face. But if that were true, she thought, why would Karyn be going back there? She decided not to ask any further questions and drove toward Hawthorne Street. A little while later, Karyn saw Jesse's Camaro parked in a driveway.

"Stop here!" Karyn said. "This is where I get out."

"Are you sure?" Mrs. Jennings asked.

"Uh-huh. I told you, I know exactly what I'm doing." Karyn was already half out of the car. Mrs. Jennings watched as Karyn walked purposefully up the sidewalk toward the seedy house. The lawn hadn't been cut and a derelict car sat in the driveway beside the house. Mrs. Jennings waited while Karyn pounded on the door. When it finally opened, she saw a young man, a very handsome young man, who gathered Karyn into his arms and then studied her face. Mrs. Jennings put the car in gear and drove straight home. She thought about calling the police, but since it was the Mathers, she decided it was a family affair and that she shouldn't get involved in family matters.

Jesse was livid. He tended to the cuts and bruises on Karyn's face with a wet face cloth, listening to Karyn tell her tale. He soothed her as best he could, growing angrier by the minute.

"I can't go back there," Karyn said as she ended her story.

"Well, I'm going back there," Jesse said, "And I'm going to tell him he can't get away with this. He's hit you before, hasn't he?"

"He hits me every time he gets mad at me," Karyn admitted.

"Why didn't you tell me before?"

"He's my dad, and I didn't want you to think —"

"That's bull!" Jesse barked. "Of all the people on this planet you should be honest with, I'm at the top of the list!" Karyn knew he was right. She hadn't been completely honest when she should have been. "Come on! We're going back to your house and set this matter straight, once and for all!"

Fifteen minutes later Jesse's Camaro roared into the driveway of the Mathers' home. Drake heard the squeal of the tires and met the kids at the door. Connie stood behind him in the foyer, crying and clutching her handkerchief to her breast.

"Mr. Mathers," Jesse began but was interrupted by Drake.

"Get inside this house, young lady!" Drake yelled, "And get off my property, you damned hillbilly!" Karyn moved in behind Jesse.

"You hit Karyn!" Jesse roared at Drake. "What kind of animal beats up his own daughter?"

"It's none of your damn business!" Drake shouted. "Karyn, get in the house *right now!*"

"No! I'm never going in there again!" she shouted back. Connie stepped to the door to look out at her daughter. She saw the swollen lips and face, and a large bruise was beginning to form where Drake had punched her.

"*Karyn!*" Drake bellowed. "I'm not telling you again!"

"*Go to hell!*" Karyn shouted.

Drake bounded off the porch, and Karyn hid behind Jesse's powerful frame.

"This is all your fault!" Drake shouted at Jesse. "I'll teach you a lesson you'll never forget!" He drew his arm back and made a fist.

"Drake! No!" Connie screamed from the porch.

Drake ignored her and swung at Jesse. Jesse's reflexes were quick and he easily dodged Drake's punch. Drake swung again, and Jesse blocked the second blow, then delivered a single, powerful lightning right to Drake's nose. Drake went down as though he were felled by an ax. Jesse, Karyn, and Connie looked at Drake's body lying spread-eagled on the lawn, the blood pumping from his nose. He didn't move.

"Let's get out of here," Jesse said, grabbing Karyn by the hand and hurrying her to the Camaro. Karyn glanced back at her father lying unconscious on his back in the grass.

As the Camaro sped away, Karyn said, "I didn't know you could fight like that. That was awesome!" Karyn was proud of Jesse and what he did to Drake. Jesse thought about what his mother would have said about the incident and knew it wouldn't be good.

"Let's get you to a doctor and have him look at your face," Jesse said. He drove straight to the emergency room of the local hospital.

At the hospital, the personnel looked at Karyn. There were a lot of questions, and Karyn told them everything. However, the interns noticed the scrapes on Jesse's knuckles and suspected Karyn was lying to protect him. Drake Mathers was an important man in town and they couldn't believe he would hit his daughter. They suspected it was Jesse who had hit Karyn and she was lying to protect her boyfriend. They had seen it all before and that scenario made more sense to them than anything else.

In the meantime, Drake had regained his senses and called the police. He lied, telling them that Jesse had barged into his house, hit Drake first, and then kidnapped Karyn. The police knew Drake Mathers' position in the community and therefore believed every word he said. Drake didn't tell them that he had hit his daughter, nor did he tell them that he had swung at Jesse twice before Jesse defended himself. The police put out an immediate all-points-bulletin for Jesse's arrest. One officer pulled Connie aside and asked her if Drake's account was accurate. Connie saw Drake glaring at her while she was talking to the officer. She remembered what Karyn had said about Drake turning on her next and a bolt of fear went through her. She made a single, slow, solemn nod and began to tremble.

The hospital personnel held Karyn much longer than usual, constantly asking the same questions over and over, trying to find a flaw in Karyn's story.

They wouldn't let Jesse in to see her. After nearly two hours, a senior doctor came into the room where Karyn was. A number of doctors had looked at her, but no one had treated her.

"Are you going to take care of me?" she asked the doctor. He looked at her in silence. She studied him. He had gray hair at his temples, and a widow's peak plunging down his forehead. He wore half-glasses for reading, his eyes looking over them at Karyn. His deep brown eyes showed years of experience and wisdom. He pretended to study the injuries on Karyn's face. She could smell his Ralph Lauren after-shave lotion as he moved closer to look at her wounds.

"Has this happened before?" he asked, his voice gentle, almost serene.

"Yes, but not this bad," Karyn said. "What are you going to do to me?"

"Nothing," he replied. "Who did you say did this?"

"My dad. You're not going to do anything? Why not?"

"Because you are a minor. I can't treat you without your parents' permission." He gently touched her swollen upper lip.

"Ow!" Karyn said. "How come everybody keeps poking my lip? Don't you people know that hurts?"

"Sorry. Just checking to see how much swelling there is, and if there's any internal damage."

"Talk to the other doctors! They've already checked it. Why can't you just take care of me? Give me something for the pain." Karyn was becoming more agitated.

"The law says I can't treat you without your parents' permission. I need to call your parents."

"No! Don't call them. I told you guys it was my dad who did this to me!"

"I'm not sure I believe that." He watched her reactions closely.

"What's not to believe? Look at me! My face is all busted up! Do you think I did this to myself?" Karyn's temper was flaring. The doctor moved back a step.

"No, I know you didn't do this to yourself, but..."

"So are you going to take care of me or what?" Karyn moaned. "If you're not, then I'm outta here!"

"Karyn, I need to ask you, are you sure you want to leave with — um — Jesse is his name, isn't it?" The doctor watched Karyn's face for the subtle indications of fear or lying. He had seen all this before over the years and knew what to look for.

"Why wouldn't I want to leave with Jesse?" Karyn retorted, shaking her head in disbelief at the question. "He's the one who brought me here after my dad hit me! What's wrong with you people? I've told you that a hundred times! So when can I leave?" The doctor was silent for a while as he studied the girl. She was beautiful, even with the swollen mouth and bruise. She had that special beauty that often attracted the worst kind of men, and he knew it. He had seen many such girls over his twenty-six years of practice, abused by their boyfriends.

However, over the years of practice, he had learned to tell if a girl was lying to him. He had developed the ability to read the body language, the tone of the voice, and the way they looked at him. He knew Karyn was telling the truth, but Drake Mathers — one of the town's most successful citizens! It was so hard to believe!

"Well, you can leave any time. There's no law that says you have to stay," he said. "All you have to do is go by the cashier's office and sign some papers."

"If you're not going to take care of me, I'm not signing anything!" Karyn said, exasperation in her voice as she slid off the examining table.

"Karyn," the doctor said. "I think I believe you, but if there's anything you want to tell me, either now or later, just call."

"What's not to believe?" Karyn harrumphed. "No wonder so many people die in hospitals. You people don't believe any one... you really don't have a clue!" The doctor thought again about Drake Mathers. It wasn't impossible, but the doctor wondered just how likely that it was that he was the culprit in this situation. He followed Karyn out to the waiting room where Jesse sat thumbing through a National Geographic magazine.

She went straight to him and melted into his arms as he stood up to greet her. The doctor couldn't hear what they were saying to each other, but he saw there was no hesitation in Karyn as she pulled Jesse as close as she could. Now he was sure Karyn was telling the truth.

As soon as the young couple left, the younger resident dialed the police and reported Karyn's visit. The police sent a patrol car to the hospital to talk to the doctors.

Jesse took Karyn to his home. As the Camaro rolled into the driveway, Willie Bob stepped out onto the porch. He had a bottle of beer in his hand and was smiling.

"Hi, Dad," Jesse said as he climbed out of the car. Willie Bob waved and went straight to Karyn's side of the car. He opened the door for her and offered a hand to help her out. She looked up to him in some surprise, but took his hand and rose out of the car.

"You must be Karyn Mathers," Willie said.

"Um, yeah," Karyn replied, surprised that he knew who she was. "Has Jesse told you about me?"

"Not a word," Willie replied. He was still smiling as he glanced at his son. Karyn looked intently at Willie. He was a lean man, a little shorter than Jesse, and worse than scruffy. He was unkempt, several days of beard growing on a rugged face. He wore a filthy baseball cap with Skoal on it. His cheap plaid shirt was stained and he wore jeans with ragged holes in them.

"So how did you know me?" she asked. Jesse was wondering the same thing, looking to Willie for an answer.

"Oh, the cops left 'bout ten minutes ago," Willie said and flashed another smile at Jesse. Jesse hadn't seen his father smile that much in a long time, and it made him wonder.

"The cops?" Jesse asked.

"Yeah," Willie Bob confirmed, his smile growing even broader. He moved to look at Karyn's face. She instinctively backed up a step as Willie reached for her chin.

"Aw, I won't hurtcha none," Willie said. She reluctantly let him approach, although he didn't smell very good, as if he could use a bath and some good deodorant.

Willie Bob gently cradled her chin with his fingertips. She could feel the calluses on his fingers as he touched her, and his breath almost bowled her over, but she stood still. Jesse came around the car as his father studied Karyn's face.

"What about the cops?" Jesse asked.

"Oh, they was here lookin' fer you an' this young lady here." He peered at the split on Karyn's lower lip. "We kin fix this up fer ya," he told her, nodding his head. "Ain't no worse'n I've done fer m' boys a few times."

"What did they want?" Karyn asked.

"They want to arrest Jesse. Seems your ol' man has filed charges agin m' boy."

"Daddy filed charges?" Karyn asked. "Why? He started it!"

"Yeah, but your daddy's a big man in town and the cops is gonna believe him a whole lot sooner than they'd believe me or Jesse." He let his hand drop from Karyn's face. "You shore got a pretty one here, Jesse. I gotta hand ya that! She's near as pretty as your mom was."

Karyn knew that was a compliment and smiled at Willie, even though it hurt to move her lips.

"I can't believe my dad filed charges!" she said to Jesse, shaking her head. "Why did he do that?"

"Because he wants to save face," Jesse replied. "He wants to make this all my fault and get even with me." Willie continued to grin at Jesse, like the cat that had swallowed the canary.

"And why are you smiling?" Jesse asked his father. "I don't see what's so funny about it."

"Oh, it ain't funny," Willie replied. "But, I gotta admit, I'm durned proud of you. You just decked the biggest dude in town. That takes guts, boy, and you got 'em in spades!"

"You're *proud* that I hit Mr. Mathers?"

"I always thought you was too scared to fight, but I guess you ain't. I mean, you just took on the biggest man in town, and laid him out like a trout ready for filletin'! That takes balls, son! Oops! I didn't mean to offend the young lady here," he said with a nod to Karyn.

"Yeah, I think Jesse has balls, too, Mr. Waller. He's the only one who has ever stood up for me in my life. Heck, even my own mother never stood up to my dad for me!" She pulled Jesse's arm around her shoulder. "I'm so proud of you."

"I am too," Willie said. "Ain't too much more manly than protectin' your woman. Let's go inside and git somethin' t' drink. We gotta look at your options."

The trio went into the house. Karyn was shocked to see how Jesse lived. The air was stale and smelled of liquor. Dishes were stacked all over the kitchen and the chairs around the table were worn and needed repairs. The window drapes also needed cleaning. Karyn thought it would take a crew about three days to clean up the place.

Willie motioned for Karyn to sit in one of the chairs while he wet a stained dishrag in warm water. Karyn was shocked as Willie pulled a chair up in front of her, sat, and began to daub at the wounds with the stained rag. However, she let him continue without comment.

"Now, you gotta look at what you're gonna do," Willie said to Jesse as he ministered to Karyn.

"I don't know what I *can* do," Jesse said as he watched his father tend to Karyn.

"I know what you should do," Willie replied. "You should get the hell outta Dodge until this blows over so's the sheriff cain't git his hands on ya!"

"What do you mean?" Karyn asked.

"He means I should leave town," Jesse explained. "It's a line from an old Errol Flynn movie."

"Errol Flynn?" she asked, bewildered. She'd never heard of Errol Flynn.

"Oh, never mind," Jesse replied, exasperated. "He just thinks I ought to take off for a while."

"That may not be a bad idea," Karyn confirmed. Willie smiled at her.

"This here's a smart young lady," Willie says. "She's got some good sense."

"And just where could I go?" Jesse countered.

"Aw, hell," Willie said. "You kin go anywhere! You're a good mechanic. I know. I taught you m'self. You kin get a job anywhere."

Karyn nodded in agreement. "I've seen what you did with your Camaro," she said. "You're a great mechanic!" Jesse thought about what Willie and Karyn were saying.

"Besides," Willie went on, "I been in similar scrapes before my own self. They's no way the cops is gonna believe you over Drake Mathers. He kin tell 'em you robbed Fort Knox and they'd believe him, even if all the gold was still there!"

"He's right, Jesse," Karyn said as Willie put the finishing touches on her face. Willie got up and put some ice cubes in the wet cloth. "And they probably won't even listen to me over Daddy," she continued, " 'cause he's got so much influence around here."

"Son, lookit. Ol' Drake Mathers is a big man. He's got the ear of ever'one that matters in this town." He gently pressed the makeshift ice bag on Karyn's face and placed her hand over it. "If'n he says you're guilty, then ever'one's gonna believe it, no matter what you say. You're gonna have t' leave for a while. That's all there is to it." Jesse looked at Karyn. She nodded in agreement.

"Karyn, I don't want to leave you," he said softly, "Especially with your father on this rampage like he is."

"Who says you're leaving me?" she asked.

"Well, if I have to leave town —" he said.

"Who says I have to stay?" Karyn interrupted.

"You'd come with me?" Jesse asked.

"I'll never leave your side," Karyn replied. Willie's smile grew broader. He remembered when Rachel had said those same words to him so many years before in West Virginia. Willie told them about the time he was in a similar situation as Jesse. He'd been in a fight with the mayor's son. The mayor's son was lying about the incident and regardless of the seven witnesses that came forward with the truth, the mayor, the police, and the judge wanted Willie in jail. He was forced to run. The mayor's son wanted Rachel for himself, which was what started the fight. The mayor's son had thrown the first punch, but Willie had thrown the last, breaking the man's jaw in the process. Rachel and Willie were married by the local preacher, then bolted for Michigan. They had never gone back to West Virginia.

"I don't know," Jesse said. "I don't have much money and if I take off, I won't have a job."

"You're a good mechanic, like your dad says," Karyn replied. "Mechanics can get work anywhere. Everybody has a car and they all need fixing sometime or another."

"I have to think about this," Jesse said.

"What's to think about?" Willie Bob said. "They're gonna come fer you and haul you off to jail. That's where you'll sit. You ain't got much choice!"

"I need to talk to Mike," Jesse said, and went to the telephone. Karyn and Willie stayed in the kitchen, talking.

"You shore think a lot o' him, doncha?" Willie asked her after several seconds of silence. Karyn eyed the scruffy Willie.

"Yeah, I do," she said.

"I felt the same way 'bout his mom," Willie said.

"What happened to his mom?" Karyn asked.

"Aw, she died 'bout two years ago. She had cancer," Willie told her. "Lung cancer."

"That's awful," Karyn said. "I knew she was gone, but Jesse never talked about it much and I didn't ask too many questions. He seemed real sensitive about it." Karyn was thoughtful. "How did she get lung cancer?"

"The doctors said it was her smokin'." Willie glanced away to hide the moistness starting to fill up his eyes. "She smoked a lot for years. We both did. That was her only vice."

"It's a known fact that smoking causes cancer, especially lung cancer," Karyn replied. "My parents don't smoke."

"Well, she knew it was the smokin' that was killin' her, so she begged me t' quit before I got sick, too," Willie said. "I quit while she was sick and promised I'd never start agin and I haven't. Jesse don't smoke, neither." In the other room, Jesse was talking to Mike.

"And that's exactly how it happened," Jesse was saying. "He swung twice before I swung back."

"You need to go to the police and tell them exactly what you told me," Mike told him.

"Karyn and Dad want me to run for it," Jesse said.

"Yeah, Dad would say that. You know he was in the same situation when he and Mom left West Virginia."

"Yeah, he told me just a little while ago," Jesse said. "It sure sounds like him, doesn't it?"

"Yeah," Mike agreed. Although Mike was the product of Rachel's first marriage, Willie Bob had accepted Mike as his own son when he married Rachel, and Mike loved his stepfather very much. However, he knew Willie was from a whole different background. Willie's culture respected work, strength, and aggressiveness, and placed less importance on refinement and education.

"I still think you should turn yourself in and get this matter cleared up," Mike said.

"Yeah. Thanks, Mike," Jesse said and hung up. Jesse headed back to the kitchen where Willie and Karyn sat.

"Mike thinks I should turn myself in and tell my side of the story," he told them.

"Mike's a great guy and pretty smart 'bout most things," Willie said, "But he's never been in a lick o' trouble with the law before and he shore don't know how it works. They say, '— justice fer all,' but that's a load o' horseshit. Mathers is the biggest man in town, next to ol' man Malcolm. I'm tellin' ya that ol' Drake Mathers is gonna lie through his eyeteeth an you're goin' t' jail. I'm willin' t' bet that he's already changed his story to git you in even more trouble."

"Your dad's right," Karyn added. "When I went to Homecoming with Harold, Daddy made it out that I'd embarrassed him at the office. Harold's dad works for my dad, and when I went with Harold, Daddy said I had undermined his authority at the office. Go figure!"

"Did he hitcha that time, too?" Willie asked.

"Yeah," Karyn admitted with a nod. "Jesse, you gotta run. Besides, I'm not staying here anyway."

"You're not?" Jesse asked curiously.

"I'm getting out of here! I can't stay with my dad any more. I'm always grounded or being punished for something. There's no such thing as discussion with him. He hits me every time we have an argument. He just keeps getting worse and sooner or later, I'm afraid he's going to kill me. I just can't stay. Besides, I'm going to show him he can't run my life!" The anger had been boiling up inside her for two years, and now she had had enough. Karyn was already angry with her father, but since he had pressed charges against Jesse, the man she loved, she was absolutely livid. "He's a dictator who doesn't listen to anybody, especially me. I don't ever want to see him again!" she declared, as tears began to trickle from her eyes. She had decided to split and there was no changing her mind.

"I still don't know," Jesse said. "Mike says —"

"Fergit Mike!" Willie interrupted. "He's a real smart guy, but he don't know nothin' 'bout this stuff. You kids better take off, an' the sooner the better. The cops is gonna come back by here lookin' fer you and they's not gonna be nice guys 'bout it. You decked a real big man an' the law don't like that, regardless of the reason. You gotta run, boy! I know what I'm talkin' 'bout!" Jesse looked from Willie to Karyn.

"I don't know what your problem is," Karyn said to Jesse. "You've been through all this before. You know with your police record, the cops are gonna believe my dad instead of you!"

"Police record?" Willie asked. "What police record you talkin' about?"

"You know," Karyn replied. "The year Jesse spent in jail."

"Jesse's never been in jail! Hell! He ain't never even got a parkin' ticket before this trouble."

"He's been in jail," Karyn retorted. "I know he has. Everybody knows it." Karyn thought Willie was lying to her and it made her angry.

"Gal, I don't know what you're talkin' 'bout, but Jesse here ain't never been in any trouble of any kind. He ain't never even been inside a police station." Karyn glared at Willie.

"Dad," Jesse said in a low voice, "It's a rumor that started at school from when I missed last year."

"But you was sick, boy, not in jail," Willie said.

"Yeah, but a lot of the kids think I was in jail because we live in this section of town."

"An' you ain't never set the record straight..." Willie asked as a statement. Karyn watched them in total shock.

"No. It kept a lot the kids away from me," he said. "I didn't feel very sociable after Mom died, anyway. I liked the space, so I didn't say anything."

"You were sick?" Karyn asked.

"Yeah. I had an awful case of mono," Jesse explained. "Every time we thought we had it licked, it came back. I missed all last year because of it."

Karyn studied his eyes and knew he was telling the truth.

"You could've told me," she pouted.

"You never asked, so I didn't think it was important," he said with a shrug.

Karyn thought for a minute and realized that she should have known it wasn't likely that a guy with a one-year jail term would have a three-point-eight-seven grade point and would be the star of the football team. She nodded and smiled at Jesse.

"I told my mom that whatever you did, I knew you wouldn't do it again," she said. "It looks like you didn't do it in the first place."

"So, whatcha plannin' t' do?" Willie asked, bringing the conversation back to Jesse's problem.

"I don't know," Jesse replied.

"Well, I'm leaving, with or without you," Karyn said. "I want it to be *with* you. Are you coming with me?" Her blue eyes practically begged Jesse to come with her. "Well...?"

"I need to borrow some money," he said. "I have about fifteen hundred bucks. I can get more from Mike."

"*Now* you're talkin'," Willie shouted, slapping his hand on the table. "Get goin'!"

Jesse and Karyn drove straight to Mike's house. As Mike opened the door, he knew immediately why Jesse was in love with Karyn. He took in her blonde hair and blue eyes, the tank top, which did nothing to hide her breasts, and her long legs. Even with the bruise and the swollen mouth, she was beautiful beyond words.

"Hi, Mike," Jesse said. "This is Karyn." Mike nodded and smiled as he opened the screen door to let Karyn and Jesse enter. Karyn stepped into a modest but immaculate house. The living room was clearly masculine, but it was perfectly clean and organized. There was a comfortable-looking couch and a Lazy Boy easy chair with one magazine lying on it. In front of the couch sat a glass-and-wood coffee table, matched with the end tables. The glass was sparkling clean. She glanced at a glass-shelved étagère that held a number of memorabilia, mostly sports and military items. It was organized and pristine, with not a speck of dust anywhere. Karyn saw the same picture of Rachel on Mike's television that she saw at Willie's house. Karyn was surprised that Mike's house was so perfectly clean while Willie's home was in total disarray. She found it difficult to believe they were from the same family.

"Gee, you have a nice house here," she said, looking around.

"You had her at Dad's place, didn't you?" Mike said to Jesse. Jesse nodded.

"Mike was a Marine," Jesse told Karyn. "He still likes to keep things squared away. You've heard the saying, 'You can take the man out of the Corps, but you can't take the Corps out of the man,' haven't you?"

"No, I never heard that, but I can see what you mean," Karyn said with a smile. Mike returned her smile.

"So what brings you two to my humble abode?" Mike asked with a twist of a grin. Mike's voice had a low, soothing quality that Karyn liked.

"Mike, I need to borrow some money," Jesse said, "and I don't know when I'll be able to pay it back."

"For bail?"

"No. To leave town."

"I don't think that's a good idea," Mike said. "They'll put out a bench warrant for your arrest. It's only a matter of time until they catch you."

"I'll take my chances," Jesse said. "Can I borrow some money?"

"I can give you a thousand bucks. Will that be enough?" Mike offered. For an instant, he thought about refusing to help Jesse to force him to go to the police and resolve the situation, but he couldn't take his eyes off Karyn's bruised face.

"It'll have to do," Jesse said. "I've got fifteen hundred. Twenty-five hundred bucks ought to get us pretty far from here, don't you think?"

"I'm still not sure this is a good idea," Mike said, "I still wish you two would go to the police first. As for the money, don't worry about paying me back. I know you'll get it to me when you can. No problem." Mike went to his bedroom and returned with a wad of cash.

"I had this set aside for a down payment on a new car, but since you and I fixed the water pump on my old one, it's been running fine. I just never got around to putting this back in the bank." He handed the cash to Jesse. "So when are you taking off?"

"As soon as we can," Karyn answered for him. Mike's eyebrows rose at Karyn's comment. "My father is probably swearing out a warrant for his arrest right now. And if I go back, he'll just beat me up again."

"*We?*" he asked

"Yes. We're both leaving — together," Karyn replied. Mike shot a glance at Jesse. Jesse nodded. Mike still would have felt better if Jesse went to the police first, but he knew Karyn was probably right about her father.

"This is going to mess things up, you know," he said to Jesse, "Taking her along. They may consider this a kidnapping and then they'll get the FBI involved."

"He's not kidnapping me," Karyn retorted. "We're going together." Mike sighed.

"Well, you're a big boy now," he said. "You know more about this than I do and you can make your own decisions. You know how to get ahold of me."

"Um, Mike?" Jesse said, scratching his chin, "You know I used your address for the colleges I applied to."

"Yeah. It was fifteen the last I remember," Mike said.

"Yeah. It's still fifteen," Jesse replied. "It doesn't look like I'll be applying to any more for a while. Let me know if any of them reply, okay? I'll call home every so often. I'm still hoping for a scholarship."

"Why are you using Mike's address?" Karyn asked.

"Because my dad doesn't want me to go to college. He wants me to get a job right now," Jesse told her. "He said he'd throw any college correspondence in the trash if they showed up at the house, so I'm having them sent here."

"Your dad's really weird," Karyn said. Mike smirked at her remark.

"Well, weird or not, that's the way he is," Jesse said.

"Sure thing, Sport," Mike said, using the nickname he and Willie often used. "I'll keep them right here."

"Mike, we need to go," Jesse said. "I need to pick up some stuff at the house and hit the road."

"Any idea where you're going?"

"None. All I know is that we have to get out of here ASAP." Mike nodded and led them to the front door. After a hug for each of them, Mike stood on his porch and waved as the Camaro backed out of his driveway.

Chapter 7

"Mike's pretty cool, isn't he?" Karyn said as they pulled away from his house.

"Yeah. He's the best thing that ever happened to me — except you, of course," Jesse said, meaning every word.

"Of course," Karyn confirmed.

"He learned a lot in the Marines, especially about discipline. He's tried to teach me discipline, too." Jesse talked as he drove. "You can see how he keeps his house in perfect order, and I mean that in a Biblical sense, too. Mike's the best person I know next to my mom."

"He's your step-brother?" Karyn asked.

"Yeah. My mom was married before she met my dad. Her first husband was Mike's dad. They tell me he was a real hell-raiser. One day she'd just had enough and divorced him. That's when she met my dad and married him. Mike was six when I was born and he took me on like I was his own real brother. He took me camping and hunting and taught me everything from how to build a model car to how to do my homework. He's the one who got me to play football. He told me to excel in everything I did. He and my mom made sure I knew the difference between right and wrong. He's pretty cool, all right."

"I can see you two get along real well," Karyn said.

"He's my best friend," Jesse said. "Mom and Mike both wanted me to go to college. Mom knew Dad didn't think anyone needed a college education, but she pushed me in that direction anyway. She didn't want me to live like a hillbilly all my life. Before my mom died, she made me promise in front of Mike that I would go to college. I'll be the first Waller ever to get a college education."

"Your mom was one smart lady," Karyn said. "I think I would have liked her."

"Oh, you would have," Jesse said with a smile. "Everybody liked Mom."

Several minutes later, Jesse stopped the Camaro down the block from Willie Bob's house. He peered ahead to the house. A police cruiser was parked in the driveway.

"Can't go there," he said. Karyn saw the police car and agreed. As they were turning around in a driveway, the police came out of Willie's house and spotted the Camaro. They ran to the patrol car and gave chase.

Jesse had a head start on them. He gunned the car and sped toward the freeway. He took several turns at high speed, using the Camaro's powerful engine and special suspension to its fullest potential. He was glad he had modified the car and installed the new tires.

"If they catch me, I'm toast," he said while maneuvering the car through a tight S-curve. Karyn silently nodded, bracing herself in the seat as best she could. She glanced out the back window.

"They're still there," she cried. "They're calling on their radio!"

"Yeah, but I'm going faster than they are!" he replied. He dodged a panel truck that was turning onto the street in front of them. Jesse glanced in the mirror, but the cruiser was hidden behind the truck. Jesse saw his chance and stomped on the brakes.

The Camaro's anti-lock braking system took over, preventing the car from skidding. Jesse spun the steering wheel to the right and bounced into a 7-11 convenience store parking lot. He gunned the engine and roared around to the back of the store, stopped, and waited.

The policemen had last seen the Camaro as it dodged the panel truck and assumed with its large, powerful engine, it had already disappeared far ahead of them. They told the backup cruisers to go far ahead of their current path, which actually sent them away from where Jesse's Camaro sat hidden behind the 7-11 store.

Karyn could hear the siren of the police car as it passed the building and began to fade. They sat in the idling Camaro until the siren's howl was gone.

"That was close," she said. "We'd better get out of here before they figure out we're not somewhere in front of that squad car."

"You're right," Jesse replied. "Let's go."

A few minutes later, Jesse cautiously approached Willie's house. No patrol cars were in sight. Jesse drove the car behind the house. Willie Bob met them at the back door.

"I saw 'em take off after you," he said. "Looks like they missed ya."

"You should've seen it!" Karyn said excitedly. "It was just like in the movies! Jesse took off and drove like a real racecar driver! It was awesome!"

Willie grinned at Jesse. "Sounds like you had fun," he said, slapping his son on the shoulder. "I guess maybe you're a man after all!"

"I can't say it was fun, but it was exciting, for sure," Jesse replied, his heart still pounding with the adrenaline. However, more than that, Jesse saw his father was talking to him as an equal for the first time in his life. Willie Bob suddenly viewed him as a man, although in Jesse's mind, it was for the wrong reasons. It was a bittersweet feeling to know his father, whose approval he had sought for so long, now lauded him for something his late mother would have disapproved of. Jesse was pleased his father was proud of him, but wished Willie's pride was based on scholastic or athletic accomplishment, rather than on vulgar fisticuffs.

"We need to get some stuff and get out of here." Willie followed Jesse to his room with Karyn close behind. She looked over Jesse's room while he packed. It was very neat and as clean as could be expected. He had a number of sports awards on his dresser and around his mirror, attesting to his sports career. A picture of him with his mother and father graced his dresser. His bed was made, the faded and worn bedspread tucked tightly all around with precise hospital corners, like Mike had learned to do in the Marines. She could see Mike's influence on Jesse in how Jesse kept his room.

"Any idea where you're goin'?" Willie asked.

"None at all," Jesse answered. "And even if I did, I wouldn't tell you because I don't want you to have to lie for me, Dad."

"That's pretty smart," Willie said. "You're right. Maybe you can just gimme a call when you get settled somewheres."

"Yeah, Dad, I'll do that," Jesse said as he packed some clothes into a back-pack. In less than five minutes, he was ready to go.

"Let's hit the road," he said to Karyn. "It's only a matter of time until the cops come back here."

Willie Bob watched from the porch as the shiny Camaro backed out of the driveway. He remembered all the hours he and Jesse spent together restoring that car, and how rewarding they had been. They had actually grown closer over the couple of years that they had worked together on the car. He felt a twinge of guilt that he didn't spend much time with Jesse any more. He didn't know when he might see his son again. Jesse waved one last time as the Camaro rolled down the street and out of sight. Willie Bob wiped his eyes clear of any tears.

* * * *

"So where are we going?" Karyn asked.

"Don't have a clue," Jesse said. "Got any suggestions?" He was thinking about California, but didn't know how far twenty five hundred dollars would get them. Then an idea hit him. "How about Florida?" he said. Karyn's family had been to Florida a number of times and in her mind, going to Florida would be just like the vacations she took with her mother and father.

"Sure!" she said. "Florida will be fun. I'm sure you can be a mechanic there. Let's go." Their minds made up, Jesse drove for the freeway.

* * * *

That evening, Karyn and Jesse found themselves in southern Ohio. They had stopped at a McDonald's and were finishing the meal at a roadside rest stop as the sun sank low into the western sky. Karyn leaned onto Jesse across the seat. Jesse felt the same powerful urges he felt when they were dancing at the homecoming dance. Soon they were in the throes of some heavy necking, with long, lingering kisses and petting. Karyn and Jesse's chemistry was in high gear, but they didn't become sexually intimate. The weather was warm, so they decided to sleep in the car at the roadside rest stop.

As they settled in for the night, the car became infested with mosquitoes. The insects attacked in swarms as Karyn and Jesse both slapped at the biting pests. It seemed the more they killed, the more that showed up. They were biting Karyn all over her body. Besides that, while she and Jesse were making out, she hadn't noticed how warm the night was. But now that there were no distractions, the hot, humid night closed in on her. She had never been anywhere without air conditioning and was soon begging Jesse to start the car to keep the air conditioner running.

"We're almost out of gas," he told her. "If I run the car for the air conditioning, I'm afraid it'll run out."

"Well, that's gotta be better than this heat," she replied. "And then we can close the windows and keep the mosquitoes out," she added.

"If we run out of gas, we'll be stuck here."

"Well, we gotta do *something*," she complained. Karyn wasn't used to roughing it, and this was the beginning of a night of endless complaining. Jesse ran the car for periods of time to cool things off and get a break from the mosquitoes.

Karyn slept little, and Jesse almost not at all, as they slapped at mosquitoes and Jesse listened to Karyn's constant bitching, first one thing, and then another.

"I don't know what to do," he said.

"Well, you gotta do something," she groaned, smacking a mosquito almost as big as a fly. "This isn't what I thought it was going to be," she said, looking at her watch in the dim light of the new dawn.

Jesse was hurt by Karyn's remarks, but he said nothing. He rubbed his eyes and stretched and looked over at Karyn who was leaning against the door, her eyes closed, a frown on her face. He started the car and backed out of the parking space.

"Where are you going?" she asked, yawning.

"It's dawn. Let's hit the road," he said.

"Hit the road?" she grumbled. "I need to get cleaned up and wash my hair. We need to find a hotel or something!"

"We can look for something on the way," he offered.

"I gotta get cleaned up right now!" she pouted as Jesse looked at her in disbelief. A car horn behind him brought him back to reality. He had stopped in the traffic lane while looking at Karyn. He put the car in gear and pulled away, heading back onto Interstate 75. The car cooled off with the air conditioning and soon Karyn dozed off. Jesse felt relieved with the silence.

* * * *

That day, the Mathers house was in turmoil. Karyn had been gone all night and no one knew where she was. Drake and Connie called the police at seven o'clock that morning. They showed up at the Mathers' residence at a little after ten.

"Well, they took their sweet time getting here," Drake said to Connie as he opened the huge front door of his house. A white man and a black woman, both detectives, stood on the porch and said nothing. The man was in an ill-fitting suit and the woman in a neat, plain dress.

"You guys *are* cops, aren't you?" Drake asked.

"Are you Drake Mathers?" the man asked.

"Who the hell else would I be?" Drake hurled back at him. "And why did it take you so long to get here? We called you at seven this morning!"

"Do you have some ID?" the woman asked.

"What do I need ID for?" Drake glared at them. "Are you going to help me or not?"

"Come on, Dana," the man said. "We don't need to take this." The Suit turned to walk away.

"Do you know who I am, for Chrissakes?" Drake bellowed. The policeman continued to walk toward the black car in the driveway. The woman watched him go and turned to Drake.

"Mr. Mathers, we're here to help in any way we can, but if you don't calm down, there's nothing we can do. I am Detective Dana Brampton, and that is my partner, Sergeant Detective Jim Fletcher." She showed her gold badge to Drake, but he only glanced at it and returned his glare to "The Suit."

"I don't care who you are — I just want to file a missing persons report and have that hillbilly arrested!" Drake continued to eyeball Jim Fletcher. The Suit was sliding into the front seat of his unmarked police sedan. "Where the hell does he think he's going?"

"Mr. Mathers, I have identified us as police officers. There is a law on the books about showing proper respect to a police officer, which you are not doing. Either you show us the proper respect and cooperate, or we'll leave." Her eyes were on Drake but he paid her little attention. Drake continued to glare at Sergeant Fletcher. Connie stepped around Drake, her eyes red from lack of sleep and crying.

"Detective Brampton, please help us," she begged. Connie was almost beside herself with worry about Karyn.

"You stay out of this!" Drake demanded and pushed Connie back inside. "I'll handle this." Connie did as he said. When Sergeant Fletcher saw Drake push Connie, he got out of the unmarked police car and walked purposefully back up to the porch.

"One more move like that and I'll arrest you," Fletcher warned.

"Like what?" Drake demanded.

"Like pushing that woman like you did," Fletcher replied in the same tone Drake had used. "And if you think you can —"

"*Hold it!*" Dana interrupted. "We can either all work together or we can take everybody downtown and spend a few hours getting all the necessary information!" she said sternly. She turned to Drake and said, "Either you calm down and clean up your act, or we can arrest you and that will make things very difficult for everybody. We're here to help if you'll just let us. Now, do we have an agreement?" She spoke with authority and Drake saw in her eyes that she meant what she said. His blood was boiling. Drake was used to issuing orders, not taking them, especially from a black woman.

"Come on in," he said curtly. He turned his back on the officers and walked into the house, leaving the huge door standing open. Connie stood off to the side of the foyer, watching the officers. Fletcher nodded politely to Connie as he entered. She motioned them to go into the large, plush living room.

"After you, ma'am," Fletcher said to Connie. She mustered a weak smile.

Twenty minutes later, the two detectives had taken statements, mostly from Drake, who was still in a hostile mood. Every time Detective Brampton tried to talk to Connie, Drake would interrupt and answer for her. Finally, Dana told Drake to shut up and let Connie answer. Once the statements were taken, the officers stood to leave.

"We can't do a missing persons for seventy-two hours," Sergeant Fletcher said at the door.

"Why not?" Drake asked, his irritation evident.

"It's just the way it's done. Generally, most people who disappear in cases like this return home in less than seventy-two hours," Fletcher said.

"Besides, your daughter is seventeen and we have to assume that she has left town at her own volition, not under duress," Dana Brampton said. "No foul play is suspected." Drake jumped to his feet and began to bellow at the police.

"No 'foul play?' Are you crazy?" Drake shouted. "That kid kidnapped my daughter and I want him arrested and put in jail. He hit me, dammit! What good are you?" he shouted at Brampton. "What am I paying taxes for?"

"That's it, Mathers," Sergeant Fletcher said as he arose. "We don't need any more of your mouth. You might be able to yell at your employees like this over at Cox Chemical, but this isn't Cox Chemical you're dealing with now. It's the Police Department, so simmer down." Fletcher put his notepad in his pocket and motioned for Brampton to follow. They went to the front door.

"Where are you going?" Drake demanded. "What the hell's going on here?!"

"We're done here and we're done listening to you," Fletcher replied. He dropped his business card into Connie's hand. "Mrs. Mathers, you can call us if you hear anything or think of anything else to tell us," he said to Connie quietly.

* * * *

At the Waller house, Willie Bob was alone in the kitchen, staggering drunk. He had sat up all night drinking, not even going to bed. Although he didn't always know how to show it, he loved his son as much as any man and he was proud Jesse had decked Drake. But now he was worried about what would happen with the police being involved with Jesse and the Mathers girl.

Willie was very proud that Mike had been a tough Marine. He wanted to see the same sort of toughness in Jesse. Jesse was great at sports — a star on the football team, in fact — but had not been a "real man" in Willie's eyes. Jesse didn't even drink. He just wanted to go to college, play football, and get a good education, which left Willie dumbfounded.

Willie Bob had a reputation at the shop for being a hard-working, hard-drinking, hard-living man with a sense of fair play — that is, when he wasn't drunk. Willie believed the worth of a man was measured in terms of how hard he worked, drank, and could street fight. He didn't finish high school and it wasn't important to him. He just didn't understand Jesse's determination to get an education and get himself some high-falutin' job.

Chapter 8

That afternoon, after being on the road for several hours, Karyn finally roused herself from a deep sleep. She looked out the window of the car to see the hills of Tennessee passing by as they rolled south on Interstate 75. Jesse cast a critical eye at her but said nothing.

"So, where are we?" Karyn asked as she stretched herself out lazily. Her back and neck ached from sleeping in the car, and she felt like she had a mouthful of cotton.

"Near the southern border of Tennessee," Jesse told her.

"Have you been driving all this time?" she asked.

"Yeah."

"Aren't you tired?" she asked, looking at him. His eyes were bloodshot, his mouth pulled down in a tight grimace.

"A little bit," he admitted. They rode in silence for another twenty minutes.

"I need to brush my teeth and get some clean clothes," Karyn said. "And I also need a hot bath and to wash my hair, too. I probably smell stinky-poo right about now."

"Yeah. Okay," Jesse replied. "We can stop at a motel tonight and you can clean up. I could use a shower, too. We're pretty close to Chattanooga. We'll stop there for the night."

Twenty minutes later, they were in Chattanooga. Jesse thought it was a pleasant city, with Southern charm.

"There's a shopping center with a K-Mart. We can get you some clothes and shampoo and stuff," he said, pointing. Karyn followed Jesse's finger and saw the K-Mart sign in the distance.

"K-Mart? I'm not going into K-Mart. Find a Hudson's or something," Karyn said.

"What's the problem with K-Mart?" he asked.

"I'm not going to wear those cheap K-Mart clothes," Karyn replied. "I don't even know what they look like."

"Well, sweetheart," Jesse said, "They look like ordinary clothes. We don't have a lot of money until we can find some work, you know."

"You have twenty-five-hundred dollars!" she huffed defensively. "We can spend a thousand on clothes and still have fifteen hundred left over! I don't want to wear cheap K-Mart clothes!"

For the first time, Jesse understood what Willie Bob meant when he had once called a woman "high maintenance," meaning she had expensive tastes and expected them always to be fulfilled. Karyn was beginning to make demands that he knew would soon deplete their limited funds.

"But, honey," Jesse countered, "Be reasonable. We've already spent over a hundred dollars on food and gas, and we're only halfway to Florida."

"I don't care!" Karyn pouted. "I'm not going to wear anything cheap that looks exactly like what it is — real junk."

"But Karyn —" Jesse began.

Karyn shook her head. "Come on, now. You have the money and I want some good clothes. Don't be so cheap!"

"Sweetheart..." Jesse began.

"Don't 'sweetheart' me!" Karyn answered back. "You want to control me just like my dad!" Jesse could feel the aggravation growing in the pit of his stomach.

"At least go into K-Mart to see what they have," Jesse implored. "They might have something you like."

"They won't have anything I want," Karyn said sullenly. "I won't go." Jesse began to wonder what he had gotten himself into. He felt like he had a tiger by the tail. They rode on, barely speaking to each other. Even when they stopped to eat, Karyn remained quiet and wouldn't look at Jesse. That evening, Jesse stopped at a Best Western motel.

"I'll get us a couple of rooms," he said as he got out of the car.

"A couple of rooms?" she asked. Her temper had settled down quite a bit, although she was still a little angry.

"Yeah. One for you and one for me," he said.

She looked at him and saw the hurt in his eyes from the day of tension between them. Even with a two-day growth of beard plus the red eyes from long hours of driving and lack of sleep, Jesse still appealed to her. The intense urge inside her rose to the surface and she softened. She looked at Jesse, seeing how sad his eyes were, and her heart melted. She hopped out of the car and went over to him and put her arms around his neck.

"How about we share a room tonight —" she said, "To save money."

"Are you sure?" he asked. She pulled him closer and put her head against his chest, holding him tightly.

"I'm sorry, baby. I guess I'm just tired," she said. He held her tightly.

"We both are," he said. "I haven't slept in a day and a half. Let's get that room."

* * * *

Karyn knew by the outside of the motel that the room wouldn't be luxurious, but this was worse than she expected. There were two double beds. Jesse flopped on one bed with a loud sigh. The bedspreads were faded and the curtains smelled of stale cigarette smoke. The lampshade was yellow with age and nicotine. However, the bathroom, as small as it was, had soap and shampoo, and it was clean. Karyn looked at the tub and hand shower and for the first time all day, felt some relief. She was going to get a bath and wash her hair.

"We can go get you some clothes," Jesse offered.

"Oh, Jesse, I'm so tired and grungy. I just want a bath. I can wash these clothes in the sink," she said. "I know I'll take a while, so you go first," she added.

"Okay," he said, as he forced his tired body from the bed and headed for the bathroom with his backpack. Twenty minutes later, he had showered, shaven, and felt much better. Karyn went to him and gave him another hug. Then she went in to wash her hair and take a bath. While she was in the bathroom, Jesse called Mike.

"I'm not sure what I did wrong," Jesse was saying to Mike as he described the argument.

"Maybe it's just because she's under a lot of stress and she's tired," Mike offered as an explanation.

"Yeah, that's what she said," Jesse replied. "Maybe we're all tired. Anyway, we're going to Florida," Jesse told him. "But don't tell anybody."

"I won't. You know that," Mike said. "I won't even tell Dad. And don't worry about that little spat today. All people have them. It's how you treat each other in the long run that counts."

"Yeah. Okay," Jesse said. "I'd better let you go. I'll call you later. I'll let you know where we'll be staying after we get to Florida." Jesse hung up and flopped back on the bed. It felt so good to be lying down.

An hour later, Karyn peeked out from the bathroom door. The television was on and Jesse was on the bed, fast asleep. She felt the cool rush of air from the cheap air conditioner that hummed under the window. She had washed her clothes in the sink and hung them over the shower curtain bar to dry. Her hair was damp and she had nothing but the skimpy motel towel wrapped around her. She was embarrassed that Jesse might see her that way, and was relieved that he was asleep.

It was already dark outside. She tiptoed to the curtain and pulled it shut, then turned on a light. The weak bulb gave minimum illumination through its yellowed shade. She studied the young man lying on his back on the bed, shoes off, clad only in his jeans, breathing deeply. His face was highlighted in the dim light. The light and shadows accentuated every feature. His nose was straight and well defined, not too big nor too small. His cheeks were angular and his eyes were set deep under his masculine brow. She knew his brown eyes so well after gazing into them so many times over the last several months. His body seemed to be chiseled from richly grained marble and made her think of Bernini's statue of David that she saw in Rome while traveling with her parents last year.

Karyn looked at him for a long time, feeling things she'd never felt before. She noticed dampness between her thighs, and her nipples stood erect under the skimpy towel that she clutched at her breasts. She remembered all the things her mother had told her about meeting the right man, about waiting for him in her heart, mind, and body. Especially her body. Her body yearned and ached and strained.

It was like a dream as she stood next to Jesse. She bent over and kissed his lips. He snorted, made a funny face and rolled to his side. She smiled at him and padded over to the television and turned it off. She returned to the bed and gazed at Jesse some more. Images were crashing through her mind as she stood there. Images of things they'd done and places they'd been. Images of things they'd talked about and planned. Images of things she wanted to do.

Jesse had rolled to one side of the bed. She gently pulled the bedspread from the other side, stood for several seconds, and let the towel drop from her. She turned off the light and slid between the sheets. She reached around Jesse and pulled him close.

In the night, Jesse roused and felt Karyn's form next to him. He squirmed to look and in the dim light he saw her there, lying next to him. Her eyes were closed and her breathing was soft and even. The dim light caressed her face, highlighting the features that he knew so well. He studied the pretty girl with the long, blonde hair cascading around her face. He touched her cheek and she opened her eyes. In the darkness, a long, passionate kiss flowed into even more passionate lovemaking.

It was the first time for both of them and they were dazzled by their wild and wonderful lovemaking experience. They explored and experimented and loved for over three hours. Finally, around 3:30 in the morning, they were exhausted and fell asleep intertwined together, their minds playing back the last few hours in wonderful, colorful dreams.

They awoke around nine in the morning, still flying high from their love-making the night before. They giggled and teased each other, and soon they were at it again. They were completely involved in each other, with not a care in the world.

"I'm hungry," Karyn said. Jesse glanced at the clock on the nightstand. It read ten-thirty.

"Yeah. So am I," he agreed. "Let's get going. I don't believe we slept in this late!"

Karyn arose and Jesse watched her perfect nude body as she strode to the bathroom. She saw him as he studied her long legs, firm buttocks, and rounded breasts. She stopped to let him gaze a little longer. She smiled, did a pirouette, and went into the bathroom with a giggle. Jesse felt the urge grow inside him again, but controlled it. He laid back and smiled at the ceiling.

Fifteen minutes later, Karyn emerged from the tiny bathroom, dressed in her still-damp clothes.

"I need more clothes," she said with a faint scowl. "These are still wet."

"Okay, baby-doll," Jesse said as he swung his feet from the bed to the floor. "First thing we'll do this morning is get some fresh clothes for you." Half an hour later, they were on the road when Jesse spotted the K-Mart.

"I still say we should look in K-Mart," Jesse said. "I don't know where we could find a Hudson's or a Saks." Karyn was annoyed for half a minute, but then nodded. She was in a much better mood after the night of lovemaking, plus she was desperate for clothes.

"Okay. Let's look in K-Mart."

They sat in the car in the K-Mart parking lot for a few minutes while Jesse took an accounting of their finances. They had been on the road for only two days and had already spent over three-hundred-dollars on food, gasoline, and lodging.

"We have less than twenty-two hundred dollars," Jesse said. "I figure when we get jobs, it's going to take at least a week, maybe even two, to get our first paychecks. We've been spending money at around a hundred-fifty bucks a day, which means even if we were to get jobs today, we'd just about break even."

"But I do need some clothes," Karyn pleaded. Jesse knew she was right and wasn't arguing that she needed some clothes. He was just worried about spending too much.

"I know, but we need to really lighten up on our spending," he said.

"But honestly! I need some fresh clothes, and the sooner the better," Karyn urged. Jesse looked at her and thought about how she looked without clothes that morning.

"I know that, and we'll get you some, but not for a few more days. I think I like the thought of you running around in the buff for the next week or so."

"Oh, yeah!" she replied with a wry smile. "And for sure we'll both get arrested and we won't even be in the same cell!" She gazed at Jesse, her wonderful lover.

"Okay, okay. Right now," Jesse laughed. "But we just have to budget what money we have left, right? Right!"

"*Budget?*" Karyn exclaimed. Karyn had never had to budget in her life, and at first resented Jesse trying to tell her how much she could spend. "You're serious, aren't you? I mean, about watching our money," Karyn asked, somewhat surprised.

* * * *

In the next thirty minutes, Jesse found that even in K-Mart, he had to constantly remind Karyn that they were on a tight budget. He had hoped to spend less than a hundred dollars. He had planned to get maybe a pair of no-name jeans, a couple of shirts, some underwear and a pair of sandals.

"Uh, Karyn?' Jesse said, breaking the silence.

"What?" she answered, still shopping around for more things.

"We can't afford any more stuff," he said in a low voice.

"But look at these bikini panties," she said with a grin. "Aren't they the sexiest?" she teased. Jesse smiled back but was thinking about their limited capital. "Just two more T-shirts? Please? Pretty please?"

Jesse sighed. "Okay," he said. "These two pair of panties and that's it. The problem is I'm not rich like your daddy."

His words stung. "My daddy's not rich," she said defensively. Jesse stared at her in amazement.

"How can you say that?" Jesse replied. "Next to old man Malcolm, your dad's the richest dude in town!"

"I suppose we're well off, but we're not rich," Karyn replied even more defensively and a little louder.

"Hey, it's no sin to be rich," Jesse said, seeing that Karyn was upset by his comments. "But there's no way you can deny that your old man's rich. He's practically a tycoon at Cox Chemical!"

Karyn took Jesse's comments personally and didn't like the implications.

She began to argue, raising her voice as she did. Jesse tried to calm her down, but the more he tried, the louder she became. Suddenly Jesse felt the other people eyeing them, and he walked away from her, heading for the exit.

"Where are you going?" Karyn called after him, not caring that she was creating a scene in the K-Mart.

"Hey, wait a minute!" Karyn shouted as she started after him. Jesse walked faster toward the exit. Karyn caught him outside in the parking lot.

"What am I missing? What are you trying to tell me?" she asked as she came alongside him.

"We can't afford all that stuff," he said resolutely. "Not if we're going to make it until we have some money coming in."

"It's not that much," she replied.

"Not to you, but it is to me. And now that we're on our own with no money coming in yet, it's a lot to the both of us." Karyn searched his eyes, trying to understand what he was trying to say.

"Karyn, look. I don't have unlimited money. I have twenty-two hundred dollars to last us until we get jobs. We have to eat, buy gas, and sleep somewhere. Even cheap motels aren't cheap, and I'm the one who has to pay for it. When you left Michigan, you left your dad and all his money there, too. All you have is me and what I have. Nothing more."

That's when Karyn understood what Jesse was saying.

"Money is a lot like air," Jesse said with a weak smile. "The less you have, the more important it becomes." Karyn had a blank look until his words sank in, then she laughed.

"Yeah," she said. "I guess I can see that. Okay, so show me what I can buy," she said with a smile and new understanding.

"We gotta keep it under a hundred bucks," Jesse said. "Tops."

"You know what you can get with a hundred bucks?" Karyn asked incredulously. "Squat! You don't get didley squat!" As much as she tried to understand what Jesse was telling her, suddenly she was getting angry again.

"You can get a couple pairs of jeans, just not the expensive ones. A couple tops, and some sandals, maybe. And get your underwear, too, but that's about it. After we get jobs, you can buy whatever you want. This will have to do until then."

Karyn again resented being so limited, but knew Jesse was probably right. He was a lot smarter about these things than she was and she knew it. A few weeks before she would have thrown a tantrum, but she was beginning to grow up fast. She swallowed her pride and nodded.

"Okay," she said quietly. "Let's get me some underwear for today and we can look for more clothes tomorrow." Twenty minutes later they left K-Mart with a couple sets of underwear and bras for her. That had taken a large chunk of the one-hundred-dollars Jesse had allowed. They hit the road again and continued traveling south.

That night they stayed in another cheap motel and made love for as long as they could before falling asleep, exhausted. The next morning, Karyn modeled her new bikini underwear for Jesse, but her clothes were damp again from washing them in the motel sink.

Chapter 9

Karyn and Jesse arrived in Miami, Florida, on May 29th. Karyn had managed to have at least one argument with Jesse each day since they left Michigan. Jesse had called Mike every night to talk about his problems in dealing with Karyn's emotional problems. Karyn was still wearing only her original set of clothes plus the new underwear. The motels, meals, and other travel costs had eaten up over $600 out of their total funds. Driving through Miami, Karyn asked Jesse about their finances.

"Well, we're doing better than before, but it's going pretty quickly," he said. "We have less than $1,900. That might last us three weeks if we really watch ourselves."

"Is there any place that has clothes cheaper?" she asked Jesse. "I don't mean just inexpensive. I mean real cheap." She was beginning to see that they did, indeed, have to budget their money. It was a new concept to her, having been raised in a household with few financial restrictions. However, she was desperate for new clothes and was ready to compromise. Jesse took another quick accounting of their limited cash and commented that they should find a Salvation Army Thrift Store.

"What's that?" Karyn asked. She had no idea what the Salvation Army was, let alone their thrift stores. Jesse, on the other hand, was familiar with them, having shopped there many times when his family was teetering on the edge of poverty.

Jesse found a Salvation Army Thrift Store. Karyn was concerned when she saw the store was in a rather seedy neighborhood. As they walked to the entrance, Karyn saw the racks of clothes in the window and was appalled. She stopped and stared through the gritty glass at the racks of nondescript clothing. Karyn turned to Jesse with tears streaming down her face.

"What do you think I am?" she demanded. "Why are you doing this to me? These clothes have been worn before by God-knows-who!"

"You said 'cheap' and this is as cheap as I know," Jesse replied, his temper finally starting to rise after all of Karyn's outbursts. He loved this girl, but the arguments and resulting tension were starting to take their toll. He wanted desperately to make their relationship work, but Karyn's constant outbursts, especially in public, were doing more damage than either one of them realized. In frustration, Jesse gave up. He dug into his pocket and counted out three hundred dollars. He handed it to her, saying, "Here. Buy what you want."

"What's this?" she asked sharply.

"It's three hundred bucks. Buy whatever you want with it."

"*In there?*" she asked in amazement. She looked at the money in her hands, knowing it wasn't a lot.

"I don't care where you go," he replied. "It's yours. Do what you want with it." She looked at the $300 and began to complain again. By this time, Jesse was tired of arguing with her every day. He pulled a $100 bill from the money he had left in his hand and handed the rest to Karyn, then walked back to the Camaro.

"Now what're you doing?" she demanded.

"I'm fed up with your 'rich girl' attitude," he said as he slid into the car and started the engine. "I can't afford you. I'm going back to Michigan."

Karyn went ballistic. She started to scream at him in the parking lot. He let her rant for a while, then drove away. Suddenly Karyn realized she had nothing but the money in her hand, which she knew from traveling the past few days, would not get her very far. More than that, she realized that she had pushed Jesse too far and he was leaving her.

"Jesse, stop!" she yelled. "*Stop!*" The Camaro continued toward the parking lot exit, where it stopped while waiting for an opening in the traffic. She sprinted to his car, yelling at him to wait for a minute, then jumped into the car.

"What the fuck do you think you're doing?" she bellowed angrily.

He looked at her and softly said, "I can't afford you. I'm not your daddy. I don't make a gazillion dollars a year so I can't buy you Gucci this and St. Laurent that. And I can't do this all by myself. I need some help. People have to work together to get anything done." Karyn looked into his eyes and it hit home that Jesse had been doing everything. Other than washing her clothes every evening, she'd not had to lift a finger. Jesse had done all the driving, they were living on Jesse's money, and he'd done all the planning and all the thinking. And sitting there in the car with him, with the man she loved, she realized for the first time that a couple has to work together. The lesson had finally hit home and it hurt. She knew she had been wrong, that she had been selfish.

"I'm sorry," she said. As she searched his eyes, it occurred to her that she could not recall ever saying she was sorry to anyone in her life before now. It was a lesson she needed to learn, and learn it she did.

Jesse looked at Karyn, as beautiful as ever. He felt the love he had for her, and remembered their passion of every evening and morning for the past few days. Jesse's heart melted.

"Okay," he said. "So what do we do now? Go look for clothes?"

"No," Karyn replied. "The clothes can wait another day. I think we need to find us some jobs." Jesse nodded in agreement.

"Let's get something to eat and then start looking," he said.

"Okay, but can we do something special?" Karyn asked.

"Like what?"

"Let's eat at a real restaurant instead of Burger King," she suggested, "And not one around here. This place is too creepy for me."

"Okay," he said with a smile. "We'll drive until we find a decent restaurant. That shouldn't be too hard."

In fifteen minutes, they had driven into a better class neighborhood. They spotted a nice-looking restaurant on a corner. A sign advertised luncheon specials for $9.99.

"How 'bout there?" Jesse asked, pointing to the restaurant.

"Yeah. It looks nice," Karyn replied as they pulled into the parking lot. The front of the restaurant was dark brick, had a sheltered entrance, and a sign that said valet parking was available during dinner hours

It was a nice restaurant and as Karyn and Jesse walked to the entrance in the hot Miami sun, she saw a small, neat sign in the window. "Help Wanted," it read. By the time Jesse and Karyn had finished eating, they had not only had lunch, but the manager had agreed to hire them both. They were to start the next afternoon.

Karyn and Jesse arrived at the restaurant an hour early the next day, both of them in good mood after a long, passionate lovemaking session followed by a quick snooze. Jesse had an understanding of how restaurants worked, but Karyn had never held a job in her life and was totally bewildered. During the training session, she argued with the maitre d' who was instructing them on how to wait tables. He tolerated her attitude only because she was so attractive.

It was the next day, Wednesday, before they were allowed to serve customers directly. Jesse was easy and comfortable with waiting tables, and functioned like he had done it for years. Karyn, on the other hand, resented people telling her what to do, especially the kitchen staff. She didn't feel they should tell her anything. Within twenty minutes, she had yelled at one of them. The chef intended to talk to the manager about this mouthy kid.

Out front, Marco, the manager, watched Jesse. Jesse was the best waiter he'd hired in years. He liked Jesse from the moment he met him and watching Jesse take orders and talking to the customers, he knew Jesse had all the right instincts. Jesse was performing for the benefit of his customers. He also noticed that the women especially liked the tall, muscular lad. After four hours of watching him, the manager pulled Jesse aside.

"Listen, kid," he said. "I want you to make a lot of money."

"That sounds good," Jesse replied. "How?"

"You know that woman you just served the coffee to?"

"Yeah. She seems like a nice lady," Jesse said, with a quick glance toward her.

"Well, you know, you turn her on," Marco said, with just the hint of a smirk.

"Well, I'm not interested in her," Jesse replied, glancing at the lady again.

"I'm not sayin' you are," Marco replied, "But you can use this to your advantage. The next time you go to the table, smile at her, but when you do, look her right in the eye. Make that smile as sincere as you can."

"Why?" Jesse asked, becoming more annoyed. "I don't want to pick her up."

"You're not gonna pick her up, kid," the manager said. "You're just gonna give 'er a thrill is all. You're gonna make her heart beat a little faster."

"Why do I want to do that?" Marco's insight was lost on Jesse.

"Because she'll give you a bigger tip. That's why."

"Because I smiled at her?"

"No, because you made her heart go pitty-pat," the manager said. "Go do it. Right now. You'll see!"

Jesse went to the lady with the coffee pot to refill her cup. He locked eyes with her and smiled, not once, but twice. He held the gaze for several seconds, then nodded and moved on. Ten minutes later he returned to the manager.

"Wow," he said. "She left me a ten-dollar tip!" Marco grinned at him.

"I didn't steer you wrong, now did I?" he said. "If you do that just five times a night, that's an extra fifty bucks in your pocket that Uncle Sam can't touch! You just listen to me, and I'll show you how to maximize this business. You just keep practicing that smile and you'll do all right here." Just then there was a commotion in the kitchen. Marco rolled his eyes and sighed, and headed for the kitchen.

In the kitchen, Karyn was arguing with another waitress. Karyn had mistakenly taken the lady's order and when she pointed that out to her, Karyn had exploded in anger.

"What's goin' on here?" Marco demanded as he strode in. Karyn began by cussing out the other lady.

"First, young lady," the manager began, "We don't cuss nowhere in this restaurant. That's our policy. We don't cuss. So what happened?"

The other waitress started to explain but Karyn cut her off and told her side of the story. Marco just shook his head.

"Look, if you got the wrong order, put it back and get your own," he said to Karyn. "It happens, but there's no reason to get so defensive about it. Now both of you get back to work!" he said as he turned to go back out front.

An hour later, Marco was watching Jesse again. Jesse carried the heavy trays with the ease and fluid motion of a big cat. His sense of balance permitted him to move quickly through the crowded dining room, tilting the trays perfectly. Since he was tall, Jesse could lift the trays over the heads of the other wait staff and keep moving. Jesse's smile was electric. Some shouting on the other side of the dining room interrupted his thoughts. This time Karyn was having an argument with one of the customers. The manager strode to the table. The steak was too rare, but Karyn had taken the complaint personally and was arguing with the customer about it.

"I'll take care of it," Marco said politely. "Karyn, please come with me." Karyn hesitated. "Come on," the manager said, more emphatically. "It's okay."

"No it's not!" Karyn replied. "You're just gonna yell at me!"

"No, I'm going to get this man another steak," Marco replied. Karyn began to argue, but Jesse showed up at her side.

"Karyn, just go with him," Jesse said. "He's a good guy. It'll be okay." Marco appreciated Jesse's help, but still assigned the table to another waiter and told Karyn to wait for him in the office. She sat in the office, stewing, until Marco arrived.

"Karyn," he said as he entered the kitchen office, "I've got a situation that I gotta deal with. Jesse's a great waiter. You seem to have a problem with some of our guests, but — and I emphasize this — I need you someplace else." He wanted to keep Jesse, but knew he had to placate Karyn before she got angry and walked out, taking Jesse with her.

"Here's what I got in mind," he said. "I need someone to run the dishwasher." Karyn came up out of her seat.

"Now hold on," he said, his hand up. "It's a raise. I'm givin' you a raise, 'cause kitchen help don't get no tips. You've been here less than two days and you're gettin' a raise already." Karyn's face softened, but she was still angry.

"So how 'bout it? You want the raise?"

"Yeah," she replied sullenly. "We need the money. I'll take it." Twenty minutes later, Karyn was working the dishwasher alone. It was mindless work that required practically no supervision, and she didn't have to deal with anyone on a direct basis except the busboys. Most of them didn't speak much English, so it was a workable situation.

Within thirty minutes after starting the job, Karyn was muttering to herself. She worked the dishwasher until after closing. She did the job well enough, but it was hot, wet, messy work.

Jesse, on the other hand, was doing very well. The people responded to him as though he was an old friend, which made his job easier, and the tips continued to pour in.

At closing time, Jesse found Karyn in the kitchen, finishing off the dishes. He helped her but she was complaining. Soon everybody was gone except Karyn, Jesse, and Marco. At almost one-thirty in the morning, Marco let them out the back door into the warm Miami night.

"I'm beat," Jesse said as they walked to the car.

"*You're* beat?" Karyn replied angrily. "You didn't do a million dishes tonight! And you didn't work in the heat. And I'm soaked! This job is awful! Tomorrow we go look for another one!"

"Why?" Jesse asked.

"Because this is terrible! I didn't know it was going to be like this when I took this job!"

"I think we ought to stay," Jesse countered. "I made a bundle in tips."

"How much?" Karyn asked. Jesse pulled a wad of bills from his pocket. Some change fell out with it and clinked across the dark pavement.

"I don't know. I haven't counted it yet, but there's gotta be more than enough to pay for our room and then some left over."

"Oh, damn!" Karyn harrumphed some more. "I forgot we still have to get a room for tonight. I'm not staying in the car again!"

"We'll get a room," Jesse assured her as they got into the car.

They drove around for over an hour before they found a Comfort Inn with vacancies.

"How long you stayin'?" the clerk asked as he tossed a dog-eared magazine aside.

"Tonight," Jesse replied.

"That'll be seventy-five dollars," the clerk said as be set the registration card on the counter.

"That's a little steep, isn't it?" Karyn asked.

"That's about the best price you'll find around Miami, especially this time of year," the clerk said. "I can cut you a break on the weekly rate."

"What's the weekly rate?" Jesse asked. The clerk eyed the pair and knew they were on a limited budget.

"About $375. I'll give you the AAA discount," the guy said.

"We'll take the one-night for now," Jesse said.

"If you want to make it a week, I'll take the night rate off the weekly price tomorrow." He smiled at Karyn. She smiled back, appreciating what he was doing for them.

Jesse counted out seventy-five dollars from his wad of tip money. There was still some tip money left, which was a comfort to both of them. While Karyn had some tip money in her pocket too, she didn't offer any of it to Jesse.

"How much of that tip money do you have left?" Karyn asked as they walked to the room.

"About fifteen dollars," Jesse replied.

"Wow! You made eighty dollars in tips just tonight?" she asked.

"Yeah. Marco told me how to work the customers for more tips," Jesse said with a smile. "He's really an okay dude." Karyn resented the fact that Marco had sided with the other waitress and didn't appreciate what the manager had done for Jesse.

Karyn bathed and washed her clothes in the sink again, as she had done for the past several nights. She didn't complain about it since she was getting used to it, but she wanted more clothes. Jesse showered and washed his clothes, too. It was nearly four o'clock in morning when they finally got to bed. They were too tired for making love and immediately fell fast asleep. It was about ten o'clock in the morning when the maid tapped on the door.

"Housekeeping," she called in a thick Spanish accent. "You stay tonight?" Jesse stumbled to the door, trying to shake the sleep from his mind.

"No. We'll be leaving," Jesse called through the door. "We got in late. We'll be out of here real soon!"

"*Esta bien,*" she answered. "I come back one hour."

"Yeah. Sure. That should be enough," he said and went to wake up Karyn. She had slept through the conversation.

"What?" she groaned as he gently shook her.

"Come on, baby. We have to pack and split," he said as he pulled the covers off her.

"Go away! I'm so tired," she said and curled back under the sheet. Jesse looked down at her, seeing her nude form under the sheet. His male juices were running hot again as he sat on her side of the bed and began running his hand along the curves of her body.

"Go away, I told you. I'm trying to sleep," she said, with irritation in her voice. Jesse continued to stroke her body as a smile grew on his face.

"I'm warning you just one more time," she said, but her voice was considerably softer now. Jesse continued to stroke her, gently reaching more intimate places.

"Or what?"

"Or I'll... I'll..." She shifted under the sheet.

"You'll what?" Jesse said as he reached a warm, moist spot.

"I'll rape you!" she shouted as she lunged up and grabbed him. They giggled and rolled over in the bed, teasing, touching, and kissing. They tumbled and writhed and felt all the passion two young lovers could feel. They plunged headlong into one another, pressing, pumping, and pulsing in their passion. They continued for most of the hour. Then it was a rush to gather their things and get out of the room before the maid returned.

Karyn was in a much better mood in the car after a bath, six hours of sleep, and some great sex. Jesse drove through the streets of Miami.

"Where're we going?" Karyn asked at last.

"Looking for another job," Jesse said.

"I'd like a new job," Karyn replied, "but I'd really like some new clothes first so I'll look good for interviews. Can we afford to take some money from the budget and get me some?" For the first time she had actually asked Jesse for the money rather than demanding it, a fact not lost on Jesse.

"Well, sure, if that's what you want," Jesse replied. "If I add what I took in tips last night, we have a hundred-and-eighty bucks in cash, plus our kitty of $1,400."

"I have twenty from tips, too," she said. "That's two hundred. Let's find a K-Mart."

"K-Mart?" Jesse asked.

"Sweetie, that's all we can afford right now," she replied. "It'll have to do." Jesse was pleasantly shocked by her complete change in attitude.

Like most young women, Karyn took a long time shopping for clothes. This time, she looked for the best bargains instead of the most expensive name brands. She spent the entire two hundred dollars, but got a week's supply of clothing. It was mid-afternoon by the time they left the K-Mart.

"Let's get something to eat and then go look for a job," Jesse said.

"Okay, but I think it's too late to look for another job right now," Karyn replied.

"So we don't work tonight?" Jesse asked.

"No, let's go back to the restaurant," Karyn replied. "One more night won't kill us. Besides, your tips were pretty good."

The evening went as well as could be expected. They were busy the entire night and it was one-thirty in the morning again when they left the back door of the restaurant.

"What a night," Jesse said. "I got even bigger tips tonight than I got last night."

"How much did you get tonight?" Karyn asked as she ran her hand up the back of her head and held her hair off the nape of her neck. She was hot, wet, and sticky from the dishwasher.

"About the same as last night, but I had fewer customers, so it's still a gain." Karyn did the math in her head. With his tips alone, Jesse was making almost twice as much as she was and it really rankled her because she was busting her chops for ten straight hours. She sighed a frustrated sigh at the thought of her working for $7.15 an hour, just two dollars over minimum wage.

"Where are we going to stay?" Jesse asked.

"We might as well go back to the same place we stayed last night," Karyn said. "We're too tired to go look for anything else this late at night." Jesse nodded in agreement.

* * * *

"You clean up first," Jesse offered as he closed the door. "Then let's get some sleep." Karyn nodded and plodded off to the bathroom. As the door shut, Jesse stepped out to the pay telephone at the corner of the parking lot. Mike was instantly awake when the telephone rang on his nightstand.

"Hey, Sport! How are you?" Mike cheerfully asked.

"We're doing okay," Jesse replied. "We just got off work. Karyn's in the shower so I decided to call you."

"You got work? Hey, that's good! You guys making ends meet?"

"If we don't get too extravagant," Jesse said. "Karyn likes the better things in life, but today she used some common sense for a change." Jesse explained to Mike about Karyn's expensive shopping habits, but how today she had willingly gone to K-Mart.

"Mike, we have a lot of arguments," Jesse said, "But it seems to be getting better."

"Yeah, I hope so, for your sake," Mike confirmed.

"Is this normal?" Jesse asked. "I mean, do people go through this all the time, or what?"

"You know Mom and Dad never argued," Mike said. "But they'd had a lot of years to sort out their differences. Maybe all you two need is time." Mike had never been married, so he wasn't sure how close relationships resolved the normal differences that exist between people. "Maybe if you give it some time, it'll work out, but don't sell yourself short."

"I don't understand," Jesse said. "Whattaya mean?"

"You shouldn't try so hard to make a relationship work that you end up losing your own identity," Mike explained. "Never do something that goes against what you know is right just because you like that person... or even if you love her, like you do Karyn. And you shouldn't let anyone do something to you that you know isn't right."

"I think I understand," Jesse said. "Incidentally, are the cops still hanging around the house?" he asked, changing the subject.

"Nope. It's like nothing ever happened. My guess is they know you're long gone and they're just as glad."

"That's good. I'd better let you go. I need to get some sleep."

"Yeah," Mike said. "Don't be afraid to call me any time."

"And Mike?" Jesse added, "Don't tell Dad where I am. I don't want him to have to lie to the cops."

"No problem, Sport. I won't," Mike confirmed, "At least until I know it's safe to tell him."

"And have I received anything from any colleges?"

"Nada," Mike said. "Zip. But I'll keep my eyes open and let you know as soon as they show up."

"Yeah. Thanks. I gotta go now," Jesse said.

"Talk to you later," Mike said and hung up. Jesse returned to the room just as the shower turned off.

Chapter 10

It had been five weeks since the kids bolted. In Michigan, Drake pushed himself further into his work, almost completely ignoring Connie. Connie was terribly worried and frustrated over the disappearance of their daughter, and as Drake began to shut her out of his life, she felt totally alone, which only made matters worse for her.

Drake's life revolved around Cox Chemical, Incorporated, a Fortune 500 company. Cox, a premier player in chemical production, supplied chemicals to various industries throughout the world, and was growing at a phenomenal rate, thanks to John Malcolm's aggressive business tactics. John Malcolm was the major stockholder and president of Cox Chemical, Inc., and Drake's boss. They had worked closely together for the past eighteen years and John treated Drake more like a son than an employee.

John was sixty-nine years old, and beginning to feel his age. When he was twenty-nine, against his family's recommendations, he had leveraged a buy-out of the failing Cox Chemical Company. He had spent the past forty years rebuilding Cox Chemical until it was now a financial powerhouse in the industry. John had no son of his own, and on that day, so long ago, when John interviewed Drake looking for a job, he saw him as filling the bill. Drake was bright and had an affable manner about him that exuded confidence, not to mention that he was tall and very good-looking. Drake was the type of young fellow that any man would be proud to call his son. There was an immediate bond between them, formed of mutual respect and admiration. John promoted Drake's growth in the company from the beginning. In the time Drake had been with Cox Chemical, he had been elevated every few years until he was now Executive Vice President and Chief Operating Officer, immediately below John Malcolm. There was something in Drake that John could identify with, something that put the pair of them on the same frequency. John and Drake could almost read each other's minds. John loved Drake so much that he had included Drake in his will. John planned to leave one-third of Cox Chemical to Drake in return for Drake's promise to always care for John's wife and daughter. John Malcolm knew something was wrong in Drake's home life for the past several weeks, even though Drake had said nothing. John gave it a couple of weeks to see if things might work themselves out, but it was apparent that the situation was getting worse.

On the first Friday of June, five weeks after the kids bolted, John finally asked Drake what the problem was. Drake hesitated, sighed and told John the whole story. Because of John's affection for Drake, he wanted to help. He invited Drake and Connie to join him and his wife, Anne Marie, for dinner that evening to talk about Drake's situation. Drake was pleased with the concern John showed about his problem. Drake called Connie at home to inform her about the dinner at John Malcolm's home.

"I don't want to be discussing personal family matters with the Malcolms, or anyone else," Connie told Drake on the telephone.

"John's like our own family," Drake countered, frustrated with Connie. "The Malcolms are the best friends we have."

"I know you and John are close," Connie said. "But Anne Marie and I have never been all that close, and I just don't feel comfortable talking to them about Karyn."

"Look, Connie," Drake said, growing irritated. "John has practically handed me the reins of the company and I frankly want to keep those feelings alive and healthy. I want you to go if for no other reason than it's good for my career. He sincerely wants to help and I welcome his interest in our family."

"I don't know how sincere he is."

"Connie!" Drake interrupted. "Just be ready at six! Just fucking do it and stop arguing with me!"

"Okay," she said dejectedly. "I'll be ready."

"That's better," Drake said. "I'll send a company car for you."

"You won't even be home to pick me up?" Connie asked, hurt that Drake wouldn't even pick her up himself.

"I don't have time," Drake replied. "You know I've been working a lot lately. Just be ready."

"Okay," she said. "Good-bye." Drake didn't wait for hear her good-bye. He'd already hung up. That evening, when John Malcolm got home, he told his wife, Anne Marie, that Drake was having some family problems.

"Oh, that's too bad," Anne said, but she was secretly pleased. She had harbored a lusty crush on Drake Mathers for several years. Anne Marie was fifteen years younger than John, and although she was in her fifties, she could pass for late thirties. She was five-feet-six-inches tall and had the shape of a model. Money and fine living helped her to stay firm and extremely stylish. She loved the life John provided for her and their daughter, Sandra. Early in her marriage to John, she was deeply in love with him, but the years of taking a back seat to John's company took their toll on their relationship. Anne Marie remained married to John only to keep the good life, but she wasn't faithful. Being in the right social circles, she met many of the movers and shakers of industry and entertainment throughout the country, especially New York and Hollywood. More than that, she had had affairs with a number of them. John was so wrapped up in running Cox Chemical that he never had a clue about her extra-marital activities. She always thought Drake Mathers was charming and handsome, and wanted to get "closer" to him. "Do you know what the problem is?" she asked.

"No, but I know Drake's worried about it," John replied.

Drake and Connie arrived at the Malcolm's home promptly at seven o'clock. Cocktails were served and they made small talk until dinner began precisely at eight. John and Anne Marie's daughter, Sandra, joined the group late. She was a twenty-three-year-old dark-haired beauty with a sensuous five-foot-eight-inch body that looked like pure sex. She always complemented her long, slim legs with short skirts bordering on the risqué. She had just completed two years of study in Paris and she was now back home, ostensibly to look for the right man. She had managed to avoid meeting him, although she avidly enjoyed the search. Like her mother, Sandra had had affairs with some of the same names as found in *People*. She took an instant liking to the very handsome Drake Mathers, whom she knew was the senior executive of her father's firm. She knew Drake was married, but that didn't stop her. It merely added to the challenge. More than that, she suspected her mother wanted Drake, too, and Sandra would do anything to upstage her mother.

As they finished dinner, John guided the conversation to the Mathers' family situation. Anne Marie was playing the role of dutiful wife to John, but she was secretly trying to figure out how to use this information to get next to Drake. However, Sandra also wanted to entice him into an affair. Although they were mother and daughter, the competition was keen, and it was already understood between them that the bragging rights went to the winner.

During the discussion, John offered to retain Huffmaster, a well-known detective agency, to find the kids. At first Drake refused the offer, but Connie realized that John was really genuine in wanting to help the Mathers family, and especially Drake.

"Why not hire detectives?" Connie asked Drake with a note of urgency in her voice. "What have we been able to do since Karyn left?"

"Not much, I admit," Drake replied. "But there has to be something else I can do!"

"And just what would that be?" John watched Drake for an answer.

"I don't know. But there must be something, I'm sure, I just haven't thought of —"

"Drake!" Connie interrupted. "They would be professionals! You're good at your job, but they would be pros at theirs. Why *can't* we use detectives?" Drake looked at Connie and wanted to scold her for questioning his decision. He never believed she could have any original thoughts that could help out. He needed to be in total control of his family at all times, but he always kept his true feelings in check in front of others.

"All right, John," Drake replied. "I accept the offer. And many thanks!"

"That's the man I know!" John said, now contented. "The Drake Mathers I know would use every means to make something happen. I'll get on it first thing tomorrow morning!"

"By the way, Drake," John added. "Have you talked to the boy's parents yet?"

"Hell, no!" Drake blurted out. Everyone blinked at the vehemence of his response since around the office he was the epitome of a gentleman. Even Connie was caught off guard by his sudden outburst in front of outsiders. "I wouldn't go to those hillbillies if my life depended on it!" Drake continued, shaking his head angrily.

"Drake," John said with concern in his voice, "They may be your best hope for finding Karyn. If they've heard from their son, you might be able to find out where Karyn is and bring her home."

"They have nothing I want," Drake replied.

"You don't want your daughter back?" Sandra asked. Drake looked at her. He had seen Sandra occasionally since he'd started working for John, but not in the past five years. From a distance, he'd watched her grow up from a knobby-kneed five-year-old to become the drop-dead gorgeous woman she now was. Drake had difficulty focusing on what Sandra had just said.

"Um, yeah. Oh, sure — I want my daughter back," Drake conceded.

"Then why not chance it?" John added. "You've nothing to lose and everything to gain."

"But those people are so — so — Well, you just can't talk to them on our level," Drake countered.

"But they might know something you don't," Anne Marie replied. "You can never tell. Isn't your daughter worth a try?" Drake now studied Anne. He knew she was fifty-four but she looked about the same age as Connie, his wife. However, she was elegant and refined, not like his wife who was so plain.

"Yeah, I guess she is," Drake answered. "I'll talk to them tomorrow."

By the time Drake and Connie left the Malcolms' house, they were both feeling better about their situation. That night they made love for the first time in weeks.

The next day, Saturday, Drake sent a lawyer to Willie Bob's house to arrange a meeting. The lawyer reported back to Drake in his office.

"He told me to get lost," the lawyer said.

"Who the hell does he think he is?" Drake practically shouted. "Doesn't he know who he's dealing with?" He waved the lawyer out of the office and picked up the telephone. Willie hung up on Drake, telling him that while he was resentful of all rich people, he particularly disliked Drake.

Drake decided to see Willie Bob in person. Slamming the office door behind him, Drake stormed down to the garage, jumped into his expensive, black Porsche and roared over to Willie Bob's house. Drake pounded on the door of the shabby house and looked around at the yard, seeing that it hadn't been cut in several weeks. Willie came to the door and peered at Drake through a worn screen.

"Who are you?" he asked, taking notice of Drake's expensive clothes and the shiny black Porsche in the driveway. Drake could smell the alcohol on Willie's breath as he spoke.

"I'm Drake Mathers and your son kidnapped my daughter."

"You the one who sent that lawyer earlier?" Willie asked, irritated.

Drake nodded.

"Go away!" Willie said and closed the wooden door in Drake's face. Drake began beating on the door.

"We have to talk!" Drake bellowed.

Willie opened the door just a crack and said, "I told you to vamoose! Git lost! Now beat it!" He again slammed the door in Drake's face again. Drake was not one to be put off and began fiercely pounding on the door again.

"What part of 'go away' don't you understand?" Willie yelled through the door. "Get off my property!"

"I'm Drake Mathers! I want to talk to you about my daughter!"

"I know who you are, but do you know who I am?"

Drake was caught off guard by Willie's response.

"I'm the guy who owns this house. Now get the fuck outta here!" Willie responded. "The next time I come to this door it'll be with a sawed-off shotgun!"

"You wouldn't dare!" Drake challenged.

"Just you try me, Mr. Big Shot Mathers! Your daughter took my son away from me and I don't like it one bit!"

"Your son kidnapped my daughter!" Drake shouted through the screen door.

"Your daughter stole my son!" Willie retorted. "I guess you could say it's a matter o' perspective! Either way," Willie continued, "we're both out a kid. Now get the hell offa my porch or I'll blow your balls off!" Drake thought for a moment.

"Hey, wait a minute," Drake said, his voice suddenly more civil. "You made a good point. You want your son back, and I want my daughter back. How about we work together?"

"I wouldn't work with the likes o' you if my life depended on it!" Willie drawled slowly.

"Would you work with me if your son's life depended on it?" Drake asked.

"Are you threatenin' my son?" Willie growled. "You plannin' on hurtin' him?"

"No! No, that's not what I mean!" Drake lied. In truth, Drake wanted to cause as much trouble for Jesse as he possibly could. "I mean, we both know it can't be good for the kids to be gone like this. Their lives would be better if they were with *us*, their parents. I'm sure your wife would agree."

"Ain't got a wife," Willie said dryly. He eyed Drake suspiciously.

"Divorced?" Drake asked.

"Dead, if'n it's any o' your business." Drake noticed that Willie's face had soured.

"Oh, sorry," Drake replied. "I didn't know." Actually, Drake couldn't care less that Willie's wife had died. He was interested only in getting any information he could from Willie that might lead him to his daughter and hopefully put Jesse in jail. "But that's all the more reason to find the kids. Your son has nobody left but you."

Willie thought about Drake's comment for a moment. Willie wanted his son back even though he knew Drake Mathers was a bullshitter.

"We'll work together?" Willie Bob finally asked.

"Absolutely," Drake replied, trying to convince Willie of his sincerity.

"You'll tell me everything you know?"

"And you'll tell me," Drake said, nodding his head. *This is going too easily*, Drake thought.

"Okay, I'll work with you," Willie said without enthusiasm. "I ain't heard from Jesse and I ain't seen hide nor hair of 'im. I don't know where he is, neither."

"What about his friends?" Drake asked. "Won't some of them know where he is?"

"Jesse ain't got many friends," Willie replied. "After his mom died and that year he missed school, he didn't socialize much. He's really a loner, but they did elect him Homecoming King," Willie said, a little pride in his voice. "I thought that might get 'im out some more." Drake had heard about the year Jesse missed school. He had heard that Jesse spent the year in jail.

"So what do *you* know, Mathers?" Willie asked. "I tol' you what I know, although it ain't much."

"Frankly, I don't know any more than you," Drake replied, shaking his head, trying to appear sincere to Willie. He really had no intention of telling Willie anything he learned about the kids. Although he wanted his daughter back, he especially wanted to put Willie's hillbilly kid in jail, and hopefully for a long time.

"Well, that's all I know," Willie said. "If'n I hear something, I'll let you know. How do I get ahold o' you?"

"Just call my office," Drake said as he produced his business card and held it out to Willie. Willie put it in his shirt pocket.

"Okay, I'll do that, and you let me know just as soon as you hear anything, okay?"

"Okay," Drake lied. Willie nodded, knowing full well that Drake was lying through his teeth. Drake left in the Porsche, Willie Bob watching from behind the screen door.

"What a sonofabitch!" Willie muttered to himself.

Chapter 11

On that same day, Jesse was serving two men who were having dinner in the restaurant. He noticed they were watching him closely. As he brought them the dessert menu he asked, "Is everything all right, sir?"

"Yes," the man replied. "Everything is fine." Jesse continued to hover over them. "What's wrong, young fellow?" one of the men asked.

"Well, I saw you were watching me pretty closely, and I was wondering if I did something wrong," Jesse said. "I always try to do my best, but if I messed something up, or I did something wrong, I'd like to know about it."

"No," the man said with a grin. "I run all the restaurants on board a cruise ship and I was just telling Jerry here that I'd like to have a waiter like you working for me. You're pretty dang good."

"On a cruise ship?" Jesse asked.

"Yes," the man said. "My name's Don Bingham and I run the ship's restaurants on a Radisson Seven Seas luxury cruise liner. You know, we're hiring right now. Think you might like a job?"

"Well, I'd have to check with my girlfriend, but it sounds pretty good," Jesse said.

"I can tell you the hours are murder, but the pay's a lot better than you get here, plus you get free room and board. Talk to your girlfriend and give me a call tomorrow."

"She's back in the kitchen," Jesse said, the excitement growing inside him. "I'll talk to her right now!"

"She works the kitchen?" Don asked. "We can use some kitchen help, too. How about we talk during your break?" Jesse went to Marco and told him about the conversation.

"I don't want to leave you in the lurch," Jesse said. "I'll turn them down right now if you have a problem with it."

Marco liked Jesse a lot and was honest. "Kid, you could stay here until you retire and even then it would be too soon for me," the manager said. "But I think this is an opportunity you shouldn't miss. The money should be good and you'll get to go places and see things you'd never see here. I'm glad for you." He smiled and held out his hand. "How soon do they need you to start?"

"I don't know," Jesse replied. "I've gotta talk to Karyn first." He disappeared into the back. Marco casually walked over and sat down with the two men and looked at them ruefully.

"You're taking my best worker, ya know," he said. "He'll work his ass off for you, then ask for more. If he ever decides to leave you, all I ask is that you send him back to me." They talked about Jesse and the restaurant business for a few more minutes while Jesse was in back.

Jesse told Karyn about the offer to work in the restaurant of a luxury cruise ship. She was thrilled with the idea. It never occurred to Karyn that she'd be working in the ship's galley, and she had no idea that it would be almost sixteen hours a day. They went over to the table where the three men were still talking.

"We'll take the jobs," Jesse said. Both men offered their hands to Jesse and to Marco. Jesse shook all three while he and Karyn smiled. "So when do we start?"

"You can start Friday," Don Bingham said. "You'll need to come by the ship tomorrow with your passports to sign on.

"Passports?" Karyn asked. "I don't have my passport."

"I've never had one," Jesse added. "How can we get them?"

"Not to worry," the man named Jerry said. "I'll go with you to the Federal Building tomorrow. If we can get your birth certificates along with your photographs, we should be able to get a pair of passports pretty quickly."

The second man turned out to be the ship's security officer, Jerry Doyle. The next day, with his help, copies of their birth certificates were confirmed at the Federal Building in Miami. Then they took passport photos and, while it took most of the day, their passports were finally obtained.

"I'm sure glad you were there to help us, Mr. Doyle," Jesse told the ship's security officer as they got into his car outside the Federal Building.

"Call me Jerry," the man said. "I owed Don a favor, and it got me off the ship for a few hours. I was glad to help." He studied Jesse and Karyn. "Normally, we wouldn't hire a seventeen-year-old, but since you're close to eighteen, we decided to give it a shot." Jerry had gone out on a limb for the pretty girl.

"Well, I'm out on my own now," Karyn said, a little indignation in her voice, "and it's not so easy."

"Yes, I know," Jerry replied. "You're what they call an 'emancipated minor.' You're completely on your own, living as an adult. Otherwise, we'd never have taken you on." He knew they should have her parents' signature to hire her, but he also knew they were running from something. He'd been in the business for years, and knew the signs. Karyn settled back onto the seat.

"'Emancipated minor'," she said. "I like the sound of that. But I was worried I couldn't get the passport since I was only seventeen," Karyn said, changing the subject.

"You were easier than Jesse since you already had one. It was just a matter of certifying that the other one was lost," Jerry told her. "Jesse, on the other hand, had to prove he was a citizen before he could get one."

They remembered the many telephone calls Jerry had made on his cell phone during the day, the trips to the fax machine, and the two trips back to the ship to coordinate the paperwork.

"I really appreciate your help on this," Jesse said.

"Yeah! Me, too!" Karyn added.

"It's all a part of my job," Jerry replied as he drove them to the ship.

"So when does the ship leave?" Karyn asked Jerry.

"We leave Miami in two days. You can stay aboard starting tonight." Karyn was pleased that they would be on the ship and out of the Comfort Inn.

"Where is the ship going?" she asked.

"Jamaica and the Bahamas," Jerry replied.

"Great! I love the Bahamas," Karyn cried. Jerry knew she wouldn't have much time to do any sightseeing in port, but said nothing.

From the ship, Karyn and Jesse went to the motel to get their things. Then they stopped at a used car lot to sell Jesse's Camaro. After some haggling, the dealer bought it for $6,000. He drove them to the docks in the Camaro. Jesse looked at it longingly for several minutes. It had been his one hobby, a labor of love to refurbish and maintain that car. It was like parting with a good friend. Finally, he shook the dealer's hand and walked toward the ship.

"Come on," he said to Karyn.

"Jesus!" she said. "You should've held out for more money!" she said as they boarded the ship.

"I got what I could," Jesse replied. "You never get as much from a dealer as you can selling it yourself. That's where they make their profit." They were on their way to Jerry Doyle's office.

"But you should've asked for more!"

"I did!" Jesse said. "I asked for ten thousand, but I knew he wouldn't go that high."

"Then you should've kept it," she said.

"And where would we put it? If we left it on the dock, it would probably have been stolen tonight and we'd be out the whole amount." He was becoming angry. "We have six thousand bucks that we didn't have two hours ago. Let's be happy with that."

"Well, I'm *not* happy about it. I think you could've gotten more and you didn't even try."

"I did so try," Jesse said. "That's a fair wholesale price for that car. Now let it go, Karyn. I don't want to talk about it any more."

* * * *

In Michigan, Drake was trying to use Willie Bob to find the kids. He invited Willie to the Mathers' home to talk, which turned out to be a bad move.

Willie arrived at the Mathers' home and parked his battered pickup truck on the circular driveway in front of the big, white, colonial-style house. Just as he pressed the door chimes, Drake Mathers opened the huge front door.

"Come in," he said with a slight scowl. "Let's talk." The foyer was almost as big as his living room at home. Willie looked at the floor, which was done in some sort of marble he'd never seen before, as were the walls, up to about shoulder height. A chair rail topped the marble and above that was some very strange-looking wallpaper that stretched to the vaulted ceiling. The furniture was obviously expensive, light wood, and attractive. Willie had never seen anything like this before and was very impressed.

Connie stepped around the corner to meet Willie Bob Waller, and saw an unshaven man wearing a White Sox baseball cap and faded jeans. His work boots were scuffed and had already left marks in the light green oriental rug on the foyer floor.

"Let's go into the den," Drake said curtly, waving toward a paneled opening on Willie's left.

"Drake," Connie began.

"Not now," Drake insisted curtly.

"*Drake*," Connie said again, more forcefully. "I don't want him in here. He looks dirty to me." Willie had stepped into the plush den and was studying his rich surroundings. His eyes blinked in amazement at the handsome furnishings.

"We need to talk to him," Drake whispered to her in the foyer.

"No. I don't want him here," she said, not realizing how loud she was, the edginess growing in her tone. Willie ignored her remarks. He peered with great interest at the 52-inch big-screen TV.

"Drake, get him out of here right now," she said, panic rising in her throat. "Look at him!" She was no longer making an effort to be quiet. "Just look at him!" she repeated.

"Connie! Be quiet!" Drake commanded.

"*Drake!*" she continued in a strident voice. "He's the reason! Look at him! He's... he's... an *animal!*" She motioned toward Willie as he walked toward her.

"*You're* the reason!" Connie cried out as Drake tried vainly to control her. He tried to pull Connie from the room but she broke his grip and charged at Willie.

"It's your fault! I can see that now! Look at you! You're — you're —" Drake caught up to Connie and wrestled her from the room while she still screamed at Willie. Willie Bob heard them arguing, shrugged his shoulders and figured the meeting was over before it even got started.

On the way down the driveway, Willie cussed to himself as he looked in the rearview mirror and shuddered at the splendid house. His thoughts turned to Jesse, who was out there somewhere with the spoiled Mathers' girl and was surely worried about his son.

* * * *

That evening, Mike called Willie Bob on the telephone.

"Hi, Dad," Mike said.

"Hey, Mike," Willie responded. "What's up?" Mike was pleased that Willie seemed to be stone cold sober. Willie had been thinking about Jesse.

"Not much," Mike replied. "I was just calling to see how you're doing."

"Doin' okay, I guess," Willie replied thoughtfully.

"Dad, what's wrong?" Mike asked, concerned.

"Aw, Mike," Willie said slowly, looking for the right words. "I jus' don't know how to say it."

"Say what?" Mike pressed for an answer. "What, Dad?" Mike repeated.

"Aw, Mike, didja ever feel like — like —" Then he paused. Mike waited in silence. "Didja ever feel like they was somthin' gone inside ya? Sorta missin'?"

"Like when Mom died?" Mike asked.

"Yeah. A lot like that. I didn't ever think I'd feel that way agin'" he said. He drew a deep breath. "You know, Mike, you're all I got now, not that it's so bad." Mike listened in silence. "I mean, now that Jesse's gone." Willie paused to regain control of his emotions as tears filled his eyes. "Now that Jesse's gone, you're all that's left." Willie Bob was finally letting some of his feelings out in the open for the first time. "You're a good boy," Willie went on. "I guess I ain't never told you that before, have I?"

"You've told me, Dad. Lots of times."

"No, I haven't. I was always proud o' you, though. You've been a good kid. I always thought o' you as my own son." The tears filled Willie's eyes again.

"You've always been my dad, too," Mike said. "I didn't really know my real dad, and I haven't missed him because you were always there for me."

"Mike, you're a stepson, and some people may not think that's so good, but you've been just about the proudest thing in my life. Why, when you went into the Marine Corps, I thought I'd bust 'cause I was so proud. You're a real man, that's for sure. Gawd, I was proud that day when your mom an' me was at your boot camp graduation! You were the best Marine there. An' when you won that award for bein' the best in your platoon... Well, that was the proudest day o' my life!" Willie paused, took two deep breaths, and then continued.

"Mike, I don't think I could love you more if you were my own flesh an' blood," Willie admitted. This was a huge step for Willie. He'd grown up in Appalachia, where men didn't admit their affection for other men, even sons.

"I've always loved you, too, Dad," Mike said softly.

"I don't think Jesse loves me any more," Willie said.

"Oh, Jesse loves you, Dad," Mike said.

"How can you be so sure?" Willie asked.

"Because he told me so a whole bunch of times," Mike insisted.

"When? It cain't have been recent!"

"Well, the last time was just a couple of nights ago," Mike replied.

"You heard from Jesse?" Willie asked, his voice suddenly excited.

"Yep. Every few days he gives me a call."

"Well, how's he doin'? Where is he? An' why ain't he called *me?*" The relief of knowing Jesse was all right caused Willie's spirits to soar.

"He hasn't called you because he's afraid the police will come by again and he didn't want you to have to lie to protect him," Mike explained.

"Well, I kin appreciate that. That's pretty smart. But then, I guess he's always been a smart kid," Willie said proudly.

"Dad, you don't have a clue," Mike told him. "Did you know he has almost straight As?"

"Straight As? How'd he do that?" Willie asked. "I didn't know he was that good!"

"Dad, he's more than good. He's got damn near a perfect record all through high school. He's really awesome!"

After a pause, Willie spoke. "Mike, I gotta ask you. Am I the real reason Jesse ran away?" Willie sat in silence while Mike carefully considered his answer.

"Well, Dad," Mike said hesitantly, "Let's just say your actions didn't make him want to stay." Willie thought about what Mike had just said.

"Go on," Willie said. "I'm listenin'."

"Dad, you haven't been very understanding. Jesse wants to go to college. He wants to get a football scholarship so he can get a college degree without it costing you any money, but you've always made him feel guilty about that. I know you don't have any use for college, but that's what Jesse wants. It's not about you, Dad. It's about Jesse. Besides, he promised Mom."

"He promised Rachel?"

"He sure did. She made him promise her that he'd go to college and make something good of himself. I was there when she asked him."

"Your mom wanted that?"

"More than life itself," Mike said. "She cried that she wouldn't live to see him graduate from college. She wanted Jesse to be the first Waller ever to get a college degree. She wanted him to be the best at everything he did, and, so far, he's doing it."

"I didn't know that." Willie said. "I didn't know it meant so much to her."

"Oh, it meant a lot, but she never mentioned it because she knew how you felt about those 'educated stuffed shirts,' as you call them. But Mom thought that was the best way for Jesse to be sure he wouldn't be a hillbilly forever."

"And you?" Willie Bob asked.

"I've been encouraging Jesse to do exactly what he promised Mom before she died." Willie's silence told Mike he was getting through. They were both silent while Mike's words echoed in Willie's head.

"I saw 'im play football a few times," Willie said softly, "but I never let him know I thought he was pretty durn good."

"You saw him?" Mike asked incredulously. "Playing football?"

"Yeah," Willie admitted shamefully. "When he was a sophomore, your Mom an' I went to a couple of his games. He was already playin' varsity then an' he was only a sophomore."

"Tell me more," Mike said.

"Well, when your Mom got sick, we didn't go no more. I never went agin 'cause I figgered if'n he did real good playin' football, he'd definitely be goin' t' college. I guess I was bein' narrow-minded."

"That's just my point, Dad. All those times you tried to slap some sense into him only drove him further away. You know how his girlfriend reacted to her father hitting her. Why do you think Jesse would be any different?"

"Naw, I guess not. I see your point," Willie confessed. "I was wrong, but I ain't like that Drake Mathers. I kin admit when I'm wrong. But Mike?"

"Yeah, Dad?"

"Mike, I followed purt'near ever single one o' his games in th' papers. I never told 'im cause I didn't want 'im t' know."

"Really, Dad?"

"Yep. I never said nuthin' 'cause I jus' didn't want 'im t' think playin' ball an' goin' t' college was more important than gittin' a job. You think I'll ever git the chance t' make it up to 'im?"

"Don't know, Dad," Mike replied. "All I can say is it's not just the cops he's running from."

"I kin see that now," Willie said. "It's the alcohol, ain't it? It's the booze that makes it so bad?"

"Well, that's not all of it," Mike replied. "It's also your attitude on education. It made Jesse feel guilty and he didn't want to hurt you." Mike paused. "And there's more."

"As if this ain't enough. What is it, then?"

"It's Mom," Mike replied, his voice as soft as possible.

"What about your mom?" Willie asked.

"You need to let her go, Dad. You need to admit she's gone and get on with your life."

"Yeah," Willie slowly drawled in his thick West Virginia accent. "I ain't done nobody no favors tryin' t' keep your mom alive," he said. " 'Specially Jesse. Mike, I gotta go."

"You okay, Dad?"

"Hell, no, I ain't okay!" he replied sternly.

"You'll be just fine, Dad, and remember that I'm here if you need me," Mike said softly. "Call any time, even three o'clock in the morning if you want."

"Yeah, an' guess what?" Willie said. "I'm here if'n you need me. Prob'ly for the first time since your mom died. An' if Jesse calls, tell 'im that I'm here for him, too."

Willie did a lot of growing up that night.

Chapter 12

Anne Marie Malcolm was an avid shopper. She enjoyed spending John's money nearly as much as he enjoyed making it. Fortunately for John, he was able to make it faster than she could spend it. Occasionally when she went on one of her shopping sprees, she would stop by John's office and entice him into going to one of the better restaurants for lunch where she would discuss some new gossip, then give him a little peck on his cheek and leave. However, since the night that the Malcolms had Drake and Connie over for dinner, Anne Marie had been coming by the office more frequently. After short visits with John, she would make a beeline for Drake's office.

The first time she visited Drake, Anne sauntered quietly into Drake's office and closed the door. He was on the telephone, his feet up on the bureau behind his desk, looking out the huge window as he talked. The window ran the entire length of the wall behind Drake's desk. It had white Venetian blinds that were raised almost to the top of the twelve-foot high windows. Drake liked to look out on the Cox factory complex while he talked. He finished talking and spun around in his burgundy leather chair to hang up the receiver. He almost froze as he saw Anne Marie leaning on his desk, her cleavage exposed.

She wore a black dress that gripped her lush female figure. She had a wispy, black scarf around her neck, pinned with an obviously expensive brooch to keep it located at the best vantage point. Drake stared at Anne, his mouth slightly agape. Anne Marie turned and sat on Drake's desk, resting her leg on the glass top.

"Hi, Drake," Anne Marie purred, her low, sexy voice, making his every nerve stand on end. "I just stopped by to see how you were doing. Is everything good?"

"Of course. I'm all right," he stammered. He stared at her exposed thigh as she sat on the edge of his desk, almost near enough to touch.

"I hope you don't mind that I stopped by," she said. "I was wondering how you and Connie are doing."

"Oh, well — we're hanging in there," Drake said.

"Well, I know problems like this can be a terrible burden on a relationship at home," Anne insinuated, shifting her body on Drake's desk. He had a full view of her well-formed breasts. His imagination was in high gear as he watched her moisten her lips with a quick, provocative motion of her tongue.

"I can't say I know what you're going through," she said. "But I'm a good listener, and maybe I can offer a different perspective." Drake chased further fantasies from his mind as he thought about his relationship with John.

"Thanks. We appreciate that. It means a lot to Connie and me," he said, struggling to regain control of himself. "I'm fine. We're fine."

"That's good," she said, and slid off the desk to stand up. "I was just thinking —" She turned and made direct eye contact with him. She got so close he could get wisps of her perfume. *Jesus,* Drake thought. *Is this woman really coming on to me or is it just my imagination?*

"You were thinking...?" Drake asked.

"Oh, yes," she said. "I wasn't sure you were listening." He was listening, but only barely. "I was thinking, maybe you and I *should* get to know each other better, since you and John are partners, and you have that business arrangement." She was referring to the fact that John had included Drake in his will in order to make sure Anne Marie and Sandra would be financially secure. Drake, almost mesmerized, continued to stare at her without a word.

"So you say Connie's taking this well?" Anne Marie continued, innocently prolonging the discussion.

"Well, not really," Drake confessed. "In fact, she's been a basket case."

"Oh? That's too bad," Anne replied. "Tell me about it."

Drake began to pour his heart out to Anne, although she didn't care in the least about what he felt or how things were going for Connie. All she cared about was that she was getting inside Drake's head and that brought them closer together. She watched Drake carefully and knew by the signs that he was hot for her body but was afraid of destroying his relationship with John.

Drake felt better after doing most of the talking for over forty minutes. It had felt good to let some of his emotions out. Then as Anne rose to leave, he thanked her for listening so well.

"I guess I really needed to talk to someone," he said.

"Oh, that's all right, darling," she said without missing a beat. "What are friends for?" She smiled and touched his cheek. "You'll be all right. John has some detectives working on this and it's all going to be okay, I'm sure." Anne smiled and blew him a kiss as she walked out of his office. He was absolutely sure his boss's wife was seducing him and didn't know how to handle it.

Anne smiled as she rode in the back of her chauffeured car on the way home. She had just taken the first step in having an affair with Drake, and she loved his state of utter confusion and obvious lust. She deliciously anticipated the conquest.

Two days later, Anne again showed up unannounced in Drake's office. He was pleased to see her and this time he showed it. Anne closed the door and moved toward Drake's large teak desk.

"I closed the door so the office staff won't hear," she explained. "They would just make gossip of it. You know how office help is."

"Yeah, I know what you mean," Drake said, nodding with a smile. "It's good to see you!" He stepped around the desk to shake her hand, but she took him in her arms and gave him a warm hug. He was surprised, but lingered there for several moments. It felt good to have a sensuous woman's body that close to his.

"Hugs are nice, aren't they?" she whispered into his ear, then stepped back. She had taken extra time dressing for him and she wanted him to get every detail. She was in a pale blue silk blouse with black velvet slacks that showed off every soft curve of her body. She wore a solid gold necklace that accented her creamy white neckline. Her earrings matched the necklace, as did her bracelet. He let his eyes wander the length of her body. *This is one sexy woman*, he thought as she moved away from him.

"Yeah. Hugs are good," he confirmed. "How've you been?" he asked.

"Well, actually, I came by here to se how *you've* been doing. Anything better with Connie?" she asked.

Drake's eyes dropped as he frowned. "No. If anything, it's getting worse."

"Oh, you poor dear," Anne replied. She wrapped her arms around him again and held him close. "You need some TLC," she purred. She was an expert at providing tender loving care. She leaned back while holding him with one arm and brushed his hair with her fingers. "As if Karyn running away weren't enough, someone has to dump more hurt on you." Her blue eyes glistened. Her lips were full and inviting, but she suddenly pushed away from him and walked to the window.

"Why do people do these things to the ones who love them the most?" she asked as she looked out the huge expanse of glass. "Your wife should be the most supportive person in your life, not someone who makes things more difficult." Suddenly she turned to face Drake, her figure backlit by the huge window behind her. "Okay, I see now. Karyn — and Connie, too. They're both part of the same problem." Anne Marie came back to sit in the leather chair next to Drake. He hadn't moved from the spot in front of his desk since she hugged him. She took his hand and continued to talk.

"I know I try to be there for all my friends, but especially John. He's older, you know, and sometimes he needs more support." Anne was lying. She never gave him any support, emotional or otherwise. She always played the part of dutiful and loving wife to perfection, but it was just a role. Not that it would matter since John's attention was focused on Cox Chemical. His family was a distant second. There was nothing else in his life. He rarely traveled, and what traveling he did was exclusively for business. He didn't particularly like the theater or even to shop for himself. All his energies went into the business.

Anne looked up at Drake. He stood there, six-feet two-inches tall, ruggedly handsome, with a few streaks of gray at his temples. Anne tried to understand why a man so handsome would have asked a woman as plain as Connie to marry him. The fact was, that when Drake asked her, he was twenty-one and honestly in love with her. It was his devotion to Cox Chemical that had taken its toll on their marriage. Besides, Connie hadn't grown with Drake. She could have enjoyed their money a lot more and made herself more attractive. She had put on some weight over the years as a housewife because her family was more important to her than her shape. Also, over the years, Drake had learned how to bully her into making the decisions he insisted on. They talked for almost an hour that day, and then Anne slipped out the back again.

The day after that, Drake was signing some papers when there was a tap on his office door. He looked up to see Sandra, John's daughter, standing in the open doorway.

"Am I interrupting anything?" she casually asked as she came in.

"Oh, no," he replied, "Not at all." He stood to greet her with a surprised look on his face.

"I was in to see Daddy and I thought I'd stop by to say hello," she said as she wandered over to the same chair her mother had sat in the day before. Her Obsession perfume filled the office with a heady fragrance that made Drake think of Connie when she was ten years younger. He studied this young lady as she settled into the chair. He noticed she wore a simple DK dress that emphasized every curve of her lithe but shapely body. It had two straps that left exposed a tattoo of a small red heart on her left shoulder. The dress went to just above the knee, and Drake was disappointed that it had no side slits. Her bare legs were wonderfully tanned, and on her feet were a pair of black sling back toeless shoes. Her toenails were painted some impossible shade of pink to match her fingernails. She had a golden anklet and a ring on one of her toes. Drake sat back down on his huge chair and racked his brain for something to say.

"Have you heard from Karyn yet?" she asked as she dug into her sling purse for a cigarette. "Oh, I'm sorry," she blurted. "You don't smoke!" She stuffed the cigarettes back into the purse. "So, have you heard from Karyn?"

"No. Not yet," Drake replied, wondering why this young woman was in his office. In the eighteen years he'd worked at Cox Chemical, he could remember only two times he'd seen Sandra in the office. She was usually away at school, and more recently, she had been in Paris. "No, we haven't heard from her," he repeated.

"That's too bad," Sandra replied. "I always call Daddy when I'm off somewhere." She did indeed call her father, which he appreciated. Sandra was like her mother in many ways, but she did love her father more than anyone else and made it a point to stay in touch with him. Besides, he paid the bills.

"She's probably all right," Sandra continued, "or the police would have called you. I think in this case, no news is good news."

Drake agreed, "Yes, you're probably right. I just wish she'd come home."

"I wish the same thing for you," Sandra said. "I know you and Connie must be worried sick." Sandra crossed, uncrossed, and re-crossed her legs. It seemed to Drake that every move she made had sexual connotations. Sandra exuded sex from every part of her being. Drake found himself uncomfortable watching her movements with so much intent. He looked at her dark hair. It was short and pert, curving over her ears and hooking back under them. It glowed with a hint of auburn in the light from the window, and perfectly framed her beautiful, angular face. This girl belonged on the cover of *Vanity Fair.*

"Sandra," Drake asked pleasantly. "To what do I owe this wonderful visit?"

"Oh, just to see how you were doing," she replied evenly. "Since the dinner at our house, I've been thinking about you and hoping things were better. Besides, I care about Daddy's executives, and I especially care about you." Drake just nodded, trying to determine if she was really on the make or what. *Wow,* he thought. *What a family of women!*

"Well, I'm glad to see you, and I thank you for your concern," he said, still not sure of her true motives.

"Listen, Drake," she said. "May I call you Drake?"

"Yes. Of course," he replied.

"I know Daddy's trying to find those two so he can put that boy in jail for all the aggravation he's caused you." Suddenly Drake felt a kindred spirit with Sandra. She'd said the right thing and she saw it in his eyes. She added seductively, "And if there's anything I can do to help, please let me know. That's *anything* at all, Drake," she continued, lowering her eyes for effect.

"I don't know what they'll do to him, but I want that kid to do some hard jail time," Drake said derisively.

"When a boy takes advantage of an innocent young girl like that, it does terrible emotional damage to her. She will need years to get over it!" Sandra said, leaning toward Drake. He watched her perfect breasts move as she talked.

"You have to — no, *we* have to make sure he never gets a chance to do something like this to anybody else ever again. Not only that, we have to make him an example to anyone else who is thinking about doing the same thing." She was talking with determination.

"You're damned straight!" Drake replied, nodding vigorously. "My whole aim is to catch this kid and make sure he can't do this again. He's messed with the wrong guy and I'm going to make him pay!"

"*Absolutely!*" Sandra said firmly. "And you should! This is your daughter, for crying out loud! But more than that, this is for every young girl in the world. They need to be protected from boys like this!" Drake completely identified with her remarks and couldn't have agreed more.

By the time Sandra left, Drake was in no condition to do any work. He was too angry and confused. He wanted to do more than just talk to Sandra. He wanted to see more of her. He sat looking out the big window and wondered what was going on with the Malcolm women. He'd never received so much attention from two beautiful women in such a short time in his life. He leaned back in his big leather chair and enjoyed the moment.

* * * *

Both Anne and Sandra continued to stop by the office on a regular basis. Anne stopped by two or three times a week, and Sandra was there at least once a week. After a few weeks of this, John made the comment one night at dinner that he'd never seen so much of them at the office. They each separately took the hint and began to go directly to Drake's office without seeing John first.

In the meantime, Drake had taken to confiding everything in Anne. He grew closer to her every time she stopped. While he enjoyed their talks, she endured them because it was all part of the game to her. She wanted Drake Mathers in bed!

Sandra, on the other hand, enticed Drake. He appreciated Anne Marie's visits, but he looked forward to Sandra's visits. Sometimes he even ached for them. While Anne was attractive, Sandra was young and absolutely, stunningly sexy. One time she came in wearing a baggy sweatshirt and jeans, but his imagination played on what was underneath and he grew huge and hard inside his pants. He didn't dare stand up from behind the desk that time for fear of embarrassing himself to death. He liked Anne, but he had a weakness for Sandra. One day, Anne called Drake on the telephone.

"Drake, darling," she said, "I'm in the area for a short while and wondered if you'd like to meet for lunch."

"Well, I'm kind of busy." he said, checking his watch.

"Oh, you poor dear," she said. "You're always so busy! I should tell John not to work you so hard! Can't you meet me? It's just for lunch. You *do* take lunch don't you?" Drake made a quick check of his calendar and found he had no meetings until three o'clock.

"Where do you want to meet?" he asked.

"How about that little bar just around the corner? You know, the one where they have —"

"I know the one," Drake interrupted. "I can be there in ten minutes. Is that okay?"

"That's fine," she said. "I'll see you there." Her car was already sitting in front of the bar when she placed the call to Drake. She told the driver that she was going to have lunch and that he should do the same, then go find a place to park nearby. He nodded, knowing her routine with all the men she'd had affairs with over the ten years he'd worked for John Malcolm.

* * * *

True to his word, in ten minutes Drake slid into the booth where Anne Marie sat. He gave her a quick peck on the cheek and smiled.

"This is a good idea," he said. "It got me out of the office for a while."

"I knew you needed a break, dear," she said sympathetically. "You work so hard every day. It's just not fair."

Drake nodded and thought of Connie and Karyn. Neither of them appreciated how hard he worked, and all for them, too.

"Well, I'm with you and that makes it all better," he said, patting her on the knee.

"So has anything improved at home?" Anne asked as she held up two fingers to the bartender, indicating she wanted two drinks. She rested her other hand on his leg.

"Not since you stopped by the office on Tuesday," he said. He began to react to her hand in his groin, but tried to appear nonchalant. "And I don't think they ever will," he continued. "Connie practically doesn't talk to me at all any more. Last night I don't think she said ten words to me.

"Just last night," he told Anne, "I mentioned that I wanted to find Karyn and put that damned hillbilly in jail. Connie just glared at me and said, '...if you feel that's the *right* thing to do...' The way she stressed the word 'right' told me she doesn't agree, but she never actually disagreed with me. You know what I mean?"

"Oh, that's just a manipulation trick she's using on you, darling," Anne replied. "She patronizes you while disagreeing. It's so infantile."

"Yeah, it's infantile," Drake agreed. The drinks arrived and he downed his right away. Anne nodded to the bartender and held up two fingers for two more drinks.

Drake complained about Connie through the afternoon. Anne badgered him about what he planned to do while she kept the drinks coming. Three o'clock came and went and no one in the office knew where Drake was.

It was close to four o'clock and Drake was still in the bar with Anne. He had removed his tie and jacket. He was drunk and complaining about Connie, Karyn, and Jesse.

"I'm tired," he finally said. "I'd like to take some time off, but I hate to go home any more."

"How about you go with me?" Anne offered. "I know a place where we can relax for a few hours." Drake peered at her. He was convinced Anne Marie was the best friend he had.

"Okay," he said. "Sounds good."

"Let's get you out of here," she said as she dialed her driver on her cell phone. Five minutes later the driver was stuffing a very inebriated Drake Mathers into the back seat of the car. Anne slid in next to him. "You know the place," Anne casually said to the driver.

"Yes, ma'am," he replied, nodding, as he drove away from the bar. Drake passed out.

Twenty minutes later, Drake's stuporous mind realized the car had stopped. He opened his eyes to see they were parked in front of a posh Hilton Hotel. Anne was coming out the door.

"We can rest here, darling," she said as she opened the door. The driver reached in and helped Drake climb out. Standing on wobbly legs, Drake wondered why they were there.

"Come on," she urged. The driver grabbed Drake by the arm and wordlessly muscled him through the lush and luxurious lobby straight to the elevators. Five minutes later, Drake was in a room on the ninth floor, lying on the bed. The driver had removed Drake's shoes and disappeared out the door.

"How are you feeling, darling?" Anne said as she caressed his head. "It seems you had a little too much to drink."

"I guess I did," he said. "I'm sorry I got so drunk."

"Oh, that's okay," she replied. "You just rest." She settled in next to him on the bed and cradled his head at her breast. She stroked his cheek and talked softly. Then she unbuttoned his shirt and began to rub his chest. He squirmed around so he could look at her. Anne was a good-looking woman, no doubt of that, but he'd never known her to look this good. She had the same blue eyes Sandra had, and her breasts were plush and alluring. He looked at her lips and wanted to touch them, to taste them, to have them pressed against his in passion. He shook his head and struggled out of the bed.

"Anne, what are you doing?" he asked. "What are we doing here?"

"We're here to rest," she replied innocently. "I got this room so you could rest all by yourself for once in your life. It's a chance for you to get away from it all." She stood up and faced him. *God, she looked good!* Drake hadn't had sex with Connie in weeks and now this wonderfully attractive woman stood in front of him like a movie star. She smiled and cocked her head to one side. "I take it you like what you see."

"Anne, you know I like you," Drake replied. "I always have, but I'm not so sure."

"Not so sure of what?" she asked. "Don't you like what you see?"

"Yeah, but —" His mind was hazy with the alcohol.

"Would you like to see more?"

"Anne —" He tried to shake off the alcohol-induced fog, but couldn't.

She slid her arm behind her and Drake heard the zipper as it moved down. He saw the dress loosen in front. She smiled and wriggled and the dress fell to the floor. She wore no bra; just brief panties. He stared at the woman before him. He knew she was fifty-four, but wow! What a fifty-four-year-old! *Her boobs!* he thought. He hadn't seen boobs like that since — Then he realized he'd *never* seen boobs like that.

"Jesus, Anne," he mumbled. She stepped to him, slid his shirt off and began to rub his chest. Then she hugged him, pressing her breasts firmly against his chest. She felt his reaction in his pants and backed up just enough to get to his belt. In a few more minutes they were in the king-sized bed, finding it wasn't big enough for everything they were doing.

It was nearly nine o'clock that evening when they walked out of the hotel lobby. Drake watched Anne's car disappear around the corner. He hailed a cab and rode back to the office, thinking about what he'd done. Drake felt guilty for having been unfaithful to Connie. He felt doubly guilty for betraying John. At the office he called Connie from work for the first time in weeks to apologize for working late. He promised to come home as soon as possible. As he drove home, his mind replayed the wild and passionate events of the afternoon. Although he felt guilty, he felt pretty good, too. It pleased him that someone as attractive as Anne wanted him, and he couldn't wait until their next date.

Chapter 13

Karyn and Jesse were in the middle of the Caribbean, working twelve hours a day. Jesse was waiting tables, and Karyn was still working in the kitchen and complaining, which irritated her coworkers.

Within a week of joining the crew, some of the waitresses began hitting on Jesse. One named Darlene was quite bold about it. She heard Karyn's constant complaining and figured Jesse had to be getting tired of it, so she made her move.

"Hey, when do you get off work?" Darlene asked casually as she and Jesse were picking up their orders.

"Same as always," Jesse replied without looking at her.

"And what time is that?" Darlene put her hand on the last plate that Jesse needed to pick up.

"Same as you," he said. "You know the schedule." He tried to take the plate but she wouldn't let go.

"Got any plans?" Darlene asked.

"What plans could we have on a ship?" he answered. "I'm tired and going to bed." He tugged at the plate. "Let go. My customers are waiting." He knew what she was doing.

"We're docking in an hour," Darlene said. "Why don't we go ashore and see the sights?" Jesse pulled the plate free from the woman's grip and walked quickly back into the dining area. Karyn had seen the entire episode from her station in the kitchen. She was jealous and came over to the pickup counter.

"Hey, bitch!" she said. "Leave him alone!"

"Mind your own business!" Darlene replied sharply.

"He *is* my business!" Karyn replied, "And if you know what's good for you you'll find someone else to hit on!" Several of the other staff were watching, and the waitress thought better of her actions. She gave Karyn a wry smile and walked away from her. That night after work, Jesse came out of the shower to see an angry Karyn.

"What were you doing with Darlene today?" she demanded.

"Nothing." He continued to dry his hair while Karyn glared at him.

"She wouldn't have come on to you unless you did something to encourage her!" Karyn challenged.

"I didn't do *anything*," Jesse replied. "Heck, I don't even know her last name!"

"You did or said something," Karyn replied, "otherwise she wouldn't have come on to you." She turned away from him, burning with jealousy.

"Karyn, I didn't do *anything*! Sometimes people hit on people. It happens. What's important is what I do, and I didn't do anything."

"You did something," she complained. "Women don't hit on men unless they're encouraged!"

"That's not true," Jesse replied, remembering the supermarket cashier. "Both sexes hit on both sexes." In another three minutes, they were embroiled in another of their almost daily arguments. Jesse couldn't seem to dodge these regular confrontations. After several minutes of trying to reason with Karyn, he left the room. She followed him, continuing the argument. Rather than be embarrassed in front of other people, he left the ship. Karyn watched him as he went ashore but didn't follow him. Once ashore, Jesse placed a collect call to Mike.

"Mike, I don't know what I'm doing wrong," he said.

"You may not be doing anything wrong, Sport," Mike told him. "Sometimes people have their own psychoses that neither you nor they can do anything about."

"What do you mean?" Jesse asked.

"Well, if I had to guess, I'd say Karyn's jealousy is based on insecurity," he said. "After years of not being able to measure up to her dad's demands, Karyn has become insecure," he explained. "She may mask it well, but the insecurity is still there and maybe she responds to it by acting out her anger on you. I think psychologists call it 'transference'."

"Well, that would explain it, but it doesn't make it any easier to live with," Jesse said. "This is getting old."

"Yeah, I bet it is," Mike said. "Just remember what I told you. Don't sell yourself short."

"I won't, Mike," Jesse said. "I'm getting tired of Karyn's temper, but you know, I like the work and we get to see a lot of cool places. And Mike, before I forget, have I received any letters?"

"Not from any colleges," Mike told him. "But I check every day. And the cops haven't been by, either. I think they've given up on you."

"That's good," Jesse said, "But I wish at least one of the colleges would write. Well, I'd better let you go. I don't need to run up your phone bill."

"Oh, that's okay. Listen, Dad's doing a lot better, too, so don't worry about him."

"Better than what?" Jesse asked.

"He's been sober now for almost two weeks."

"Sober? Are we talking about Willie Bob Waller here?" Jesse couldn't believe his ears.

"Yeah. No bull. I'm telling you, he's been straight as an arrow for almost two weeks."

"What happened?" Jesse laughed. "Did they stop making booze?"

"Nope, not at all. We talked about you," Mike told him. "He knows you left to dodge the cops, but now he also knows you left because of him. He's been doing a lot of growing up these past two weeks." Mike went on to tell Jesse how well Willie Bob was doing, and the fact that he and Mike were talking practically every night.

"You think this is a permanent change?" Jesse asked incredulously.

"Too soon to tell, Sport," Mike said, "But they say a journey of a thousand miles begins with one step."

"Yeah," Jesse replied. "But I'd like to know just who 'they' are and what makes them experts."

Mike laughed and said, "I just wanted you to know. You might want to give him a call sometime. I'd make it sooner rather than later. He would really appreciate that one helluva lot."

"Yeah. I might just do that," Jesse said. "It would be refreshing to talk to him sober sometime. Now if I can just get him to understand about me going to college."

"Done," Mike said. "He finally understands now and really hopes you get that scholarship."

"Who is this guy and what have you done with my dad?" Jesse joked again. "This doesn't sound like the William Robert Waller I knew!"

"Well, he's pretty different, I'll give you that," Mike said. "He even had those cars towed out of the yard and he's cleaning the place up. It's starting to look pretty good now."

"That does it!" Jesse said. "This isn't my dad. He wouldn't have parted with that old Cadillac for all the gold in Fort Knox!"

"It's gone," Mike confirmed. "It's history as of yesterday!" Jesse could only shake his head in disbelief.

"Now I'd like to come see him," Jesse said softly, reflecting on the good times they had when he was younger.

"He'd like that," Mike said. "He'd like that a lot. He thinks you're a man now, you know."

"Yeah. He told me." Jesse remembered feeling so grown up when his father said he was a man. Although Jesse didn't completely agree with Willie Bob's definitions of a man, he appreciated Willie's assessment nonetheless. "Hey, Mike. I gotta go or there'll be hell to pay when I get back to the room."

"Sure thing, Sport. Call me when you get a chance."

"Yeah. 'Bye for now!"

Jesse went straight back to the ship, pleased to have heard the news about Willie Bob. That was almost better than a scholarship.

He returned to the room to find Karyn sitting in the dark. He turned on the light and saw she had been crying. He knelt in front of her and put his hand on her knee. She didn't say anything but she wrapped her arms around him and pulled him close. Five minutes later they were in bed, making up with wonderful lovemaking.

* * * *

It was the second week of July when a sexy twenty-something college student made a blatant play for Jesse in the dining room. Darlene saw it happen and decided to drive a wedge between Jesse and Karyn.

"Wow! You should've seen Jesse!" she said as she sauntered into the kitchen, glancing at Karyn to be sure she heard it. "When that girl hit on him he was so sweet to her! He had her eating out of his hand! But she wanted more than his hand," she added snidely.

Karyn glared at her, but Darlene continued as though Karyn wasn't there. The rest of the kitchen crew knew what she was doing and was hoping to see Karyn lose it. They were hoping for an old-fashioned woman-to-woman, hair-pulling catfight, but Karyn was too angry with Jesse to do that. She merely glared at the waitress.

Darlene continued her diatribe, sparing none of the details about how attractive the woman was, nor how obvious her play for Jesse was. The only thing she left out of her account of the action was how deftly Jesse had deflected the woman's offer. That evening in their room, Karyn and Jesse had another fight. It was the worst one to date and Jesse was near the end of his rope with Karyn's temper. As the argument escalated, Jesse stalked out of their cabin to cool off. Karyn sat in the room, stewed for several minutes, and soon left the room, also. She walked the deck in the warm tropical evening. She paced from one end of the ship to the other, then back. She had walked the length of the ship three times when she spotted Jesse some distance away at the bow of the ship. The bow of luxury liners had become a popular spot for lovers since the movie *Titanic*. They all wanted to experience "flying" like Kate Winslet in the movie. Jesse was talking to a woman.

"No, I can't go with you," he said, but Karyn couldn't hear that. "I won't go anywhere with you. I already have someone in my life." The woman reached out to touch Jesse. He caught her hand and pushed it aside. When he let go of her hand, she reached right back to his chest. He took her hand and held it to keep her from touching him again.

Karyn knew that this was the woman who had hit on Jesse in the restaurant earlier because the description the waitress had given was so explicit. She was in a very short red sundress and sandals. The waitress didn't describe the woman's figure, but she was certainly more endowed than Karyn. All Karyn saw was this sexy redhead and Jesse was holding her hand.

Karyn could not hear Jesse refusing the slinky redhead with groping hands. Karyn watched for what seemed like an eternity, furious with Jesse.

A male passenger spotted Karyn. She was not in her ship's uniform so he figured she was a fellow passenger. He approached the lone, slim, long-legged blonde with sex on his mind.

"Hi," he said as he sidled up next to her. "Waiting for someone?" He followed her eyes to Jesse and the redhead. In an instant, he knew what was going on in Karyn's mind and set his plan in motion.

"No. Go away," she said, still watching Jesse.

"That's no way to treat a friend," he said. She turned to glare at him.

"You're not a friend," she snapped. "I don't know you and I don't want to know you. Just go away."

"And if I don't?" he asked.

"You'd better leave me alone." she said, and turned to look for Jesse again, but he and the redhead were gone.

"You look like a lady who has a lot on your mind," he said. "I'd guess it's man trouble." He had just put out the bait.

"How would you know, and why should I tell *you*?" she asked. He had her hooked now because all he had to do was keep her talking to him.

"That's what I thought," he said with a knowing nod of his head. "Man trouble. Why do men do the things they do to the important women in their lives?" He shook his head and looked over the water.

"Have you ever done bad things to a woman?" Karyn asked. He had just set the hook as surely as if he were landing a trout. All he had to do was reel her in.

"Yes, but I've learned not to do that any more. I'm Rick. How about we go some place and talk about it? I'd like to hear what's on your mind."

"I'm Karyn," she said.

Karyn was hurt and angry by what she'd seen between Jesse and the sexy redhead. This man seemed to be concerned about her and he apparently knew how to treat a woman. His attentions were flattering so she agreed to have a drink with him, more out of spite than anything. *After all*, she thought, *Jesse's having a fling*. The ocean liner had several bars, some more exclusive than others. Karyn was led to a VIP bar that was very private, reserved for only passengers that had suites. In two hours, the seventeen-year-old was fed more liquor and told more lies than ever before in her entire life. It was almost nine o'clock when Rick leaned over to a very drunk and disoriented Karyn and suggested they go get some fresh air.

"Yeah," she slurred. "Fresh air might be good." She could barely stand, so he helped her up. She leaned on him, staggering out of the bar with his arm supporting her.

Outside she tried to walk, but the deck seemed to be pitching. She looked up and saw the moon, and wondered why the ship would be rolling so much if there wasn't a storm.

"I need to sit down," she said, feeling nauseous.

"Come on," Rick said. "I know a quiet place where we can sit." She held onto him as he guided her into the ship and through the corridors. A few minutes later, she watched him unlock a door. She peered inside to see a rich and luxurious room. It had windows that looked out over the open sea.

"Is this another lounge?" she asked. "Is this for special passengers, too?"

"It's just for you," he said as he picked her up and carried her in. She didn't resist as he took her to the bed and gently laid her down on it. He lifted her legs onto the bed and untied her shoes. "Let's make you more comfortable," he said. She felt the shoes come off and heard them hit the floor.

Her head was reeling. She closed her eyes and felt the ship move beneath her. She felt like she was floating. Rick's voice was soft and gentle, and it seemed so near, but so far away. She felt him pull her up to a sitting position.

"You're such a nice guy," she murmured. It felt like he was rubbing her shoulders and arms. *That's nice*, she thought. *No one has ever done that before*. She opened her eyes and saw him drop something on the floor. *That looks like my top*, she thought. She fell back on the bed.

It wasn't until she felt her pants moving that she knew something was wrong. She opened her eyes again to see him pull off her panties and toss them aside.

"Uh — uh — " She tried to resist. "Stop. I can't — "

"It's okay," he replied. He stroked her breasts. *Where's my bra?* she wondered, but it felt good. He stroked and touched and caressed them. She felt her nipples rise. *Maybe it <u>is</u> okay*, she thought. *Jesse never did anything like this.*

Shortly, they were in the deep throes of sex. He was powerful and passionate, and he did things that felt so good, things that Jesse never did. They rolled and thrust and pushed. And it went on for so long. Jesse never went that long. He just kept going and going and it felt so good. *Jesse thinks he's so hot, going with that other broad! It serves him right for me to have Rick*, she thought. *He's got that other bitch, but I've got Rick. Jesse needs to be here to learn how to make love to a woman!* Her body responded like never before. She came over and over again.

Some time later, Karyn forced herself to consciousness. It was like she was having a dream. Part of it was a fairy tale, how she felt and how her body reacted, but part of it was a nightmare. She had been unfaithful to Jesse. Rick was lying next to her, awake, naked, and watching her. She looked at her own naked body and knew the dream had been real. She'd had sex with this man! She'd gotten drunk and had sex with him! She couldn't believe it, but she knew it was true.

"God! What was I thinking?" she lamented as she grabbed for her clothes. "Jesus help me — I've gotta get outta here!" Rick casually watched as she hurriedly and clumsily got dressed. She felt like she was going to throw up as her mind raced over the events of the evening. What had she done to herself? What had she done to *Jesse*?

It was after midnight when Karyn silently opened the door to their room. The light was on and Jesse sat on the bed, waiting for her.

"Where have you been?" he asked. "I've been worried about you."

"I had to work late in the kitchen," she said distantly. "Last minute stuff." She couldn't bring herself to look at him. She didn't feel good about Jesse because she still thought he had gone with the redheaded bimbo, although in fact, he hadn't. He'd looked for Karyn for hours, checking the kitchen regularly. He could only surmise that she'd been in someone's room.

As bad as she felt about Jesse, she felt even worse about herself. She was still drunk, and she'd given herself to another man. She felt cheap and dirty and headed for the shower. Jesse knew she was lying, but said nothing.

Chapter 14

It was two days later in Michigan, and Drake was still working late every night. Connie was very depressed and lonely and had lost a lot of weight. Since he was spending all his time at the office, Drake hadn't noticed.

By this time, Drake had been with Anne Marie twice more. His liaisons with Anne were exciting and refreshing. Anne knew sexual tricks that Connie had never dreamed of. However, Drake knew that even if Connie had been as sexually eager, he still would have preferred being with Anne. Along with that, Sandra was still coming by the office and he looked forward to seeing her. Sandra hadn't let the game stop by any means. She intended to show her mother up by taking Drake away from her, thereby winning the bragging rights. One day Sandra stopped by Drake's office and closed the door.

"Drake, I know you've been with my mother," she said without any emotion in her voice.

"Why, yes," Drake replied, trying to be as innocent as he could. "She stops in to see me once in a while. We even had lunch once."

"Don't bullshit me, Drake Mathers," Sandra said matter-of-factly. "I know you've been fucking her."

Suddenly, Drake's heart started pounding like a jackhammer. "Now — now wait — " he stammered. He was trying to think of something to say.

"Just shut up and listen," Sandra went on. "It's okay. Mom does this all the time." Drake stared at her, his mouth agape. "Oh, don't give me that shocked look," Sandra continued. "You didn't think you were the only one, did you? Hell, she's bedded down half the producers in Hollywood, and probably as many of the politicians in Washington! Let's just say she gets around — a lot!" Drake couldn't believe his ears. He honestly thought Anne had been true to John until she began her affair with him.

"Your mom's a good —"

"Lay!" Sandra interrupted. "You were going to say she's a good woman, but she's not. A good woman doesn't fuck around on her husband. She only stays with Daddy because she likes his money." Drake could only stare at Sandra. He couldn't believe his ears.

"What do you want from me?" he finally asked after several moments of silence.

"I'm glad you asked," she said. "I'll tell you what I want. I want you to stop seeing my mother. She may not love Daddy any more, but I do. I want you to leave her alone."

"That's all?" Drake asked.

"No. Instead of seeing her, I want you to be my lover." Drake nearly fell out of his chair. Here sat Sandra, the foxiest woman he'd ever laid eyes on, demanding that he start seeing her. Things couldn't get any better than this.

"You mean an affair?" he asked for confirmation.

"I'd prefer to call it a 'consenting adult relationship'," she replied. "You and me. Grown ups. Having real, live, grown-up fun." Drake's mind immediately pictured all the things he wanted to do with Sandra between the sheets. Finally, he regained control of himself.

"I don't think your mother's going to take this very well," he said. "She's used to getting her own way. I can't imagine she'll take this calmly."

"That's your problem, not mine," Sandra said, like she was in a business meeting. "But I'll tell you this: that problem is minor compared to the one you'll have if I have to tell Daddy about you and his wife." Drake knew that if John were to find out about him and Anne Marie, not only would his career be in the dumpster, but his entire life. John would cut him out of his will, Connie would probably leave him, and the story was sure to become public.

"So it's simple," Sandra went on. "Either you stop seeing Mom or I tell Daddy. I love Daddy and I want what's best for him." She did, indeed, love her father as much as she loved anyone, but it really wasn't John's best interests she was looking out for. She wanted to drag Drake away from her mother in a classic game of one-upmanship. She and her mother had competed for men before. Sometimes she won, sometimes her mother won, but the competition was always keen. However, never had they competed for someone so close to home. It was frightening and yet delicious, and for Sandra, it would be even more delicious to best her mother under these circumstances.

Drake was flattered that two attractive women wanted him, and although he was thrilled with the idea of having sex with Sandra, he didn't want to give up what he'd already known with Anne Marie. It was a delectable dilemma.

"So what do you have planned for this afternoon?" Sandra asked as casually as if she was asking what time it was.

"I can clear my calendar if something important comes up," he said with a silly grin. He was daydreaming again about what he was going to do with her.

Two minutes later Drake and Sandra slid out the back door of the office and drove away in her red BMW Z3 roadster. Later, Anne Marie stopped in to see Drake. She learned from George Peoples that Drake and Sandra went out the back door together an hour before. She wasn't happy with her daughter.

* * * *

The next morning, Anne awakened in the bed next to John's. Although they still shared the same bedroom, they'd had separate beds for years. John still occasionally had sex with Anne, but his stamina wasn't good. Anne never rejected him, but for over a decade, there had been no pleasure in it for her. John was sleeping, but his breathing was heavy and labored. She looked at the sixty-nine-year-old man with a mixture of contempt and pity. She resented him for putting his business ahead of her. She considered him a fool because he had made it so easy for her to have one affair after another over the years. Even so, she had loved this man so many years ago, and lived on his success. This was the father of her daughter, the man who had picked her up off the streets so many years ago. Sometimes she had regrets, but then her thoughts returned to Drake and the anger boiled inside her. He was playing her for a fool and she resented it.

It was mid-morning and Drake was sitting at his desk when Anne stalked in. She slammed the door behind her just to get his attention. It also got the attention of the entire office staff.

"You son of a bitch!" she shouted. Even her eyes were raging at him. Drake stared in shock.

"Anne, what's wrong?" he asked.

"You know exactly what's wrong, you cheating bastard!"

"Anne, pipe down! You're attracting attention." He waved his hand at her as he glanced out the window of his office to the desks and people in the main office. They were all staring at Anne and him.

"Don't you tell me to pipe down, you arrogant piece of shit!" She was pacing back and forth in front of his desk. More office personnel came to see what was going on.

"Anne, stop it!" he said more firmly, embarrassed that the employees were watching. In the main office, they couldn't hear the words, but Anne's muffled shouts and actions carried her emotions.

"You slimy bastard! You stay away from Sandra," she demanded. "You will never see her again!"

"Anne, I don't know what you're talking about," Drake lied.

"You know *exactly* what I'm talking about! You left with her yesterday at two o'clock! I know because I was here at three!"

"Yeah, but nothing happened," Drake said. His face showed that he was lying. They had, in fact, gone straight to her apartment and had some great sex.

"*Liar!*" Anne shouted and threw his pen and pencil set at him. By now, the entire office staff was watching through the window of Drake's office, trying to make out the words. Drake went to close the blinds.

"All right," he said, trying to take control of the situation. "That's enough! We're through! Get out of my office!"

"Get out of *your* office?" Anne said. "*Your* office? This is my husband's office and he just lets you use it! As his wife, it's more my office than it is yours!"

"Yeah, and what kind of a wife are you?" Drake challenged. "What kind of wife would screw her husband's best friend?"

Anne went red. "You slimy bastard! You *slimy bastard!* Look who's talking! His best friend! And you're married, too!"

"Get out of my office!" Drake demanded again. "We're through. Go ahead and tell John if you want. I may lose my job, but John will dump you like yesterday's trash!" Drake's words hit home in an instant. Anne knew Drake might be right. John loved Anne dearly, but would he keep her if he knew about her affair with Drake — or the others? She could lose the wonderful lifestyle she loved. Even so, Anne was not one to be put off so easily. She was used to getting her own way and she wasn't about to give up without a fight.

"Yes, you're right," she said, her voice lower. "But just how much are you willing to give up? Are you willing to give up your salary and bonuses just to get rid of me? Is it worth all that?" It was now Drake's turn to think because Anne had a point, too. Drake was rich and powerful because of John. It never occurred to him that it could be cut off one day. Drake loved his salary and bonuses, but, more than that, he loved the status and power that came with his position at Cox. If he lost his job that would all disappear. Anne had him over a barrel and he knew it, but he didn't know how to handle the situation between Sandra and her mother.

"Anne, look. I'm sorry. I didn't know she would — we would —" He was desperately trying to find the right words to tell her.

"Save it, you lying son of a bitch! I know my daughter and I know you. You fucked her and if you ever do it again, you can be sure I'll tell John so fast your balls will fall off! I may have problems, but they won't compare half to yours! You'll be out in the cold, my darling, without your nice cashmere coat to keep you warm!" Drake stared at her in silence for a moment, thinking about what she'd just said. He looked at her contritely.

"Okay. It won't happen again." But even as he said it, he was already trying to figure out a way to continue seeing Sandra without Anne finding out. After just the one time, he knew he preferred Sandra to Anne. Anne glared at him.

"It better hadn't!" she said, her voice calmer. "And incidentally, you be here at six tonight — or else."

Drake was in his office at six, as Anne Marie had instructed. A few minutes after the hour, Anne came through the door, dressed in a suggestive black dress. Her hair was perfect, her eyes were perfect, even her fingernails were perfect. He was entranced by what he saw, but after the fight earlier that day, he was afraid to move.

"Are you busy?" she asked. She moved slowly around his desk to stand beside him.

"No more than usual," he said. His heart was beating rapidly and his breathing was short. He didn't know what Anne Marie might do next.

"Good," she replied. "How about a break?" She spun his chair to face her and knelt to the floor. She began to run her hands on his legs, starting at his knees and slowly and deliberately working up. He felt himself responding to her touch.

Quite some time later, Drake left the office. He and Anne had had sex on the couch, in the chairs, and even on the desk. It took him twenty minutes to straighten the place up after she left. He was smiling as he finished. *Keeping Anne instead of Sandra might not be so bad,* he thought. *She's a lot more woman than I ever imagined.*

On his way home from work, he thought about Anne and Sandra, and occasionally, Connie, but Karyn was out of the picture. It was like he'd never had a daughter.

When he arrived at home, the house was totally dark except for a dim glow coming from the family room window. He figured maybe Connie had gone out and thought no more about it. He walked into the family room to see her sitting there beside a low lamp. He noticed that recently she didn't look so good, especially since she wore no makeup. Connie glanced up at him then looked away, deeply buried in her own thoughts.

"Is there anything for dinner?" he asked. Connie had no appetite and it hadn't occurred to her that Drake might be hungry when he got home.

"Sorry," she said. "I wasn't hungry. I'll fix you something." She rose and trod toward the kitchen. Drake's eyes followed her, wondering what was wrong. He was so self-centered that he hadn't realized that for several weeks, Connie had been severely depressed over losing their daughter. All he knew was that Connie had never been like this before. After having sex with a flashy, attractive woman, he was turned off by this older-looking woman.

"Never mind," he said. "I'll go out and get something myself." He wanted to get away from her as quickly as possible.

"I don't mind," Connie replied in a monotone. "I can get it."

"No," Drake said firmly. He didn't want this woman doing anything for him, least of all fixing food. He brushed past her in the hallway and out of the house. Connie stood in the dark hall for several minutes, trying to understand what was happening. At last, she climbed the stairs to her bedroom, sat on the bed and began to cry.

* * * *

Drake drove away in his Porsche, dialing Sandra's number on his cell phone before he'd cleared the driveway.

"I've got to see you," he said. "Something's come up."

"Well, you can't come here," she replied. "It's not a good time." She didn't tell him that she was lying naked next to a man. They agreed to meet in a small bar near Sandra's apartment. At the bar, Drake told her about the fight he had with Anne at the office.

"It was terrible," he said. "She was yelling and all the people were watching. You wouldn't believe what she did. She threatened to tell your dad about us."

"I told you to stop seeing her," Sandra demanded. "If you'd stopped, you wouldn't have gone through this."

"It's not that simple," Drake said. "She comes to the office. I can't tell her not to come to the office."

"You can and will," Sandra replied. "It's your office!"

"I told her that, but she said it was more hers than mine since she's married to your dad." Sandra could see there was more to the story and pushed the issue.

"You're not telling me everything," she said. "What else happened?"

"Nothing," Drake lied. His eyes said otherwise.

"You had sex with her, didn't you?" Sandra challenged, glaring at him. He looked away. "You did! You had sex with her again!" she said, louder.

"Quiet!" Drake said, afraid somebody would hear her in the bar.

"Don't tell me to be quiet," Sandra retorted, even more loudly. She enjoyed making Drake uncomfortable. "I told you to stay away from my mother and you had sex with her again!" Drake glanced around. Several people were looking at him and Sandra, listening to every word.

"Let's get out of here," Drake said, embarrassed. "Let's go someplace where we can talk more privately." He was hoping to go to her apartment.

"Let's not," she said. "Let's get this sorted out and finished now." The people nearby were eagerly listening in. Drake didn't know what to do.

"Sandra, I don't want to talk about it here. There are too many nosy people." Sandra looked around.

"Fuck them. I don't care about them. I just want you to stop seeing my mother!"

"All right!" Drake conceded just to shut her up. "I'll stop. I tried to stop today, but it didn't work out too well."

"You didn't try hard enough," Sandra countered. "You got into her pants. That's not trying hard enough!"

"All right, all right, all right!" Drake said, seeing that even the bartender was beginning to enjoy their conversation. "It's over. It's done. Now, can we go?"

"Where do you want to go?" Sandra asked. "I told you we can't go to my place."

"Anywhere. Just out of here." Sandra enjoyed being in control. She enjoyed watching Drake squirm while strangers listened to the intimate and embarrassing conversation. She was a fox and she knew it. She knew every guy in the place noticed her and was listening to everything she said, just because she was so attractive. She used that to control Drake.

"Okay, let's leave," she said after he'd squirmed enough to suit her. She led him out to the parking lot.

The summer night was warm, the humidity high. The bugs were flocking around the sodium vapor lamps. A convertible sped by in the night, the top down, radio blaring, as they walked to Drake's Porsche. The Porsche was parked in the end slot, furthest from the door of the bar. She faced Drake, holding eye contact with him.

"Are you going to see my mother any more?" she asked, sounding almost like a little girl asking for a favor. She smiled and fluttered her eyes as she ran her forefinger into the placket of his shirt.

"No. I told you that."

"You promise?"

"Yes, I promise," Drake said.

"Good," she said, smiling for the first time since she walked into the bar. She slid her arms around his neck, stood on her toes and kissed him. She pressed her breasts extra hard into his chest. He returned her kiss and pulled her as close as he could. She responded by slipping her tongue into his mouth and probing deeper than he ever thought possible. They had sex in the hot, sticky, cramped leather passenger seat of Drake's Porsche. For the next hour and a half, Drake had the most exciting sex he'd ever had in his life.

Chapter 15

John Malcolm's secretary spoke to him on the intercom.

"The call you've been waiting for has come in," she said. "Line two."

"Thank you, Irene," John replied as he punched the button for line two and pushed the speakerphone button.

"Mr. Malcolm, this is Bruce with Huffmaster Associates." Huffmaster was a full-service security and detective agency that John had used for years. He had called them to find Karyn Mathers and her boyfriend.

"Hello, Bruce," John said. "It's good to hear from you. Tell me, what have you learned?"

"Well, sir, they didn't leave many traces behind. These kids don't have credit cards or checking accounts. It can be difficult tracking someone who deals in cash only."

"Bruce, I don't care about that," John said. He was a businessman and dealt in facts. He wanted results, not excuses. "I know you guys do a good job. What do we know?"

"Well, we traced them to Miami. They apparently worked there in a small upscale restaurant for a few days. The manager said he hated to lose Jesse Waller. Said he was the best waiter he'd hired in years." John took that information as good news. John appreciated anyone who was good at his job and willing to work, although he thought it was odd that such a boy would kidnap a teenage girl.

"Go on," John said.

"Well, Mr. Malcolm, after just the few days, they got a job on a cruise ship. You know, a luxury liner."

"Which one?" John asked.

"That's the hard part," Bruce said. "The manager didn't know which one. They just took the job and left. He didn't know which ship, or even which cruise line. We've checked with all the companies that dock in Miami and none of them will release any personal information about their employees." The truth was, Marco had become suspicious while talking to the Huffmaster investigator. He asked why they wanted to find Karyn, and they told him that Jesse was under investigation for kidnapping Karyn. Marco knew that wasn't true. He knew if it were really a kidnapping, it would be the FBI looking for Jesse, not a private investigating firm like Huffmaster. Marco liked Jesse and decided to "forget" everything he knew.

"Anyway," Bruce went on. "We know they were in Miami, and in good shape, for the most part. We learned there were some marks on the girl's face, which brings me to a significant point. Did you know her father hit her, and that's one of the reasons she left home?" John couldn't believe what he heard.

"Oh, you're wrong," John said. "It was the boy who hit her. He's known to be violent. Why, he hit Drake Mathers and knocked him out cold."

"Yes, we know about that, too, Mr. Malcolm," Bruce said. "We pulled the police report. But the boy's father, a Mr. William Robert Waller, told us that it was her father that hit the girl, several times, in fact."

"That's impossible!" John countered. "I've known Drake for years. He's not that way."

"Well, we talked to the hospital staff, and they all said that's what the girl told all of them, too, that her father hit her repeatedly. Her story was consistent. We even talked to the doctor who was in charge. He personally examined her and felt she was telling the truth based on the relationship he saw between the two kids."

"That just can't be," John said. He was having a difficult time believing the detective. "I've known Drake Mathers for years and this doesn't make sense."

"Mr. Malcolm, I've worked for you for years, and I know you're probably disappointed from what I've told you, but let's look at the facts. Kids don't run away from home for no reason. They always feel there is no alternative when they bolt. I grant you that sometimes they run for foolish reasons, like Dad won't let them start wearing makeup at age twelve, but most of the time, there's a major problem in the family."

"Well, why would the Waller boy run?" John asked.

"His father is an alcoholic and tends to get violent when he's drunk," Bruce told him. "He admitted that himself."

"So the Waller boy had a reason to run away from home, too," John said.

"That's right, sir," Bruce confirmed. "It seems the Waller boy's mother died a little over two years ago from cancer. He's been a little backward socially ever since, probably grieving, until the Mathers girl walked into his life."

"You make it sound like a movie romance," John huffed.

"It's a lot more complicated than that," Bruce said. "I think we have two kids who were in bad situations at home, who both decided to run away to find a better life. We see it all the time." John was still having difficulty believing Drake would ever raise his hand against anyone, especially his daughter.

"Well, I still think you're missing the boat," John said. "You know the Waller boy is an ex-con."

"We heard that, Mr. Malcolm, and checked it out, of course. Well, the problem was, he wasn't in jail."

"Not in jail?" John asked.

"Not in jail," Bruce confirmed. "That boy hasn't even had a parking ticket. Mr. Malcolm, I don't know how to say this without making you angry, but you know I have a daughter myself, and I'd rather she was dating this Jesse Waller than some of the animals she's brought home."

"I don't believe I'm hearing this!" John said.

"Well, we heard he'd been in jail, but it turns out that he was sick with a recurrent case of mono for a year after his mom died. He's never even seen the inside of a police station. Not only that, he had better than a three-point-eight grade point until they bolted. He was going to graduate in the top three percent of his class. Plus, he's been nominated as an All-State football player two years in a row, and the school counselor told us he's looking for a four-year scholarship to college. This kid's a real surprise."

"I just can't believe this," John said.

"It'll all be in my report," Bruce said. "I can back up everything with hard proof."

"Okay, Bruce," John said. "I'll wait for your report. And thanks. Send me the bill."

"Yes, sir," Bruce replied. "At least the kids are safe for now. Not much can happen to them on board a ship in the middle of the ocean."

"Yes, I believe you're right about that," John agreed. "I'll let the girl's parents know. Thanks again, Bruce." They hung up, but John didn't call Drake into his office. He had to digest what he'd heard first. After some thought, he decided to call Connie instead.

The telephone in the Mathers home rang several times before Connie forced herself into the kitchen to answer it. She'd been upset all morning, not only about Karyn, but also because of the way Drake had been treating her lately.

"Hello?" she said in a low voice, heavy with emotion.

"Connie? It's me, John Malcolm. I just heard from the detective agency about the kids." Instantly, Connie felt better.

"John! Oh, John, what did they say?"

"Well, the last we know, they were in Miami and doing fine. They'd found jobs in a restaurant."

"Oh, John, that's great! Can we go get Karyn right away? Tonight? We can be on a plane in a few hours!"

"Well, it's not that easy," he said. "But the news is good because they left the restaurant for jobs on a luxury liner."

"Why is that such good news?" Connie demanded. "Now they're going even farther away! They could be anyplace by now!"

"Connie, take it easy," John said. "There's not much that can happen on a ship. They'll be working almost all the time and there's no place to go. I believe it's good news."

"John, that's awful! They could end up anyplace. Ships go everywhere!" She began to moan and her sobs upset John. He was great at manipulating people, but he had no experience dealing with a sobbing, hysterical woman. He didn't know what to do.

"Connie, I thought that would be good news," John said softly. "I guess it's not. I'm sorry I upset you." Connie hung up without a word of good-bye. She wandered aimlessly through the house, sobbing uncontrollably. Her grief and anger were more than she could bear. She wanted Drake to come home to comfort her, but he'd only been growing more distant. Her parents were gone and she had no siblings. She had no one to turn to now. She felt totally alone and collapsed on the family room carpet, weeping bitter tears.

* * * *

Connie Mathers had always been quiet and demure in high school and college, someone who was always in the background, never up front. She had never taken a strong stand on anything and never rocked the boat. She always chose to go with the flow, to bend with the wind. However, after an hour of bitter tears, something began to happen inside her. Indeed, she was angry with Drake, but what about Jesse? What about the Wallers? Who were they to destroy her life and get away with it? The anger was starting to rise up inside her. Her jaws were clenched so tightly they ached.

"The Wallers," she muttered to herself. "*The Wallers!*" she cried. "Just who are they to do this to me?" She dug out the telephone book and looked up the number for William Robert Waller. She was going to give Willie Bob Waller hell for raising such an awful son. Mike happened to be at Willie's house when the telephone on the kitchen wall warbled its electronic tone.

"Hello?" Mike said as he answered the telephone.

"You piece of shit!" Connie screamed, thinking she was talking to Willie. She proceeded to yell at him, venting frustration and rage. She told him what she thought of him, Jesse, and his efforts as a father. She let him know that her life was disintegrating, that she was alone and lost, and that it was all his fault. Finally, exhausted after having vented for several minutes, she became quiet.

"You must be Connie Mathers," Mike calmly said.

"That's right!" she practically roared back. "I hope you're happy!"

"My name is Mike Andrews."

"You're not Willie Bob Waller?" she asked, suddenly very sheepish.

"I get the feeling you're not entirely pleased with him," Mike said, deliberately trying to keep her calm.

"You weren't meant to hear... I mean... I didn't mean to..." Connie stammered with embarrassment.

"Hey, it's okay," Mike said in his usual, calm manner. "I understand. I also understand you don't know Jesse very well."

"I know him well enough," she shot back. "He took my daughter away."

"How did he take her?" Mike asked, hoping to get Connie to think about what had happened.

"He took her. That's all," Connie replied, her anger growing again. "She's gone and it's his fault."

"Did he tie her up?" Mike asked. "Did he hit her over the head and drag her off?"

"No, of course not," Connie replied in frustration. "He just — just took her. That's all."

"You mean she didn't run away?" Mike asked. "You mean he forced her to go?"

"No, he didn't force her. He *took* her!" Connie's temper was growing again.

"I need to get this clear in my mind," Mike said using his calm voice to its fullest potential. "What I'm hearing is that Jesse forced Karyn to go with him."

"No! I told you that," Connie said, almost shouting. "What are you trying to do?"

"I'm trying to get this clear in my mind," Mike repeated calmly. His voice was low and Connie found it a little comforting, in spite of the situation. "I haven't heard your side of this story and I'm trying to make sure I understand it. You say he took her, but he didn't force her to go. How is that possible? How can that happen?"

"He didn't *force* her —" Connie began.

"So she left of her own free will," Mike interrupted.

"Yes, but he made her!" Connie said.

"Then he forced her," Mike said.

"*No!*" Connie cried. "He didn't force her! He took her! He *took* her!" Connie couldn't understand why Mike seemed so confused. It was all so clear to her.

"Mrs. Mathers, I'm wondering if it's possible that Karyn wanted to run away."

"Of course she wanted to run away," Connie said, remembering that Karyn had said she needed to get out of there before Drake killed her. "She felt like she had to leave."

"Why?" Mike asked.

"Because she was afraid."

"Of what?"

Connie was silent.

"Of what, Mrs. Mathers?" Mike asked again, more insistently.

"Her father," Connie said quietly.

"Isn't it true that her father hit her?" Mike asked. "Repeatedly?"

"Yes," Connie said, her voice quieter.

"And you were there. You saw it, didn't you?" Mike said.

"Yes." Connie's voice was even quieter.

"And you didn't do anything to stop it, did you?" Mike asked. He listened to the silence for a long time.

"No. I didn't," Connie finally answered. Her voice was barely audible, and she knew by doing nothing, she was partly responsible for losing her daughter. "I'm sorry," she said. "I shouldn't have bothered you."

"Well, I'm glad you did," Mike said. "Do you know Jesse?"

"Yes," Connie replied.

"How well?" Mike asked.

"Pretty well," Connie told him.

"How many times have you spoken to him?" Mike asked.

"Oh, I don't know. Quite a few," she said and then she stopped. "No, maybe four or five times." She thought again. "No, wait. I've spoken to him once. It was in the supermarket last fall."

"You've talked to him once in a supermarket and you know him?"

"Well, I know all about him," she countered, growing defensive again.

"What do you know?"

"Well, I know for a fact that he spent a year in jail!"

"No, he didn't."

"I know for a fact he *did*," she retorted.

"No, he was sick with mono," Mike said. "He had mononucleosis. He missed a year of school because of it. But because he grew up on the wrong side of town, the kids just assumed that he must've been busted and spent that time in jail. But he was just sick and that was all just a nasty rumor."

"I don't believe you," she said indignantly.

"Oh, I'm telling you like it is," Mike replied, "And I can prove it. Do you know about his grades?"

"What about his grades?" Connie asked. Mike almost chortled as he began to brag about his kid brother. He spent another half hour telling Connie all about Jesse and his super grade point average. He told her about his athletic ability. He told Connie that his mother had died, and that Jesse had promised her that he would go to college and make something of himself. Then he explained to her about Willie Bob. He spared no details, being honest about Willie Bob's philosophies of life, his drinking, and his violence. That's when Connie interrupted.

"That's the common ground, isn't it?" she asked.

"Common ground?" Mike asked.

"Yes. Between Karyn and Jesse. It's the violence from their fathers, isn't it?"

"I suppose so," Mike said. "Anyway, odds are Karyn would have run away anyway, even if Jesse decided not to." Mike's calm logic had forced Connie to settle down and think more rationally.

"Yes, you're probably right," Connie finally conceded. "She said she was going to run away before she went to Jesse that night."

"And since she did, I think she's better off being with someone like Jesse than with anyone else I can think of, or, worse yet, on her own." Connie wasn't totally convinced of that, but Mike made it sound better that she was with Jesse.

"Maybe you're right," she said. "I just don't know."

"Look, Mrs. Mathers," Mike said. "They're gone, and gone together. There's nothing any of us can do about it right now. They're doing okay. They have jobs and they're making ends meet. They're healthy and staying out of trouble. Maybe we should count the small blessings."

"Maybe you're right," Connie said. "Thanks for talking to me, Mike. I really appreciate it since no one else has talked to me through any of this.

And I'm sorry I blew up at you. It wasn't meant for you anyway. It was meant for that slob, Willie."

"He may be a slob, but he's at least part of the reason Jesse is as remarkable as he is. I didn't raise Jesse, but I hope that when I do raise a son, I can do as well as Dad did, even with all his faults."

"Dad?" she asked. "I thought you said your name was Mike Andrews."

"Willie's my step-father, but the only dad I've known. He raised Jesse and me. He's really a good guy under all that rough exterior."

"I'm sorry," Connie repeated.

"Don't worry about it," Mike said. "He *is* a slob, but that seems to be changing. When Jesse and Karyn ran away it seems to have been a wake-up call for everybody."

"It seems so," Connie said. She was still confused. How could a slob like Willie Waller raise a boy with Jesse's credentials? And this Mike Andrews seemed to be the perfect gentleman on the telephone. "I have to go," Connie suddenly said. "I have some thinking to do."

"Okay," Mike said. "Call any time. In fact, let's schedule the next call right now." Mike wanted to keep Connie in the loop and knew if he let her go right now, he may never hear from her again. "How about we talk the day after tomorrow? Let's exchange telephone numbers so you can call me at my house."

That evening, Drake came home late as usual. He picked his way up the steps to the bedroom. It was dark and he assumed Connie was asleep. He was relieved whenever he came home and she was already in bed. That meant he didn't have to suffer her stares and sullen silence, or worse yet, her snide comments. However, this evening, he found Connie sitting up in the bed, wide awake in the dark bedroom. He switched on the light and was shocked at the sight.

Sitting on the bed was a scarecrow of a woman, her nightgown and robe draped loosely on her thin frame. She had lost so much weight that her cheekbones were angled and stood out sharply in the light from Drake's nightstand. She glanced up at him for a second, then went back to staring at nothing.

He couldn't believe what he was seeing. *Can this truly be Connie?* he wondered.

"Are you okay?" he asked. "Connie? Are you okay?" he repeated. She looked up at him again.

"Uh-huh. I'm all right," she replied.

"Do you want me to call somebody?" Drake asked. "Should I call a doctor?"

"No," she replied, the vacant look still in her eyes. "I don't need a doctor. I'll be okay." She had been thinking about what Mike had told her about Jesse. She felt better thinking that Jesse was a responsible young man, and that Karyn was probably well cared for, but she still wanted her daughter back home. Connie knew she should have reported Drake to the police months ago and in part was responsible for Karyn leaving home.

Drake continued to look at her as if she were a stranger.

"Can I get you anything? Maybe a cup of tea?" he asked. She glanced at him briefly and nodded in assent. Several minutes later he returned with a cup of herbal tea. For the first time, Drake had taken the time to see his wife's depression. He sat on the bed beside her and handed her the tea.

"You want to talk?" he asked, sincerely concerned about her.

"Not much to talk about," Connie replied without much expression. For weeks, she had wanted Drake to talk to her, to support her, and to allow her to support him in their time of turmoil, but he'd been hostile and aloof. Now his ministrations were too little, too late.

"I'm sorry I've had to work so much," he said, trying to apologize. He wanted to make things better between them, although he knew he would rather be with Anne or Sandra than here with Connie.

"John called," Connie said. A start went through Drake. Why would John call Connie unless he found out about him and Anne?

"What about John?" Drake asked. Connie noticed the nervousness in his voice.

"He said the detectives have traced the kids to Miami. They were fine the last anyone knew." She looked at him hopefully.

"That hillbilly shit!" Drake growled as he got off the bed. He slammed the closet door shut and began to rant on about Jesse.

"Drake, wait," Connie said.

"What?" Drake shouted.

"Jesse's not as bad as you think," she said.

"Not as bad?" Drake bellowed. "Not as *bad?* He hit me! He's a common criminal!" Drake stood over Connie as he bellowed.

"Drake, why do you always have to start yelling?" she asked. "Why can't you just talk and listen to somebody else?"

"What? About raising our daughter? I know what's best for her," he said, barely controlling his voice.

"Hitting her?" Connie asked. "How is that best for her?"

"Spare the rod and spoil the child," he said simply.

"You hit her, Drake, like she was a punching bag!"

"Don't!" he interrupted. "Just don't even go there! When kids do something wrong, they should be punished."

"By *punching* them?" Connie replied. "Drake, there are other, less violent ways to correct a child."

"Like what the hell would you know?" he challenged. "You didn't even finish college!"

"And whose fault is that?" she countered. "Within three months of our wedding you told me to stay home. Then when I started taking classes to finish my degree you objected and made me quit.

"Drake, what happened to us?" she went on. "You used to say I was one of the best cooks you knew, but now you haven't complimented me on my cooking in years. It seems you don't like anything about me these days, and it's obvious you don't like how our daughter has turned out. Why do you even stay around here any more?"

"Sometimes I wonder!" he yelled, losing control of his temper again. "Aw, to hell with it!" he finally said, shaking his head. "I'm going to bed." A few minutes later, he was sliding into bed. Connie continued to sit on her side of the bed.

"Connie, get in bed. It's late and I'm tired." As she lay in the bed, she smelled the faint aroma of perfume. It was Opium. She wore Opus 1. Drake had been with another woman.

Connie was shattered. She knew things were not good between her and Drake since Karyn had bolted, but she never dreamed that he would run to another woman. She *had* to know who the other woman was! She finally drifted into a restless sleep two hours later.

* * * *

The next morning, Drake got up and casually went into the bathroom to get ready for work. After he left the house, Connie was still in the bed when the telephone next to the bed rang.

"Hello, Mrs. Mathers, this is Mike Andrews. I just wanted to tell you that Jesse called last night."

"Oh, Mike," Connie said. "You say the kids called? How are they? Where are they?" She wanted to find out anything she could about Karyn.

"They're fine," Mike told her. She could feel relief begin to flow through her body. "They were in Nassau last night. They have jobs on an ocean liner." Connie knew about the ocean liner from John's call just the day before.

"Are they okay?"

"They're fine. They've got jobs on this big ship. They're working in the restaurant, so you know they're not starving. Jesse says it pays well and there's no place to spend it, so he's saving a lot of it." Mike paused. "Are you all right?" he casually added.

"Yes. I'm a lot better since you called," she said. "I just didn't sleep much last night. This is good news. Thanks for letting me know." They talked for a couple more minutes. After the call, Connie felt better and took a shower. For the first time in days, she washed her hair and put on some makeup.

Chapter 16

What Mike didn't know was that when the ship docked in Nassau, Jesse and Karyn had been apart for two nights. She was angry with Jesse and ashamed of herself because of her one-night stand with Rick. She had difficulty even looking at Jesse so she had asked to be transferred out of her kitchen to one of the other three kitchens on the ship. That evening when Jesse got off work, he went to see Karyn where she was now working.

"Karyn, we need to talk."

"No, we don't," Karyn replied tersely.

"Yes, we do," Jesse said firmly. "We've got a problem and we need to work it out." Other people in the kitchen were watching Karyn and Jesse while they talked, making Jesse feel uneasy.

"What we need is for you to go," Karyn said. "I'm busy. I've got a ton of dishes to do here or they're not going to have enough chinaware out front."

"Karyn —" Jesse began.

"Get lost!" Karyn insisted. That's when two Hispanic guys left their positions and came to Karyn's side. They'd noticed the pretty girl the moment she arrived, but she had an attitude and kept their distance until now. Now it looked like they could help, and maybe, in the process, gain some points with the sexy blonde.

"Hey, hombre," one said. "The lady don' wan' you here. Now get outta my kitchen!"

"Yeah," the other said. He still held his chopping knife causally at his side.

"You guys fuck off!" Karyn shouted at them. "I can handle this myself!"

"Cheez," one said. "Maybe we should've let him have her. Who wanna a bitch like thees anyways?" The other shrugged and they ambled off together.

"You fuck off too!" Karyn said to Jesse. "Just get outta here!" Jesse looked at the two Hispanics. The one doing the chopping was still watching him and Karyn. Jesse didn't understand why Karyn was so angry, but he didn't want to start a scene. He went to their room and waited for her.

That night, when Karyn finished work, she roamed the decks for a while, trying to think things through while she cooled off from the hot, sticky work. A group of two young men and a young woman were coming her way. They were making a lot of noise and having a good time. As they got closer, one of the young men saw Karyn and casually said, "Hey, we're going to a party on shore! Want to come?" Karyn thought for a moment.

"Yeah. Sure. Why not?"

"Hey! All right!" he said, grabbed her hand and rushed to catch up to the other two.

"You got a name?" he asked as they trotted onto the shore.

"Karyn," she replied without much enthusiasm.

"I'm Joe," he said, excited and pleased Karyn had joined them. "That's Chaz and Dina. Dina's my sister." The four of them packed into a waiting taxi. Joe made casual conversation as they wound their way through Nassau's deserted streets and out of town. They rode for almost twenty minutes until the cab stopped at an iron gate supported by a pair of large stone pillars. Next to it a smaller gate stood open, illuminated by two burning torches. They were well out of town on a lonely stretch of two-lane asphalt pavement. With the exception of the gates, both sides of the tiny road were lined with dense foliage, colorful jacaranda and other tropical flowers. To Karyn it appeared that the taxi had stopped in the middle of nowhere, miles from the nearest civilization. Karyn heard the thump-thump-thump of music coming through the trees. Chaz and Dina disappeared through the gate between the torches. The greenery was so thick their light barely penetrated to the road. Karyn and Joe followed. The haunting, flickering torchlight illuminated a paved path that led through the lush vegetation. There were more torches that led the quartet through the trees and bushes like the Yellow Brick Road had led Dorothy to Oz.

They came to a huge house set on the high ground above a beach. The moon was a sliver in the western sky and all Karyn could see from the house was black water and a dim beach lit by groups of torches. The only lights in the house came from randomly placed flaming torches. Dozens of people milled around, their ages ranging from early teens to late twenties. They were laughing and talking while raucous music thumped from hidden speakers inside and outside the house. Karyn could smell alcohol and marijuana. She stayed at Joe's side as they explored the large house. They made their way into the kitchen where several beer kegs sat in big tubs of ice. One of the large, black granite counters was virtually covered by a selection of booze that rivaled the bar inventory on Karyn's ship. Large bags of plastic cups were piled on the counter. Joe poured himself a beer while asking Karyn, "What'll you have?"

"Same as you, I guess," she said. He poured a plastic cup full of Guinness Stout and handed it to her.

"Drink up!" he said. "There's lots more and we're gonna party all night long!" He took a long draw from his cup. She lifted hers to her lips and took a sip. The dark liquid was bitter and she grimaced as she set the cup aside, then looked around. Outside the kitchen window she saw a girl wearing nothing but her bikini bottom. Her breasts wiggled as she danced to the reggae music in the torchlight.

"Hey, come on, Karyn," Joe said. "Let's go to the beach!" Karyn followed him, leaving the Guinness on the counter.

They stumbled down the dimly lit path and onto the beach. There were a number of people there, all making noise and drinking from their colorful plastic cups. As they got closer, Karyn could see they were all naked. Suddenly, one of the guys jumped up and sprinted to the water. One of the girls chased him, splashing into the surf behind him.

"I don't like it here," Karyn said. "Let's go back to the house!"

"Huh? Okay," Joe replied. "Whatever floats your boat." They made their way back to the house and wandered around, looking at the house and talking occasionally. Joe didn't seem to know any of the people they met.

"Who lives here?" Karyn asked.

"Don't know," Joe said. "They're gone and we have it for the weekend."

"Are you renting it?" Karyn asked. Joe looked at her in disbelief then broke into laughter.

"Rent? You gotta be kidding!" He tossed the empty plastic cup aside and said, "I need another drink. Where's yours?"

"Gone," she said blandly.

"Well, we both gotta get more. Come on!"

They returned to the kitchen where Joe poured another Guinness. Karyn poured herself a half glass of vodka and poured some orange juice in it. She'd seen her father do the same thing and figured it must be good.

"Let's see the rest of the house," Joe said. Karyn followed him down the hall, sipping on her drink. They passed several doors, which Karyn saw were bedrooms. The doors stood open, and Karyn saw naked couples writhing on the beds. She followed Joe the length of the hall and out onto a large verandah that overlooked the beach. There were two other couples on the verandah, necking.

"This is a cool house," Joe said. "I'd like one just like this some day." Karyn just looked at the two couples. One guy was unbuttoning his girlfriend's top as she smiled down on her large breasts. The other girl was reaching unabashedly into the crotch of her boyfriend's pants. Karyn was about to tell Joe she was leaving when he grabbed her by the hand and said, "Let's see the rest of it!"

They went back down the hall, past the bodies in the bedrooms, and down the broad staircase at the opposite end of the house. The lower level was a huge expanse of workout room, sauna, and great room. There was a huge big-screen TV and a hot tub. The hot tub was packed way beyond capacity with naked bodies. To Karyn, they looked like a can of worms writhing and sliding against each other.

"Joe, I'd like to go," Karyn said.

"Can't," Joe replied.

"Why not?"

"We're here until dawn. No cabs, no cars, no nothing. Just party, party, party!"

Karyn surveyed her surroundings and wished she'd never come. She was tired, uneasy with what she was seeing, and wanted to leave. While Joe was talking to someone else, she slid away into the darkness. She went outside and found a bench away from the activity. She sat there and sipped on her drink, watching the goings on. She had been there perhaps fifteen minutes when a voice spoke behind her.

"Having fun?" he asked. She turned to see a tall, blond, blue-eyed young man. He wore an unbuttoned shirt with colorful tropical flowers printed all over it. He was tanned and had sun-bleached hair, and he wore some sort of island talisman around his neck. He spoke with an accent.

"Not really," Karyn said. He was a handsome young man, about as tall as Jesse.

"That's too bad," he said. "Parties are to have fun. May I sit?" he said as he nodded to the space on the bench next to her.

"If you want," she said. She studied him in the dim light. The dull, golden glow of the torches flickered on his face. His clear blue eyes seemed to smile at her.

"It looks like you are nearly done with your drink," he said. "How about I get you another one?"

"No, thanks. I've had enough." The screwdriver wasn't as good as she'd hoped it would be and the vodka was already taking effect on her. They talked for fifteen minutes about where they were from, nothing else. He was from Sweden and his name was Lars. He was charming and pleasant company. As they talked, a couple ran by them, shouting and practically naked. Karyn kept looking at the handsome Swede and the more they talked, the more comfortable she felt. He slid closer to her and put his arm around her.

After a while longer, he pulled her closer to him and kissed her. She didn't particularly want to be kissed, but she didn't fight it. In another five minutes, she was bare from the waist up as he kissed and licked her breasts. Everything was going out of control in a hurry. Then he effortlessly picked her up and carried her inside the house. Nobody seemed to notice as he carried her upstairs and into one of the bedrooms.

She began to protest when he undid her jeans, but he paid no attention. Then he slid his shirt off and dropped his swimsuit onto the floor. It was difficult to see one another in the dark room, but his hands studied every little nuance of her body. He took her hands and placed them on his body and rubbed them in the most sensitive places. Then he picked her up and laid her on the bed.

Twenty minutes later, he got up and said, "Well, I have to go. Maybe I'll see you later."

"Where are you going?" she asked.

"Back to the party," he said as he casually got into his swimsuit.

"But we've just made love," she said. "Don't you want to stay with me?" She gathered the sheet around her as she spoke. It didn't seem right to her to lie there naked while he was getting dressed.

"Yes, we made love, but now it's time to find someone else to make love to," he replied.

"Someone else?" she asked. "What do you mean, 'someone else'? What about me?"

"Yes, you were fun, but not very good, I admit. Now I want another."

"Now wait a goddamn minute," Karyn said, growing angry. "If you think you're just going to have sex and walk out of my life..."

"That's exactly what I'm going to do," he said. "I made you no promises." Karyn bolted out of the bed and stood in front of him.

"If you think you can just use me for a good time and then leave, you're wrong!" She grabbed his arm.

"Let go. You had as much fun as I had, maybe more, because I am a better lover than you are. I want another one now."

"*NO!*" she yelled and slapped him. He slapped her back, knocking her across the bed.

"Yes!" he replied. "If you didn't want to get laid, why did you come here?"

"How many girls have you had?" she asked from where she lay sprawled on the bed.

"You were the fourth one tonight. That's all you American girls are good for anyway. You're all too easy to get into bed." He left the room, not bothering to close the door on his way out. People glanced in the room as they passed, seeing Karyn naked on the bed, but not caring. She quickly gathered the sheet around her. One couple stopped and came in.

"Hey, you done here?" the man asked. "All the other rooms are busy."

"Yeah. Sure," Karyn said as she gathered her clothes while clutching the sheet around her. The woman grabbed the sheet.

"Hey! Leave the sheets!" she said as she gave it a hard yank. It snapped free of Karyn's body, leaving her naked in the dim light. The man looked at her and grinned.

Karyn got dressed in the corner of the room while the man and woman proceeded to undress each other, oblivious to Karyn.

Karyn wound her way up the path and onto the lonely road. She had no idea which way was back toward Nassau. She made a calculated guess and started walking. She had walked for about half an hour when a car approached from behind. It slowed as it got near her. When it was alongside, the driver called out.

"Hey, lady! It not good you be walkin' the road like this!" he said in a rich Bahamian accent. She saw that it was a police car and the man inside was in his uniform. "You get in, now, I take you into town!" She got into the police car.

"Am I arrested?" she asked quietly.

"Heck, no, pretty lady! You jus' don' wan' to be walkin' alone like this at night. Someone do somethin' bad to you and feed you to the sharks!" Against his rich, dark skin, his teeth glowed white in the light reflected from the headlights. *He's too late,* Karyn thought. *Someone has already done something bad to me.* She sat silent and sullen until they were on the outskirts of Nassau. Faint traces of dawn were glowing in the distant eastern sky.

"Where you stayin', pretty miss?"

"I'm on board the ship," she said.

"No problem," he said, his voice cheerful. "That be only two blocks from the police station. I drop you off!"

Karyn boarded the ship as the policeman waved at her, but she didn't notice. She went to her room and was relieved to see Jesse had already gone to work. She pulled the sheets back and slid into the empty bed. After work,

Jesse returned to the room to find Karyn was still asleep. He woke her and asked where she'd been.

"I don't want to talk about it," she said, pushing him away.

"Well, I think we'd better talk," Jesse said. "We've got a problem and we need to work it out."

"*You've* got a problem and *you* need to work it out, not me," she replied sullenly as she pulled the sheets over her head.

"Karyn, get up!" Jesse demanded. "We're in trouble. I want to fix it!"

"The only trouble I have is with you!" Karyn shouted from under the sheets. "Get lost and leave me alone!" Karyn didn't want to face Jesse. She thought he had been with the woman from the restaurant who had hit on him, and she'd been with Rick and Lars, so in her mind they were even, but she couldn't understand why she felt so awful.

"Aw, Karyn. Let's not fight," Jesse said as she began to get out of bed, still in her clothes from the night before.

"We're not going to fight," Karyn said. "It's none of your goddamn business where I've been!" She walked out, slamming the door behind her. She stormed to the main deck and looked at Nassau. It was night again. She'd slept through the entire day, missing work. As she stood there, a friend of Rick's came up to her.

"You're Karyn, aren't you?" he asked.

"Who the hell are you?" she asked in a sultry, angry voice.

"I'm Dave, a friend of Rick's," he replied. "He said nice things about you." She remembered Rick and how nice he was to her, at least in the beginning. He bought her drinks and treated her well until they landed in bed.

"Why don't we just go to your room?" Karyn said. She knew what he wanted and decided not to fight it. She wanted to get even with Jesse and this was one way to do it. She'd show Jesse that for every woman he could get, she could get three or four men. Dave stared in shock, then smiled.

"O-*kay*!" he replied. He put his arm around her shoulder and guided her away. At the same time, Jesse was in Karyn's galley talking to the steward.

"I'd like to see about having Karyn Mathers moved back to her old galley," Jesse said to the steward.

"I haven't seen her since the first day she worked here," he replied. "I'm replacing her."

"She hasn't been in at all?" Jesse asked.

"Only the first day, and she complained the whole time she was here," the steward told him. "I can't say that anyone misses her."

Jesse left, shaking his head. After a fruitless search for Karyn, he went ashore to search for her there. He wandered the deserted streets of Nassau for almost two hours before he gave up and went back to the ship. It was late when he spotted Karyn on the deck drinking with a male passenger.

"Karyn, come on. Let's go to our room to talk." He stared at the blonde with her bloodshot eyes and her hair in disarray. She was drunk and hadn't fixed her hair after having sex with Dave.

"Get lost," she said. "We're through."

"Karyn, you don't mean that," Jesse said.

"Oh, yes. I mean it." She looked at the man with her, then glared at Jesse. "I want you out of my life. I don't need you or the bullshit you dump out."

"I haven't given you any bullshit," Jesse said defensively.

"You're nothing but bullshit," Karyn said, louder. "Just go away and leave me alone."

"Aw, Karyn," Jesse pleaded.

"You want me to get rid of this guy?" the man with Karyn asked. Jesse looked at him. He was shorter than Jesse, nearly as old as his father and stocky.

"No, he was just leaving," Karyn said.

"Karyn, come on," he said again, and tried to pull her by the hand. She snatched her hand out of his and slapped him. She took the older man's arm and stormed away. Jesse stared after her in shock, then silently turned and walked away.

Jesse went ashore and wandered the streets of Nassau until he spotted the lights of a bar. He went in and called Mike from the pay phone.

"Mike, I don't know what's wrong," Jesse said, fighting to contain his tears.

"Sport, sometimes things just go haywire and there's nothing you can do about it," Mike said. Based on what Jesse had told him, Mike was pretty sure he knew what was happening. He'd seen it all before. "So what are you going to do now?"

"I don't know. I know I can't stay on that ship with her," he said. "I don't think I can take seeing her every day with someone else. I know I can't work with her and act like there's nothing between us."

"Well, you may have some options," Mike said. "There's some letters here for you from a couple of universities."

"Really? What do they say?" Jesse asked, his mind skipping over Karyn for the moment. "Have you opened them?"

"No. I wanted to wait for you," Mike replied

"Well, open them and read them to me!" Jesse said. They continued to talk as the letters were opened, one by one, and the contents read. Most were rejections, but one, from Miami University in Oxford, Ohio, was an offer for a full-ride football scholarship.

"Miami of Ohio?" Jesse asked. "I only applied at Miami because my English teacher went there and she said I should apply. I think I'll hold out for a better offer."

"Are you nuts?" Mike countered. "Don't you know what Miami is? It's one of the best schools for football, especially if you ever want to be a coach! It's been called 'the Cradle of Coaches' because they've graduated some of the best in the business. Heck, Woody Hayes originally coached there before he moved to the Big Ten!"

"The big honcho who was at Ohio State for so many years?" Jesse asked incredulously.

"Exactly!" Mike said.

"He was at a punky little school like Miami?" Jesse asked, just to be sure they were talking about the same place.

"One and the same, and it's not punky!" Mike told him. "It's a full-scale university that can teach you just about anything you want to learn." Jesse was quiet for a moment. He thought about his promise to his mother about going to college. He also thought about his love for Karyn and weighed that against their recent problems.

"I'm going to take it," Jesse said. "I'm going to Miami."

"Attaboy!" Mike shouted over the phone. "You won't regret it!" Jesse smiled as a painful lump rose in his throat because he knew he would have to leave Karyn. After he hung up the phone he wandered to a table where he sat nursing Cokes until the sun rose, then went back to the ship.

In the meantime, Karyn awakened next to the heavy-set man that she'd slept with out of spite for Jesse. She remembered how he wheezed while he was on top of her. It had been a terrible experience.

She lay there for a few moments, wondering how things could have become so bad. Wasn't it just a few weeks ago that she and Jesse were so happy together? What went wrong? How did she wind up here in this bed with this fat old man? She couldn't even remember his name.

She got up and dressed and suddenly she hated all men. She remembered the countless times her father had slapped her and the time he actually knocked her out in the foyer. She recalled Lars and his comment about how easy American girls were. *I guess we are*, she thought. *I sure have been, but that's going to change right now. God, how I hate men!* she thought.

She closed the door behind her and went up to the deck. She stood at the rail and, for the first time, really thought about her life. She thought about where she came from and how she got to where she was. She knew she had done terrible things and the more she thought about it, the more depressed she became.

Jesse was in their room getting his things. He saw the bed hadn't been slept in and knew Karyn had been gone all night again. He went to the galley to tell his boss that he was quitting and he would be leaving the ship in Nassau. The boss wished Jesse good luck, shook his hand and promised to mail Jesse's last paycheck to Mike's house. Then Jesse went to look for Karyn. He didn't expect to find her, but wanted to try anyway.

He found her at the rail of the fourth deck, looking out toward the open ocean with red, teary eyes. She knew she'd been stupid with Jesse. She hadn't made life easy on the only person she had ever truly loved. Worse than that, she knew she'd cheapened herself terribly. She was terribly ashamed of herself.

"Hey," Jesse said softly as he came up behind her. He was moving slowly, not sure she would even talk to him.

"Hi," she replied with a hitch in her voice. She wished that she could take back all the terrible things she had done over the past few weeks.

"I've been looking for you," he said.

"Well, you found me," she responded, looking directly into his eyes.

"Yeah. Well —" He paused. He stepped to her side and looked out at the same expanse of blue-green ocean. He was quiet for several seconds then said, "Karyn, what did I do wrong?" She looked at him in amazement.

"What did you do wrong?" she asked. "I saw you with that bimbo from the restaurant! I saw her pawing you and you really seemed to like it! And you were holding her hand!"

"Karyn, I *didn't* like it and I told her to get lost," Jesse said. "I was holding her hand to keep her from pawing at me."

"Bull!" Karyn replied. Her voice was barely audible because it was so weak from emotion.

"No, it's the honest truth," Jesse said sincerely. "Karyn, there's never been anyone in my life except you since the first time we went out." Karyn faced him.

"You didn't go to bed with her?" she asked.

"Nope. I went back to our room to wait for you," he said.

"You didn't go anywhere?"

"Just to our room, like I said."

"With anyone?"

"Never."

She studied his eyes and knew he was telling the truth. The tears welled up in her eyes. She'd been getting even with Jesse for something he'd never done. In the end, she had only made a cheap fool of herself. Now she felt worse than ever. She gazed at the open sea with tears filling her eyes.

"I have some news," he said.

"Yeah?" she said in a quiet voice.

"I got a football scholarship," he said. A chill went through her and she turned toward Jesse.

"I got a four-year scholarship to Miami University in Ohio," he continued. "I'm taking it." She looked back at the ocean. She was confused, panicky, and didn't know what to do.

"Um, Karyn?" he said. "I've been thinking."

"About what?" she asked.

"Well, things haven't been too good between you and me lately, and maybe it's a good thing I got this scholarship. Maybe you're right that we need a break from each other."

"A break?" she asked. A bolt of fear went through her. Her heart pounded harder than ever before in her life. Even though she'd told him to get lost, she never believed he would really go. She had only said that to get even with him. She had always thought that she would have Jesse forever, but now he was talking about breaking up.

"Yeah," he said and sighed. Her tantrums were bad enough, but Jesse knew she had been spending time with other men.

"Maybe you need some space — you know — to grow some."

Karyn was crushed, her heart was aching and her hands shaking. She gripped the rail to hold herself up.

"You think this is the best thing to do?" she asked.

"I think it's best for the both of us."

"Are you sure?" she finally asked, her eyes flooded with tears.

"Yes."

Jesse's conviction wasn't very strong, and if Karyn had asked him to stay, he would have forgotten about the scholarship and stayed on board the ship with her. He wanted to be with Karyn forever, but it was her affairs that drove Jesse away. After several seconds of silence, he took her hand and looked deeply into her eyes, nodded a silent good-bye and walked away.

"Jesse?" she called after him. He looked back.

She desperately wanted to keep some contact with him, however distant it might be, so she asked him, "Can I call you?"

"Of course, any time you want," he said. "I'll be staying at Mike's until college starts." She nodded, the tears glistening in her eyes.

"Well, I gotta be going," he said. "The ship is leaving in a few minutes."

She went to see him off the ship. From the dock, he waved at her. She mustered a smile and returned his wave. Tears brimmed in each one's eyes.

Chapter 17

Karyn went to the room where she and Jesse stayed. She was shocked to find that all her things were gone and the room had been given to someone else. She went to the galley to report for work.

"Work?" the galley steward exclaimed. "I saw you one miserable day and you complained the whole time! Then you never came back! What makes you think you have a job here?" Karyn looked at him in silence.

"And another thing," he went on. "That guy of yours came by here trying to get you moved back to his galley. He's a good dude and you should be treating him better 'cause if you don't, you're going to lose him in a hurry." Karyn bit her lip and walked out of the steward's office.

"One more thing," he called after her. "You don't have a job, so you'd better have a ticket or you could be considered a stowaway. That could mean big trouble for you."

Karyn wandered around the deck. She had no ticket, no cabin, and no money. All her things were gone and so was Jesse. The ship was sailing to Miami but it would take all night to get there. She stood at the railing, peering into the dark, swirling water below her, her thoughts rolling wildly about her last two weeks. She had certainly fucked everything up. She had been standing there for about twenty minutes when behind her, two men were talking. One was the heavy-set man and he was telling the other how easy she was. The second man decided to give it a try.

"Hi," he said as he casually walked up. Karyn continued to stare into the roiling water below.

"Get lost," Karyn said without looking at him.

"Hey, I'm just trying to be friendly," he said, smiling. She looked at him in disgust.

"I don't feel like being very friendly," she said, "Especially with you. Now leave me alone!" She walked away from him. A few seconds later, one of the guys from the galley saw her and came up to her.

"Hey, Karyn!" he said. "I thought you quit. What are you doing here?" he asked.

Karyn had hoped to hide out until the ship docked in Miami so she could get off but now she had been discovered. She suddenly bolted from the crewman, leaving him staring in surprise. The galley man went straight to

Jerry Doyle in the Security Office.

"Mr. Doyle, I think we may have a hooker on board," he said. This had happened before and Jerry knew exactly what to do.

"What makes you think she's a hooker?"

" 'Cause she was with a man and when I talked to her she ran away, leaving him standing there."

"You know who she is?" Jerry asked.

"Yeah. Her name's Karyn and she used to work in my galley as a dish-washer."

Jerry Doyle couldn't believe what he heard. He remembered helping Karyn and Jesse get their passports in Miami. He knew Jesse was a pretty straight young man, and although Karyn had an attitude, he didn't think of her as being the type of girl who would be a prostitute.

"I know who she is," Jerry said. "I'll take it from here. Thanks." Jerry went to Don Bingham, the ship's restaurant manager, and asked him about Karyn and Jesse.

"They quit," Don said. "The steward was really sad to lose Jesse. Said he was the best."

"Why did they quit?" Jerry asked.

"I understand Jesse got a football scholarship to some college in Ohio. I guess I'd quit for that, too." He smiled at Jerry. "It doesn't surprise me a bit. That kid excels in everything he does."

"What about the girl?" Jerry asked.

"What about her? She left at the same time."

"Then why would she still be on the ship?" Jerry asked.

"No reason I can think of," Don told him. "I thought they were tight. I figured they're a pair of young lovers and she went with him. Why? Did somebody see her?"

"Yeah. I got a report she was on the ship with a passenger."

"Maybe she's taking a vacation after working. Some of our people do that, you know."

"I don't think so," Jerry said. "Especially if they were as tight as we thought they were. Something's wrong. But I'll check to see if she bought a ticket anyway. Thanks, Don."

"Don't mention it," Don said. "And let me know if there's anything I can do. You know, like if she's in trouble or something. A girl that pretty can get herself in real deep, real quick."

"Don't I know it," Jerry said as he walked out of Don's office.

In ten minutes, Jerry had checked the passenger manifest and determined that Karyn didn't have a ticket, at least not in her real name. He put his security team on full alert to detain her when they found her. Jerry knew she was probably planning to hide out until they hit Miami, then she'd get off and they'd never see her again. He was a retired police officer and knew the signs of a runaway girl.

It was nearly dawn and Karyn had been wandering the decks all night. She was on the fourth deck when two security men spotted her.

"Karyn Mathers?" one of the security men asked. She nodded. She knew she was caught and didn't try to run.

"You need to come with us," he said. Karyn silently walked between the two men as they took her to Jerry Doyle's office. Soon she was sitting in front of Jerry's desk, crying and wiping her nose with the back of her hand. Jerry came in a little later.

"How are you?" he asked as he sat in his chair behind the desk.

"I'm okay," she said softly. Jerry produced a box of tissues from his desk drawer and handed it to her. She took it without comment and began to wipe her nose. Her tears were flowing non-stop.

"I'm in trouble, aren't I?"

"Well," Jerry said thoughtfully, "I gotta admit, I'm not sure what to do with you. I mean, here you are on my ship without a job or a ticket. You're legally a stowaway."

"Am I going to jail?" she asked. In some ways, she would have welcomed it. At least she would have a place to stay and something to eat.

Jerry studied the pretty blonde sitting in front of his desk. Based on what the crewmember told him, and the facts that she had no ticket and Jesse was gone, he was afraid she'd been hooking on his ship, although he couldn't prove it. She stared at the floor while the river of tears grew. Her breathing was so shallow it seemed she wasn't breathing at all. Jerry thought of his own daughter, now grown and married with children. He recalled the times when she was young and some lad had broken her heart. Still, Karyn was a stowaway, possibly a prostitute, and who knew what else?

"Karyn, we're docking in a little while. I have to take care of some things. I want you to stay here. Can I trust you to do that?"

"I'll be here," she said without looking up. She pulled another tissue from the box and pressed it against her eyes to absorb the tears. Jerry left the office half hoping that she would be gone when he came back so he wouldn't have to deal with a potentially messy situation. He almost hoped she would leave his office, slip into the departing crowd and disappear forever, but he was also afraid that if she did, he would read about someone finding her lifeless body in Miami a few days later. He was out of his office for over an hour. He returned to find her still sitting in the same position on the same chair. She hadn't moved and the tears still slid from her eyes.

"Karyn, what are you doing here?" he asked as he walked into his office.

"You told me to stay," she said.

"That's not what I mean. Why are you still on the ship? Why didn't you leave with Jesse?"

"We broke up," she said.

"I can see that," Jerry said. "Why don't you tell me the whole story? Let's start at the beginning." He sat down in the chair next to her. His Irish good looks included a thatch of red hair with gray streaks at the temples and there were wrinkles at the corners of his eyes. His eyes were sincere.

"Not much to say," Karyn said.

"Just tell me what you can," he responded. "Tell me about your home in — Michigan, isn't it?"

Karyn started by telling him about her home town. He asked occasional questions and got her to loosen up. Before long, the whole story began to flow from her in a torrent. She told Jerry about Drake and how he would hit her, and how her mother would never defend her from him. She explained about Jesse and how his drunken father would hit him, too. She spoke of Mike, saying that she wished she had a best friend like Mike. Then she said that she and Jesse ran away together to find a better life.

"But I guess I kind of blew that, didn't I?" she said.

"How did you blow it?" Jerry asked. She sighed and told him about all the men she'd partied with. She laid it all on the line with no omissions. For the first time in her life, she was completely honest not only with someone else, but herself as well. Her story and tears flowed like a river. She sat in Jerry's office, talking and crying for over two hours. Finally, the tears stopped, and she said, "That's it. That's the whole story." She was relieved that Jerry seemed to understand the situation and didn't judge her.

Jerry Doyle had been in police and security work for three decades. He'd heard almost every story there was and this one wasn't new to him. Normally, he wouldn't get involved but there was something about this young woman that touched him. She wasn't like so many of the other girls who'd gone bad. Maybe it was because he caught her before she'd gone too far down the path of self-destruction. He knew it was a gamble, but he decided to try to help this girl.

"Karyn, I want you to wait here. I may be a while, but I'll be back." Jerry rose and smiled at her.

"Are you going to call the police?" she asked.

"No. I'm going to get your things. They were probably taken to the Lost and Found." She mustered a weak smile as Jerry disappeared out the door. It was the first smile she'd had in a long time. Karyn leaned back and dozed off in the chair. She had been asleep for over an hour when Jerry came back in.

"Here's all your things," Jerry said, as he set two cardboard boxes on the chair next to Karyn. "I'm sorry I took so long, but I had to find the paymaster so he could cash your last paycheck." Jerry handed her about $500 in cash. Karyn blinked at the money.

"I didn't know I had anything coming," she said. "Thank you!" Jerry sat behind his desk and smiled.

"Karyn, now that we're docked, there's not a lot for me to do. I've got some time on my hands. Why don't you let me take you to the airport? I can loan you whatever you need to get a ticket back to Michigan."

Karyn considered his offer. She knew if she went back home, Drake would hold her mistakes against her forever; plus, she wasn't sure about Jesse anymore since he'd enrolled in college. She felt completely helpless.

"No, I think I'll just stay here in Miami," she replied. "It's just that I don't know what to do. I guess I'm pretty bummed out," and as she looked at him, the tears started to flow again. Jerry remembered that same vacant look from a young lady he'd known a few years before named Catherine Bixby. She had come into Jerry's life in much the same way as Karyn did. Catherine was a young girl on her own, hiding out on the ship with no place to go and at the end of her rope. Men had used her too, like Karyn. Then Karyn's stomach growled and interrupted his thoughts.

"When was the last time you ate?" Jerry asked.

"I don't know," she said. "Sometime yesterday."

"Let's you and I go get some dinner," he said. "I'm calling my wife to let her know where I'm going." Karyn heaved a sigh of relief. "There's a bathroom through there if you want to get cleaned up a little," he added, motioning toward a door on the far wall of his office. Karyn nodded and trod off in that direction. Jerry really wanted Karyn out of the room so he could talk to his wife, Maggie, privately.

"Maggie, I think we have another Catherine Bixby on our hands," he said.

"How bad is she?" Maggie asked.

"Well, she hasn't tried to kill herself yet, but she's in bad shape without much self esteem. She's damn near hysterical and she can't stop crying for more than a few minutes at a time."

"Do you know what her problem is?" Maggie asked.

"Well, she's been used a lot, and she's pretty close to the bottom of the barrel." He paused. "Her father used to beat on her quite a bit," he added. "Strange, too, since the family seems to be quite well off. Based on what she told me, he must've been making a couple hundred thousand bucks a year, plus bonuses. Can't figure it out at all."

"You know money doesn't eliminate abuse," Maggie said. "But you're right. It sounds like Catherine all over, although her family didn't have that kind of money," she confirmed. "Are you bringing her home?"

"If that's all right with you," Jerry said.

"You know we never turn any kid away," Maggie replied. "Should I hold dinner?"

"No, I'm taking her out. I need to gain her complete trust to get her to come home with me."

"Okay. I'll see you later, dear," Maggie said and hung up.

"Well, it's all set," Jerry said to Karyn when she returned to the chair. "Maggie said we should have dinner while she runs some errands."

"That sounds good," Karyn said with another weak smile. "I'm pretty hungry." They continued to talk at dinner.

"Karyn," Jerry said, "I might be able to get you a job on another ship. You know our ships go all over the world."

"Like where?" she asked.

"Well, they go to Alaska or the Med, for instance."

"The Med?"

"Yes. The Mediterranean. They stop in Spain, France, and Italy among other places, but I'm not sure of all of the stops. I've never worked that cruise. It's a pretty exotic trip."

"That sounds nice but I'd like to think about it," Karyn said. Her tears had stopped during dinner. "I may try to find a job here in Miami. I have some money to tide me over. I should see if I can make it on my own."

"And where will you stay?" he asked.

"Don't know," Karyn replied. Her wrinkled brow showed that she hadn't thought that far.

"And how will you get there?"

"I guess I don't know that, either," she replied. Jerry decided to take the chance.

"Karyn, why don't you come home with me to meet my wife? I'm sure you'll like her. And you can stay with us tonight and get a fresh start tomorrow." Karyn considered her options, although she knew she really didn't have any.

"Come on, Karyn," Jerry said. "Let's take you home to meet my wife." Karyn nodded and followed Jerry from the restaurant, fighting back the tears.

* * * *

Mike and Willie Bob were at Detroit Metro Airport when the Northwest 747 approached the gate. As Jesse came up the ramp, the first thing he noticed was that Willie had shaved, his hair was cut and brushed neatly back against the side of his head. And while his shirt was still rumpled, he wore fresh jeans and his boots were new. He looked pretty good, especially compared to what he looked like when Jesse had left home a few months back. At dinner that night the three of them had a serious talk.

"Jesse, I gotta say some things to you," Willie Bob said between swallows of the chocolate milkshake he was drinking.

"First of all, I gotta say I'm sorry," Willie said, staring Jesse right in the eye. "I was thinkin' o' myself an' not you. I wanted you t' be like me, instead o' bein' what you wanted t' be." He smiled. "I come t' realize that you're a differ'nt person than me. You got your own wants an' maybe they don' line up exactly to what I want, but I kin see now that that's okay. I sure am proud o' how you handled that mister high-an'-mighty Drake Mathers." Willie paused and looked thoughtfully into the nearly empty milkshake glass.

"Jesse, I was wrong t' hit you. I was wrong t' argue with you all the time. It was the booze that made me do it, but now I know I was usin' the booze t' fergit your mom." He sighed and went on.

"When you took off, it made me do some thinkin', an' well, I was holdin' on to your mom's memory when I shoulda been lettin' her go. I hope you kin fergive me fer bein' such a dope." Willie's eyes were misty, but his voice didn't waver. "I wasn't lettin' her go and it was eatin' me up inside. I kept drinkin' t' keep the hurt out, but all it did was cause more hurt fer you. Y'know what I mean?"

"Yeah, Dad," Jesse replied. "I know exactly what you mean." Jesse smiled and put a hand on his dad's shoulder. "I knew you were hurting. We all were, but you didn't have to carry it by yourself. Mike and I were here for you."

"Yeah, I figgered that out after you left," he said, flashing a grin at Mike.

"Mike here's been th' best friend a man could have." Jesse already knew that.

"Dad hasn't had a drop of booze since the night after you left," Mike said to Jesse. "He's been dry as a bone!" Mike was proud of his stepfather. The old Willie Bob Waller was gone, a different man was inside his skin, and he looked pretty damn good.

They continued to talk about a number of things. Jesse told them about his last few months, including the cruise ship. Finally, he began to talk about Karyn. Both Mike and Willie Bob saw the distress on Jesse's face when he talked about her.

"Sport, that's the way some women are," Willie said after listening for almost half an hour. "That's why when you git a good one like your mom, you hang onto her the best you kin."

"But Dad," Jesse said. "I think that basically she's a good girl, but confused as all get out."

"Well, you cain't blame her fer bein' confused," Willie replied. "Lookit the home she come from, an' that ol' man o' hers! Hell, if'n she'd stayed here, she'd prob'ly be dead by now! Ain't no real man what beats up womenfolk like that!"

"I just wish there was some way to work things out with her," Jesse said sadly.

"Maybe you kin and maybe you cain't," Willie told him. "Only time'll tell. Most times when girls mess up like this, they don't come to any good. I wouldn't hold my breath if I was you."

"Dad's right," Mike added. "When someone goes that far off the deep end, they don't usually come back very soon. But you can never tell." Jesse sat looking at his hands.

"Your best bet is to go on with your life," Mike added. "Go to college and make something of yourself like you promised Mom. Then if Karyn comes back, you'll have something to offer her."

"Yeah. Git yourself off to that learnin' school," Willie agreed. "I didn't completely understand why you wanted t' go t' college when they's lotsa good jobs out there, but I know I was bein' narrow-minded when I tried t' talk you outta that. Maybe your mom was right. Maybe if'n you git an education, you won't be workin' as hard as I do fer practic'ly nuthin'." Jesse nodded and forced a half-hearted smile.

"I know I have to go to Miami University," he said. "It's the Cradle of Coaches. It's the best place for me. Actually, I can't wait. I've saved almost ten thousand dollars. If I add that to the scholarship, it should be easy as pie."

"I'll be proud t' come see you play football there," Willie said. "I'm sorry I didn't make it to many of your games in high school, but I'll go see you play in college!" Then Willie made a face. "I ain't never been to no college b'fore. Think they'll let me take a look around?"

"Sure they will, Dad," Jesse laughed. "Just tell them you're with me!"

Chapter 18

In the Mathers household, Connie still didn't know whom Drake was seeing. It was driving her crazy to think Drake was with a strange woman and she was driven to find out who she was.

At the same time, Drake was treading an emotional tightrope between Anne Marie and Sandra. Each was demanding that he stop seeing the other and was threatening to tell John if he didn't. By this time, Drake was spending most of his nights away from home. The affect on Connie was devastating. The day after Jesse returned to Michigan, Mike called Connie to tell her Jesse was back in town.

"What about Karyn?" Connie immediately asked.

"Well, she and Jesse have broken up," Mike told her. "I don't have a lot of information about Karyn, but I'm sure she's fine. Tell you what, though. Meet us for dinner so we can talk."

"Will your dad be there?" she asked.

"Yes, but don't let that stop you. I think you'll be surprised. Come on," he pleaded. "Give it a chance. Why don't you meet us?" Although Connie didn't want to be anywhere near Willie Bob, if she could learn anything about her daughter she thought she could weather it.

"Okay," she finally said. "I'll meet you."

That evening, Connie walked into the restaurant. She saw Jesse right away. She expected him to be tanned from being in the Caribbean sun, but he was actually rather pale. His long hours on the job prevented him from getting out during the daylight hours. Next to Jesse sat Mike, whom she'd never seen before, and Willie sat with his back toward her. She approached the table and was surprised to see Willie was shaved, his hair was cut and neatly brushed, and he wore a pressed plaid shirt. The sleeves of the shirt were rolled halfway up his forearms, showing lean, well-defined muscles. His hands were clean. Even his fingernails were clean and clipped short. She looked at him in wonderment. He smiled and nodded to her as he arose. He wordlessly offered her his hand and then a place for her to sit. The man she was looking at wasn't at all the man who left tracks on her carpet. He stood ramrod straight, and was, in fact, quite handsome. She couldn't take her eyes off his face. Before her stood Jesse, only older by thirty years. He was as ruggedly handsome as Jesse. She could see Willie's manly features in Jesse's face, only Willie was closer to her age.

"Am I late?" she asked. "Have I kept you waiting?"

"Oh, no," Willie replied. "Not at all, ma'am. We was just a little early 'cause we didn't want t' make *you* wait." He again waved for her to sit. She gingerly slid into the seat as Willie held the chair for her. He casually took the last chair and sat looking at Connie with clear eyes and a warm smile. "I'm glad you came to have dinner with us," Willie said.

Connie immediately noticed there was no alcohol on Willie's breath. She looked at the table and saw two coffees and a Coke. She didn't know how long Willie had been sober, but judging by how clear his eyes were she knew he had been clean for at least several weeks.

They made casual conversation for a while and then began to talk about Karyn. Willie, Mike, and Jesse had all agreed beforehand that they would not tell Connie about Karyn's transgressions. They knew it would do no good for Connie or Karyn.

"I don't know where she is right now," Jesse said in reply to Connie's question. "The last I knew, she was still on the ship. I guess she's still working in the galley."

"Is that hard work?" Connie asked, concerned for her daughter.

"It's not hard, but the days are long. We'd work twelve to sixteen hours a day. But the pay was good, and we had all the food we wanted. It was good food, too."

Connie was relieved that Jesse was all right. She figured if Jesse was okay, then the odds were good that Karyn was okay, too. Perhaps John Malcolm was right to think there was not much trouble Karyn could get into on a ship.

"Miz Mathers," Willie said. "You mind if'n I call you Connie?"

"Connie is fine," she replied, surprised and pleased that Willie was gentleman enough to ask.

"Connie, I know I'm pryin' an' you kin tell me t' go t' hell if'n you want, but I feel the need to ask. Is ever'thin' okay for you at home?" Connie hesitated. Her eyes told Willie everything he needed to know.

"That's what I thought," he said, nodding slowly. "I —"

"It's not what you think," Connie interrupted. She didn't want to talk about her home life, especially with three men. It was bad enough that Karyn had run away, but Drake's infidelity really compounded her inner pain. Finally, Connie began to talk slowly, but in the next few minutes she opened up like a floodgate and soon was pouring her heart out to them, telling them the story.

Karyn was the most important thing in her life and the only good news for Connie was that Jesse was all right, which indicated that Karyn might be all right, too. After Connie talked about Karyn for a while, she felt a lot better. It appeared that she had a job, a place to stay, and she could take care of herself.

"How are you doing at home?" Mike asked during a lull in the conversation.

"What about my home?" Connie replied.

"I'd say things weren't so good there if'n you ask me," Willie said with some hesitation.

"I'd rather not talk about it," Connie said, looking away.

"Why not?" Mike asked. "Holding it all in only makes it worse."

"It's nothing I can't handle," she said. The three men stared at her in silence. Connie looked from one concerned face to another. Everyone at the table knew Connie was in deep trouble at home. She slowly stirred her half-empty cup of coffee and began to talk incessantly again.

She told them about how Drake was treating her, how he was staying out late, and sometimes not coming home at all. She intentionally avoided saying Drake was having an affair. She didn't want to say it to these three men, no matter how concerned they seemed to be.

They listened intently to Connie. Their hearts went out to this lady, knowing she was hurting deeply over more than losing her daughter. It was Willie's blatant honesty that brought Connie back to reality.

"So you think he's foolin' around," Willie stated.

"Fooling around?" Connie asked. The words didn't make sense to her.

"Yeah. You know, gittin' some on the side." Connie was naive and stared at him blankly.

"What Dad means is your husband is having an affair," Mike explained. Connie's face dropped. She seemed to stare right through the table.

"Yes," she said, barely audible. "He's having an affair," she admitted for the first time as the tears began to flow down her cheeks. She just sat there and openly cried in front of them.

Willie Bob pulled a clean, white handkerchief from his pocket and offered it to her. She just pushed it away and continued to cry.

"I don't need your sympathy!"

"We're not offering sympathy," Mike said. "We're offering support. There's a big difference."

"And just how can you give me support?" Connie responded defensively. "Just what can you do?"

"I don' know what we can do," Willie said, offering the hankie again. This time she took it and buried her face in it, sobbing. "But I'll tell you this, you gotta find out who this other woman is. What with AIDS an' all the other diseases out there, you gotta find out if'n she's clean. An' then, you gotta get away from that asshole b'fore he kills you with somethin' he picks up from one of his girlfriends!" Mike glared at Willie because of his coarse language.

"But don't you think this is just a fling and he'll get over it?" she asked hopefully.

"Naw, I think he found someone with big hooters an' a small mind," Willie said.

"Dad!" Mike interrupted angrily.

"Well, I've seen it b'fore!" Willie retorted. "He's thinkin' with his —"

"*DAD!*" Mike shouted. "Knock it off! That's enough now," he said sternly as he glared at Willie. "She doesn't need to hear that! She needs our support right now!"

"No, your dad's right," Connie said, blowing her nose. "Drake *is* fooling around and I need to find out who it is."

* * * *

Karyn was sitting in her bedroom at the Doyles' house. It had once been their daughter's room and was now decorated to accommodate a houseguest like Karyn. Karyn had put her things away and was now looking out the window into the back yard. She saw Maggie carry two glasses of iced tea toward Jerry as he sat on a lawn chair. Karyn couldn't hear their words, but she was sure they were talking about her.

"Yes, she reminds me a lot of Catherine," Jerry was saying. "They've both been hurt pretty badly."

"Well, I'm glad you brought her here," Maggie replied, taking a sip of her sweetened iced tea. "Maybe we can help."

"Maggie, if anybody can, I know you can," Jerry replied. He smiled at his wife. They'd been married for over thirty years and raised two boys and a girl of their own, and had been foster parents for two more troubled girls for several months.

The next morning, Maggie found Karyn asleep in the chair by the window where she'd been all night. Maggie saw the damp tissues lying in Karyn's lap and on the floor around her.

"Karyn, sweetie. It's time for breakfast," Maggie said gently. Karyn roused.

"Oh, thanks," she said, "But I'm not hungry."

"Come on anyway," Maggie replied, tugging gently on Karyn's hand. Karyn got up and followed Maggie to the kitchen.

"Where's breakfast?" she asked as she entered the kitchen.

"We have to make it," Maggie replied calmly.

"I told you I wasn't hungry," Karyn said and started for the bedroom.

"I heard that, but we still have to make breakfast for Jerry and me."

"Well, if I'm not hungry, why should I make breakfast for anyone else?" Karyn asked selfishly. She was so depressed she didn't feel like doing anything, let alone make a breakfast that she wasn't going to eat. Then she realized she was being rude to the people who were being nice to her.

"Oh, I'm sorry, Maggie," she said. "You've been good to me and I should help." She went to the sink to wash her hands. "So what do you want me to do first?" Karyn asked.

* * * *

That day, Maggie kept Karyn busy doing all sorts of menial chores around the house and in the small garden Maggie kept in the back yard. Maggie knew that one of the best ways to fight depression is to keep a person constructively occupied. They stopped for lunch, chatting about girl things, but went right back to work afterward. At six o'clock that evening, Karyn was worn out but happy to see Jerry when he came home from work.

"How are my girls?" he asked as he came in the front door. Karyn was pleased that he called her one of his girls. Jerry gave Maggie a hug and a peck on the cheek, then gave Karyn a brief hug, too. Karyn felt awkward, but didn't protest.

Over dinner, Maggie chatted away about their day, recounting everything Karyn had done, even the little shopping spree at the supermarket. Karyn didn't feel much like talking and merely played with her dinner, but she was becoming more comfortable with the Doyle family. Karyn volunteered to help with the dishes without Maggie even asking her. As she picked up Jerry's plate, Maggie nodded at him with a slight grin, indicating that everything would be okay.

Two days passed at the Doyles' and Karyn grew used to the routine. By the third day, she was making breakfast by herself and enjoyed participating with a real family. She was talking to Maggie more and more, and found herself liking her a lot. Maggie had a warm and sensible personality that Karyn found reassuring. One day Maggie came in to the kitchen while Karyn was making breakfast.

"Why do I have to make breakfast if I don't eat it?" Karyn asked without rancor or any emotion. "I'm not sure I understand."

"Well," explained Maggie patiently, "Because we all have jobs around here and that is one of yours. We all do chores in life that we really don't want to, but that's the way it is and always will be."

"Well, I guess I don't mind the chores too much, but I don't think I should have to make breakfast if I don't eat it," Karyn said. Maggie was pleased as she studied Karyn. This was the first reaction she'd seen from Karyn other than silence and tears. It was a good sign because it meant that Karyn was beginning to heal her emotional wounds.

"Karyn," Maggie said as she came to stand next to Karyn. "Did you know that when you complain about a particular job, it makes others around you very uncomfortable, like you want to be treated differently than everyone else. It makes it hard for people to like you."

"That's their problem," Karyn replied without looking up from the skillet of frying bacon. "I guess I just don't care if they like me or not."

"Oh, I think you do," Maggie countered. "I think you care a great deal."

"I *don't* care," Karyn repeated. "I guess I don't *need* to care since I've always had a lot of friends at school." Karyn continued to push the rashers of bacon around the skillet.

"Because you're so pretty?" Maggie asked.

"That's part of it, I guess," Karyn conceded. "I get along okay with most people." Maggie shook her head, a wry smile on her face.

"Karyn, your good looks will only get you so far," Maggie told her. "And one day, they'll be gone. But the real problem with your looks is that they'll get you in trouble."

"How can being pretty get someone in trouble?" Karyn asked.

Maggie already knew some of Karyn's history and replied, "Because you'll attract a lot of the wrong kind of people. Your good looks will attract the worst users and takers in the world, but also some pretty nice guys — like Jesse," she added.

Karyn was listening to every word and remembering the last several months of her life. Jesse had fallen in love with Karyn at first because of her beauty. Then, when she betrayed Jesse, he left her in spite of her good looks. Yes, Maggie was right. Her good looks would only get her so far. As she thought, the tears started to flow again. She had stopped pushing the bacon around and it was beginning to scorch in the hot skillet. Maggie turned off the burner and took Karyn into her arms as she began to cry again.

"Oh, Maggie," Karyn moaned. "I'm so tired of crying! I just can't seem to stop!" She melted further into Maggie's arms. "Maggie, no matter what I try to do, I just seem to keep messing everything up."

The rest of that morning Karyn and Maggie sat in the backyard talking about life in general. Karyn opened up and Maggie just listened to her, injecting a few words now and again. By mid-afternoon, Karyn was completely worn out from the emotional strain. Maggie tucked her in for an afternoon nap. Karyn finally relaxed enough to really sleep for the first time in weeks. She was still asleep when Jerry got home from work.

"Where's Karyn?" he asked.

"Asleep," Maggie replied as he gave her the usual hug and peck on the cheek.

"Asleep?" Jerry asked.

"You remember when Catherine finally started to get better?" Maggie reminded him.

"She slept for two days!" Jerry replied. "You got Karyn to open up already? That has to be a record!"

"She still has a ways to go," Maggie said as they walked toward the kitchen. "But she's on her way. Do you think you can find her a job? She needs something constructive to do with herself."

"Oh, I have an idea," he said

"And that is?"

"Why don't we put her on the ship with Catherine?" Jerry asked hopefully. "Karyn already has galley experience and you know Catherine's now the steward." Maggie was silent for a minute thinking, and then she nodded.

"Yes. That's a good idea. Catherine will be good for Karyn and it would be good for Catherine to help someone else." Maggie continued to nod.

"It's already taken care of," Jerry said, pleased with himself for coming up with the plan.

* * * *

Karyn awoke around seven that evening. She found Jerry in the garage fixing a lamp.

"Where's Maggie?" she asked.

"She's out running a few errands," Jerry replied. "Are you hungry?"

"Yeah. I guess I slept right through dinner."

"Not to worry," Jerry replied. "Maggie left you a plate of food in the fridge. You can warm it up in the microwave."

"I'd sure like to talk to Maggie," Karyn said, watching Jerry as he plugged in the lamp to test it.

"Seems you did a lot of that today," he commented, turning on the lamp switch. "You really like her, don't you?"

"Yeah. She reminds me of my mom in a lot of ways, but Maggie's a lot stronger."

"From what you told me, I'd guess your mom never got the chance to develop any real self-confidence married to a man like your dad." The lamp glowed, highlighting Jerry's face.

"No, I guess not," she replied. "Daddy didn't give her much of a chance. Anyway, do you know when Maggie will be back?"

"Probably in an hour or so," Jerry answered. He turned off the lamp and set it aside. Then he stared at the young woman before him. It seemed to Jerry that Karyn had grown up a lot in the last few days.

"What?" she asked. "Why are you looking at me like that?"

"Well, I was just wondering. Think you're ready to try for that job on the ship?"

"Tell me more about it," she said. In twenty minutes, Jerry had told Karyn all she wanted to know. She learned that she would be working for a lady named Catherine Bixby. Based on Jerry's personal recommendation, Karyn had already been hired. All she had to do was fill out the application and accept the job. Later that evening, Karyn found Jerry in the family room.

"I'll take that job," she happily announced and then after a lot of soul-searching, decided to call Jesse and tell him about her new job. They talked for over an hour.

Chapter 19

In Michigan, Drake had been away from home for two nights in a row. He hadn't had sex with Connie in more than six weeks. Connie was thin and pale, had no energy, and stayed home alone almost all the time. However, she had been thinking about how she could find out whom Drake had been seeing. One evening while Drake was gone, she called John Malcolm.

"John, you remember when you offered to help find Karyn?"

"Yes, of course, Connie," John replied. "Why do you ask?"

"Well, John, I need your help on another matter. It's very important, but I need you to keep it absolutely secret." John could hear the tension in Connie's voice.

"Sure, Connie," he replied. "I'll help you any way I can. And I promise to keep anything you say completely between us."

"John I need you to have your detective find out something for me."

"Why don't you and Drake just hire them yourselves?" he asked. "Drake knows I always use the Huffmaster Agency."

"That's just it, John," Connie confessed sadly. "I want them to investigate Drake."

"Go on," John said slowly, wondering what this was all about.

"John, I think Drake is running around. He's having an affair, and I want to know with whom."

John sighed. He recalled what Bruce Huffmaster had told him about Drake hitting Karyn. It didn't make sense to John that Drake would hit his daughter but there it was, and cold evidence doesn't lie. Now he was hearing that Drake might be having an affair. What had happened to Drake? John wished he hadn't already promised to help Connie because he didn't want to be put in the position of checking up any more on Drake.

"What makes you so sure?" John finally asked.

"John, I just know," Connie replied sullenly. "He doesn't talk to me any more, and he stays out late at night. He keeps telling me that he's working late, but sometimes he's gone all night. And, when he does come home, his shirt collar has lipstick traces. You know the signs, they're all in front of us. And sometimes he smells like Opium perfume and that's not my brand." John listened carefully without responding. "John, I just *have* to find out who this other woman is!" she said. "She can have him, honestly! But I would like to give her some advice, though, based on twenty-five years of experience."

"And just what good will *that* do?" John asked her.

"John, I just *have* to! There's just no other way, for me at least." Connie waited for a few seconds and went on. "So, are you going to help me or not?" Connie heard John sigh deeply.

"Okay, I'll help you, but my heart's not in it," John conceded slowly. "I'll get on it first thing tomorrow morning. I'll let you know what I hear just as soon as Huffmaster tells me anything."

"Thank you, John," Connie said sincerely.

Drake had become casual about his affairs with Anne Marie and Sandra. He liked showing off the two glamorous women wherever he went. He made no effort to hide the fact that he went to hotels with Anne Marie, and that he spent nights in Sandra's apartment. It took the private detectives only two days to have a complete dossier on Drake's activities. The telephone in John's office rang around ten o'clock in the morning of the third day.

"Mr. Malcolm, it's Bruce Huffmaster on line one."

"Thank you, Irene," John replied and stared at the blinking light on his telephone. He hesitated to pick up the line for fear of what Bruce would tell him. Little did he know.

"Hello, Mr. Malcolm," Bruce said.

"Hi, Bruce. How's your wife and family?" he asked, attempting to be pleasant.

"They're fine, Mr. Malcolm," Bruce replied. "My wife is still talking about that turkey you sent over to us last Thanksgiving. That really made a hit."

"I'm glad you liked it," John replied. "So what do you have for me?"

"Mr. Malcolm, I think we should meet privately for a few minutes," Bruce replied, careful not to give any details.

"What's the matter with talking on the phone?" John asked. "We've never had to meet privately before. What's this all about?"

"Mr. Malcolm, I really don't want to discuss this over the phone. Can I come to your office right away?"

"Sure, Bruce. Come on over. I'll cancel all my appointments and wait for you."

An hour later Bruce reported to John with the sordid details and photos to back them up. John was shocked. How could his protégé do this to him? How could his own wife and daughter be willing culprits? He thanked Bruce and paid him what he owed on the spot. As he wrote out the check, John told him to continue the investigation, but now Bruce was to report directly to John via cell phone, and he was to report events as they were happening. Then John sat in his office and stared out the window. His own wife *and* daughter were having an affair with Drake, and he felt sick.

* * * *

The next morning, John Malcolm reluctantly called Connie.

"Hello, Connie," he said sadly. "It's me, John."

"Oh, hi, John," Connie replied, "I take it you must have some news."

"Yes, my dear, I do," John said resolutely. "Can we meet someplace? We have a lot to talk about."

"John, just tell me straight out," Connie said. "I'm a big girl and I'm ready for whatever you tell me, good or bad."

"Can't we meet someplace?" he pleaded. "I don't really want to discuss this over the phone."

"John, tell me!" Connie demanded softly. "I already know he's having an affair. What could be worse than that?"

"He's having an affair, all right," he said. "But not with one woman. He has two women."

"Two?" Connie exclaimed. "*Two?!* He needs *two* women?"

"Connie, that's not all," John interrupted.

"Okay, so who are they?"

"You're sure you really want to know?"

"*YES!* John, *talk* to me!"

"It's Anne Marie and Sandra."

She couldn't believe what John was telling her. Connie was silent for several seconds before responding. It *couldn't* be them — not Anne Marie and Sandra! Why, Anne Marie was John's *wife*, and Sandra? *His daughter!*

"John, this *can't* be true," Connie said quietly. "Not them. It *can't* be them! There has to be some mistake!"

"Connie, Bruce Huffmaster is one of the best in the business. He doesn't make mistakes. He's got photos and copies of hotel registrations to prove it. All the details are there."

"But John, it doesn't seem possible." She felt tears running down her cheeks, partly for herself, but also for John as well.

"Okay, John. I guess we'd better get together and talk."

* * * *

John and Connie met at a restaurant. John hadn't known that Connie had lost so much weight over the past three months. Her cheekbones were angular on her thin face and her clothes were loose on her slight frame. However, John could sense immediately that something had changed inside Connie because for the first time in the twenty-some years he'd known her, she had fire in her eyes. John could tell she was ready for combat and Drake was the target. He felt the same way about the three of them.

* * * *

Karyn stood on the dock next to the luxury liner, appreciating the sleek lines. She knew she was on her own and had to work hard. Her job would be bussing tables. She knew it would be messy, dirty work, but she knew it wouldn't kill her. She smiled to herself and hoped maybe she could work up to being a waitress because the money was a lot better. She drew a deep breath and boarded the ship with her one suitcase.

"I'm here to meet Catherine Bixby," she said to the man who was greeting everyone as they came aboard.

"Yes. She's expecting you," he said as he checked his list. "You'll be working in the galley?" the uniformed man asked.

"No, sir," Karyn replied. "I'll be bussing tables in the main dining room." He nodded and pointed as he told her where to find Catherine.

Fifteen minutes later, Karyn was in the galley, looking things over while the kitchen crew gave her a close once-over. The young men were taking special note of the pretty girl.

"You must be Karyn," a voice said behind her. "I'm Catherine." Karyn turned to see a smiling young woman who didn't seem too much older than she was. Catherine held her hand out. Karyn shook it.

"Yes, I am," Karyn replied. "I was expecting someone a lot older."

"Sorry to disappoint you," Catherine laughed. "I'd like to think I hide my age well. Come on, I'll introduce you to everybody." Catherine was only twenty-seven years old, but she had worked hard and had earned herself the galley manager's position in just two years. She called everyone together to introduce Karyn and make her feel welcome.

* * * *

Within a week, Karyn had adjusted to the dining room routine as though she'd been there for years. She made it a point to never complain about anything and consequently, everyone treated her like she was an old friend.

It seems that Maggie was right, she thought.

Bussing tables was mindless work, which allowed her long hours to miss Jesse and to think about her life. Occasionally the patrons would talk to her, and she always responded politely and respectfully, often refilling their coffee or doing other chores just to make things easier for the wait staff. The waiters and waitresses soon began to ask to have Karyn work their areas because she made their jobs easier and she was pleasant to work with. Catherine carefully watched Karyn's progress. One day after a particularly heavy Sunday crowd Catherine came up behind Karyn.

"Ready for a break?" she asked.

"No, I'm okay for now," Karyn replied, loading the last of the dishes onto the cart. Catherine pulled Karyn around to face her.

"Let's take a break," Catherine insisted. "You're done here anyway." Karyn nodded and they went to Catherine's office.

"Karyn, I've been watching you and I can tell you've been through a lot. What's your story? You want to tell me about it?" Catherine asked as she set a cup of coffee on the desk in front of Karyn.

"Not much to tell," Karyn replied.

"Really?" Catherine said, her eyebrows raised. "Then let me tell you a little story."

"When I was seventeen like you I was pretty, too," Catherine said.

"I think you still are," Karyn commented.

"I'm attractive," Catherine agreed, "but nothing like you, but it still got me in a lot of trouble." She took a deep breath and went on. "My dad died when I was twelve. God, I loved him! He was the only thing that stood between Mom and me. Mom was an addict, mostly coke, but sometimes heroine, too. She'd get blasted and Dad would try to get her clean. It never worked, and when he died, she got worse than ever. I was pretty and all the guys liked me, and I had pretty low self-esteem, I guess, because pretty soon I was sleeping with them. One night I got banged by half the guys on the basketball team. I was only sixteen when I got pregnant and Mom pitched me out on the street. I wound up in a Catholic home for unwed mothers. They took me in only because I had agreed to give the baby up for adoption." Catherine paused while her eyes grew moist.

"Anyway, as soon as the baby was born, they said I had to leave so I wound up on the street again. I was alone, had no money, nobody in my life, and worst of all, no education. I couldn't even get a job good enough to feed myself and keep a roof over my head. I began to do a little prostituting just to eat. I got busted twice for that, but I didn't have enough schooling to do anything else. Heck, I didn't even have a high school diploma. I always went back to prostitution. I finally hit on a scam that seemed foolproof. I started buying tickets on luxury liners and turning tricks. I was making more money than I'd ever made in my life until I got busted the third time.

"Well, there I was, sitting in Security, looking at this guy who I just *knew* was going to toss me in jail."

"So you went to jail again?"

"No, he called his wife and took me home — to *his* home, but it's my home now, too."

"That was *Jerry?*"

"One and the same," Catherine answered with a smile. "I don't know why, but he tried to help me. Every day of my life I make sure I don't disappoint him and Maggie.

"Karyn, it's no accident that you're here on this ship. Jerry called me to arrange the job for you. You and I are truly kindred spirits," she laughed. "Almost sisters!"

"I can't believe this," Karyn said. "They've taken care of everything, haven't they?"

"Not everything. You're still out on your own and have to make good choices, but at least you're not alone. You have me and everyone in the galley. We're all here together — practically a family. We all know you've been hurt, but that's all."

"Catherine, I guess I've been feeling sorry for myself because my dad used to beat me up," she said as she began her own story.

"And that's about it," she said some forty minutes later. Catherine nodded sympathetically.

"But I sort of wondered why none of the crew guys were hitting on me," Karyn went on. "I figured you'd told them to stay away from me, which was fine by me. I don't trust men any more."

"Brothers don't hit on their sisters," Catherine said. "Those guys will be like your brothers. You can trust them to be gentlemen. You'll see."

"Family sounds pretty good right now," Karyn said. "I haven't had one for a long time."

"Family is nice," Catherine agreed, "But I want to point out one more thing to you. Education is important. Maybe it's the most important thing in your life, besides your relationships with other people."

"Yeah, I'm beginning to see that," Karyn replied. "I know it meant more to

Jesse than anything, even more than me. It sure meant a lot to his mom, too. His dad didn't think much of it, though."

"Some people are like that, but that's just because he hasn't been exposed to all the benefits of it," Catherine explained. "You need all the education you can get because one day your looks will be gone, but you'll always have a diploma. Jesse knows that. I got my GED and then an Associate's in Restaurant Management. That's how I got to be the boss here."

"I understand, Catherine," Karyn said solemnly. "Thanks."

"You're welcome. You know you can talk to me any time. And I mean that — any time, day or night." Karyn smiled and nodded as she stood up and left Catherine's office.

Up to that point of the cruise, every day after work Karyn had gone to her quarters and stayed there, but that evening, after her talk with Catherine, she decided to go out for a walk on the decks. She was looking over the railing at the open sea when a man approached her.

"Hi. Waiting for someone?" he asked.

"No, just looking at the ocean," she replied without looking at him.

"Want to go get a drink?"

"Nope, I was just leaving." she said.

"Oh, come on," he responded. "Just a drink."

"Forget it, mister. My fiancé is a 235-pound, six-foot-four running back for the Green Bay Packers. He eats guys like you for a breakfast snack!"

"Hey, I didn't mean anything," he stammered.

"Yes, you did!" Karyn retorted. "Now get lost!" The man beat a hasty retreat.

Chapter 20

In Michigan, two hotel maids were staring wide-eyed at each other as they listened to the couple inside the suite. For the last twenty minutes they'd listened to Drake and Anne Marie groaning with pleasure as they were having some torrid sex. Anne had been groaning in ecstasy while Drake thrust himself into her body in hot, sweaty passion. They'd finished together in a climax that left them breathless. The maids giggled at each other as they returned to their cleaning chores.

Drake and Anne Marie lay naked next to each other, beads of sweat on their foreheads as Drake stared at the ceiling, thinking. They had already been together twice this week and it was only Wednesday. Monday was really good, he remembered, because she had started with oral sex that had really turned him on. But as soon as they were done having sex, she began to argue with him about seeing Sandra. After a heated argument, she stormed out. Then today she'd called and asked him to meet her at the hotel, but they argued for a full twenty minutes before tumbling into bed.

Over the last few weeks it had always been the same. Arguments about Sandra, then sex, or sex, then arguments about Sandra. What Drake didn't know was that now Huffmaster detectives were photographing his every move. Bruce Huffmaster knew every minute Drake spent with Anne or Sandra and immediately reported it to John. Even while Drake lay in the bed next to Anne Marie, John was sitting in his office, already aware that they were together. It tore him apart inside. John's health was deteriorating faster than ever before, and he knew he didn't have much time left. As he sat in his office watching the sun go down in a blaze of orange, yellow, and purple sky, he finalized his plan.

* * * *

John had taken to calling Connie every other day, regular as clockwork. He said it was to see how she was doing, but it was as much to get support as it was to give it. He knew she was an innocent victim of circumstances and he cared about her welfare. Connie had gone for days without seeing Drake and appreciated John's concern.

Along with John's calls, Mike or Jesse called her on occasion to see how she was doing and to talk about Karyn. Connie appreciated their interest and even began to like Willie Bob better in spite of his rough edges.

* * * *

It was the last week in August when Karyn's ship arrived in Gibraltar. Her eighteenth birthday was that week.

"Hey, Karyn," Catherine called to her as she was stacking the last of the breakfast dishes in the galley. "We're going ashore for a while. Why don't you come along?"

"Oh, that's okay," she replied. "I think I'll just hang out on the ship." However, Catherine had other plans for Karyn.

"Karyn," Catherine began as she strode toward Karyn. "You need to get out for a while. You've been holed up here or in your quarters since we left Miami. Girl, you gotta get out and get some fresh air." After several minutes of convincing, Karyn relented and agreed to go ashore with Catherine and a few other members of the staff.

Once ashore, she was delighted to see the Port of Gibraltar and learn about its mixed Spanish and British history. She hung out with Catherine and two of the galley crew all day, wandering about, talking and laughing together. Finally, Catherine pointed to an attractive restaurant overlooking Tangiers across the straits.

"Hey, I'm hungry," Catherine said. "Let's get something to eat!"

As they went into the restaurant, the entire dining room and kitchen crew shouted "Surprise!" as they stood around a big birthday cake with Karyn's name and eighteen candles on it.

The party went on for a couple of hours, complete with gifts. Catherine looked at the clock and suggested it was time for everyone to head back to the ship so they would be ready for work tomorrow. As they walked back to the ship, Karyn saw some pay telephones and asked Catherine if there was time to make a couple of quick calls.

"I'd like to call Maggie and Jerry first, and then maybe Jesse," she explained to Catherine.

"I think that's a great idea," Catherine said enthusiastically.

Karyn and Catherine joined in together for a happy conversation with Maggie for about fifteen minutes. Then Catherine went over to an outdoor café across the street so Karyn could have some privacy with Jesse. They talked for almost half an hour about a lot of little things. Jesse decided not to tell Karyn about the problems with her family back in Michigan.

"Well, it's getting late," Karyn finally said. "I've got some friends waiting for me and besides, I've run up your phone bill way too much. I'll send you some money to pay for it."

"Don't worry about it," Jesse replied. "I've got enough to cover it. Besides, it was worth it to hear from you, Karyn. I've been thinking about you quite a lot lately."

"Me, too, Jesse. By the way, exactly when will you be leaving for college?" she asked.

"In ten days," Jesse answered.

"That soon?" Karyn asked, and then paused. "Ummm, Jesse?"

"What?"

"Can I call you at college too?"

"Sure. Any time. I'll make sure Mike has the number as soon as I know what it is. Just call him and he'll give it to you."

"Thanks," she said, relieved that he wanted to hear from her at college, too.

"Well, I gotta go," she said at last. "Bye."

They hung up and Karyn went across the street to the café where Catherine was waiting for her. All the others had now gone back to the ship.

"I take it that the call went well," Catherine said, noting the smile on Karyn's face.

"It sure did!" Karyn replied. "He wants to hear from me while he's at college! Isn't that great?"

Catherine smiled and nodded. She remembered being in love and what a high it was for at least the first several months. They walked back to the ship together in silence, each with her own thoughts.

* * * *

Jesse called Connie immediately to tell her about Karyn's call. Connie was relieved and pleased to know Karyn was all right. She and Jesse talked for quite a while, mostly about Karyn. It seemed that maybe Karyn knew what she was doing after all. And Connie's affection for Jesse was growing each time they talked.

* * * *

On the first of September, Karyn's ship docked in Nice, France. After her last talk with Jesse, she had some bad days struggling with the sad memories about their time together a few months ago. She thought about him now as she cleaned up the tables after the lunch crowd. It would have been so much better if only she had been smarter. It could have been much different now. Catherine watched sympathetically from a distance and finally decided to take some positive action. Half an hour before quitting time Catherine went to Karyn.

"I've made an appointment at the ship's hair stylist for you," Catherine said casually.

"Why? I don't want a haircut," Karyn said as she brushed sodden strands of her long, blonde hair away from her eyes.

"Honey, I've been watching you all day, and one of the best things for an old attitude is a new look. Ginger and Jenn have agreed to stay late. They're expecting us at six."

"But—"

"No 'buts'," Catherine interrupted. "That'll give you time to get a shower. Be in my office at five 'til six."

At six o'clock, Catherine and Karyn walked into the ship's salon. Ginger and Jennifer went right to work. They chatted happily for forty-five minutes as they did her nails plus a complete makeover. Then they stood back to look at her hair. Karyn trembled as they studied her and discussed what they were going to do.

"It should be short, but how short?" Ginger said.

"Yeah," Catherine agreed, nodding. "Short hair is a lot easier to take care of in the dining room."

"She could do a pixie style," Jennifer offered.

"Pixie's *too* short," Ginger said, much to Karyn's relief. "But *Dixie* would work."

"Dixie?" Karyn asked.

"Dixie, as in Dixie Chicks! Natalie Mains' hair style would be *perfect* on you!"

Ginger and Jenn went to work. After another forty-five minutes, Karyn studied herself in the mirror. Her hair was short and pert, highlighted and bouncy. The makeover on her face was professional, and made her look like she should be on the cover of the magazine *Seventeen.*

"Is that me?" she asked, blinking.

"That's you, honey," Ginger replied. Ginger, Jenn, and Catherine all grinned at the new Karyn. Karyn continued to study herself. It was still her face, but there was a new feeling and a new sparkle that came with the new look.

"I like it," she said. "I *really* like it!"

"Cool!" Catherine said happily. "Now it's time to go try it out!"

"Try it out?"

"Sure. We're going ashore into Nice tonight and you're coming with us."

"Aw, Catherine —" Karyn began.

"Don't 'aw Catherine' me, girl! You're going and that's final!"

Karyn knew it was useless to argue, so she smiled and nodded.

* * * *

It was still early in the evening when Karyn and her friends on the kitchen staff went ashore. They walked around Nice, chatted in the warm Mediterranean evening as they looked in the shop windows and listened to the French people talking on the streets. The Negresco Hotel, old and elegant, was still the focal point of the "in" crowd as it had been for over five decades. The city charmed Karyn. She couldn't speak the language, but it didn't matter because the French people were warm and friendly. Later that evening the dining room crew stopped in a restaurant for a bite to eat. The locals were pleasant and they laughed together with Karyn and her friends. A little later, the restaurant began to do karaoke. The emcee made it a point to pick people from the audience to sing. He quickly noticed Karyn and walked over to her. As he approached he heard everyone at the table speaking English.

"American, *mes amis*?" he asked.

"I'm sorry, we don't speak French," Catherine replied with a smile.

"You are Americans, no?" he said without taking his eyes off Karyn.

"Yes, *oui*. We are Americans," Karyn answered, using the only French word she knew.

"Ah, good!" he said with a smile. "Sing?" he asked, pointing to Karyn.

"Oh, I don't sing," Karyn replied, shaking her head.

"Oh, get up there, Girl," Catherine demanded.

"No, really," Karyn protested. "I don't sing. I don't know how."

The emcee dropped a booklet on the table in front of her and pointed to the stage.

"Find ze song, *mademoiselle*. You sing ten minutes from now, *n'est pas?*" He walked back to the stage to introduce another singer.

"We'd better find you a song," Catherine said. Everyone checked out the song list, finally finding a few songs that Karyn might know. Her favorite was the old song, *Superstar*, by the Carpenters. She knew the words because her mother used to sing it around the house. Catherine waved the emcee over to the table and pointed to the song. He grinned, nodded, and returned to his stack of CDs. Karyn was growing more nervous by the second.

"Catherine, I've never sung in front of anyone in my life."

"And you've never been to Gibraltar or France in your life, either. Kid, it's time for some adventure!"

"But what if I mess up?" Karyn worried.

"So what?" Catherine replied with a wry smile. "Everyone will get a good laugh out of it and no harm's done. Get your ass over to that stage! You're on next! Maybe you'll even win us a bottle of champagne!"

Karyn stood up and looked at Catherine and her friends. They all grinned and waved her on. She looked across to the stage where the emcee was waving at her to hurry up. The emcee pulled Karyn into the spotlight and introduced her.

In the audience happened to be a young man named Karl Jones, a band-leader on Karyn's ship. He'd never seen Karyn before but as soon as he laid eyes on her he was smitten. He stopped talking to his pals and watched the blonde girl intently.

What happened next was magic. As the emcee started the music, a very nervous Karyn began to sing. At first her voice was shaky and soft, but the emcee nodded and motioned for her to sing out. No one was more surprised than Karyn at how good she sounded. As her nerves faded, she began to get into the music. Her voice became clear and powerful. The crowd responded with cheers and applause. Karl was swept off his feet. He knew he had found new talent that night. The crowd gave her a standing ovation, and called for more. Karyn sang five more songs that night, each to hearty applause. She won two bottles of champagne so the crew was in a great mood as they headed back to the ship.

On the way, Karyn spotted a telephone and asked if she could call Jesse and tell him all about it. Catherine and Sam, a galley cook, stayed to wait for her.

"Oh, Jesse, you should have seen it," she said. "It was just like in the movies! There was this big crowd and they all clapped for me and then they wanted more!"

"Sounds like you were a big hit," he replied. "Congratulations!" he said, happy for her.

"Wow," she went on. "It was just super!"

They talked another few minutes, and then she said, "Jesse, I have to go. Catherine and Sam are waiting. We have to get up early for work tomorrow."

"Sure! That's cool," Jesse replied. "I'll let you go. I sure wish I could've seen it."

"Me, too," Karyn said. "Well, 'bye for now."

"'Bye, sweetheart. I love you."

Karyn froze at his words. He had just said he loved her, even after all that had happened. And she knew he wouldn't use the word "sweetheart" with her unless he meant it. The seconds ticked by as her heart pounded.

"I love you, too," she finally said, and then hung up. Jesse immediately called Mike to tell him about Karyn's wonderful evening.

"Mike, she sounded great!" he said.

"You make it sound like she was the star of the show," Mike told him.

"Oh, she was! The audience made her sing five more songs!"

"Why don't you call Connie and tell her all about it?" Mike suggested.

"That's a good idea!" Jesse agreed. "Talk to you later!"

Three minutes later Jesse was telling Connie all about Karyn's evening. The excitement rang in his voice and it elevated Connie's spirits to a high she hadn't known in months.

* * * *

The next day, two men came into the dining room and approached Karyn.

"Hi, I'm Karl Jones," the younger one said as he introduced himself. "I was at the karaoke show last night."

"I'm Karyn. Nice to meet you," she replied. She glanced at Catherine who stood nearby, eyeing Karl. She came to Karyn's side and ignoring Karl, reached out to the other man.

"You're Myron Goldstein, aren't you?" Catherine asked.

"Yep. I sure am, and I happen to be the Director of Entertainment for the ship. Karl told me about Karyn and said I should give her an audition. So, how about it, young lady? You want to do an audition?" he asked, turning to Karyn. Karyn, speechless, looked to Catherine for help. Catherine and Karl looked at each other for a brief moment as both remembered when they'd first met a couple of years ago. Then Catherine nodded as a smile curled at the edge of her mouth.

"You think I should?" Karyn asked Catherine.

"I think you'd be crazy not to," Catherine replied. "Do it!"

"Oh, Catherine, I don't know if I can."

"Just do it!" Catherine commanded. "She'll do it, Mr. Goldstein, if I have to bundle her up and take her there myself."

Karyn reluctantly agreed. Karl promised to help her practice for her upcoming audition and suggested several songs for her. That afternoon after the lunch crowd, she began a regular rehearsal schedule that was to happen every day up to her audition.

Chapter 21

John Malcolm was in declining health and was working only half-days and sometimes didn't come in at all. Drake gloated in the knowledge that John had promised him one-third of his stock and that the other two-thirds would be divided between Anne Marie and Sandra. With the stock Drake already had, that meant he would gain control of Cox Chemical after John's death. Drake was soon to be a very wealthy man. Two weeks later in mid-September, John Malcolm called Connie from his bed. He'd been so weak that he didn't even try getting to the office.

"Connie, I think my time is finally running out."

"Oh, John, I don't want to hear that. Maybe things will improve in the next few weeks."

"Well, that's not likely, my dear," he said. "But don't you worry. Everything's been taken care of."

"I'm not sure what you mean by that," she replied.

"I'm saying that everything will work out right for everybody. You just need to do as you're told by the attorneys from here on out. Beyond that, I can't say any more." John's voice was raspy and he stifled coughs.

"John, I'm not sure I understand what you're saying, but I trust you to make everything right. I'll do as you say. And John?"

"Yes, my dear?"

"I've decided to leave Drake."

* * * *

The day for Karyn's audition came. Karl had worked diligently with Karyn and he felt she was ready. He arranged to use the main lounge. Catherine got permission to close the dining room for an hour right after lunch so all her friends could be there. When Myron Goldstein ambled into the lounge, Karl motioned for two of the crewmembers to close the doors and then he struck up the band.

The music began to reverberate through the lounge as Karyn stood in the muted light of the stage with her face lowered toward the floor. The lights slowly came up, the intro to the first song grew in volume, and Karyn raised her face to the small crowd seated before her.

Karyn sailed through the ballads. All the while the audience took quick glances at Myron to see his reaction.

After the sixth song, Karyn was finished and the crowd roared with approval. Myron remained stone-faced and non-committal. Finally, a smile formed and Myron began to clap slow and steady, indicating his approval. Then he asked when she could be ready for her first show. Karyn ran over to hug Karl first, then bounded off the stage to hug Catherine. Later that day, Myron stopped by the galley and had Catherine call Karyn into her office. Catherine stood at Karyn's side.

"Karyn," he said. "I'm prepared to offer you $600 per week to be in one of my shows. What do you think of that?" Karyn's mouth went agape and all she could do was stammer.

"That means she'll take it," Catherine answered for her.

Karyn was bubbling with excitement when she called Jesse that night and told him all about her new show business career.

* * * *

One day, John called to invite Drake and Connie to come to his house for another meeting. At John's house, Anne Marie met them at the door. Connie almost retched when Anne gave Drake an innocent-looking hug and peck on the cheek. Anne Marie ushered Drake and Connie upstairs, straight to John's bedside. He was lying in his huge king-sized bed, looking wan and very feeble. Anne Marie sat on the bed next to her husband and held his hand.

"Drake, you've been a wonderful employee," he began in his weak voice, stifling a cough. He took Drake's hand with his other hand and held it as he talked. "And I know Connie has been a wonderful wife to you. A good wife is a wonderful thing, don't you think?" John cast loving eyes toward Anne Marie and she smiled back at the frail man on the bed. Connie began to wonder what was going on.

"Yes, John," Drake replied. "A good wife is a wonderful thing." He cast a quick glance at Anne Marie, ignoring Connie. All the while, John was holding Anne Marie's hand in a loving way.

"Drake, you know I have big plans for you and the company," John went on. "And it's no secret that my time is near," he said, coughing some more. "But —" he shot a meaningful glance at Connie, "— the arrangements are made for when I'm gone and I'm sure they'll be clear to everyone, especially the lawyers." Drake nodded again, and Connie smiled to herself knowing that John had made some huge decisions that would surprise everyone. "You'll just have to wait until I'm gone to get the details," John continued, "but rest assured that everyone will get what they deserve."

Then John asked, "Have you heard anything about Karyn?"

"No, we haven't," Drake replied sullenly.

"Oh, she has a job singing on a ship," Connie corrected. "She's fine and really loves her new job."

"How come I wasn't told about this?" Drake leveled his eyes at Connie with an angry glare.

"If you were ever home, you'd know," Connie retorted.

"I'm home every night," Drake lied, trying to look good in front of John.

"That's bull and everyone knows it," Connie shot back, staring directly at Anne. Anne shrank back from Connie's damning eyes.

Drake couldn't believe Connie was talking to him like this. John watched the scene unfold and, although he didn't show it, he was pleased. He could see Connie would be able to take care of herself when she and Drake parted. Anne Marie remained silent.

"John, if you have nothing more to tell us, and it's okay with you, I think we'd better go now," Drake suddenly said, taking Connie by the arm and pulling her toward the door. Connie wrenched herself free and strode over to John's bedside.

"Yes, I think we should," Connie said as she bent to give John a kiss on the forehead. "You need your rest. I hope we can see you again soon."

On the ride home, Drake began to berate Connie again

"Just what the hell do you think you're doing, embarrassing me like that in front of John?" he shouted.

"I didn't embarrass you," she countered. "You embarrassed yourself by not coming home and being a part of our family!"

"You could've called me at work!" he bellowed.

"I tried! You're never there!" she shouted back. She wanted to scream out "because you're always out with your whores!" but she held her tongue for now.

"I'm her father and I should know everything that's going on in her life! You should've told me!"

"How can I? Like I said, you're never home!" she looked at him defiantly. To Drake's surprise, Connie wasn't backing down. The more Connie stood up for herself, the more furious he became with her.

The traffic light turned red at the intersection ahead and when the car came to a stop, Connie got out of the car and stalked purposefully away.

Drake got out and raced to catch up to her. In the meantime, two policemen in their patrol car noticed Drake's car idling at the intersection with both the doors wide open and came to investigate. Drake didn't notice them pulling up behind him as he argued with Connie. They approached just in time to see Drake punch her in the face. Connie went down hard and the police jumped out of the cruiser with their batons drawn. In seconds, they had Drake on the ground and cuffed. As one dealt with Drake, the other officer radioed EMS.

"What's your name?" he asked Connie as he helped her to sit up on the grass.

"Connie," she replied. "Connie Mathers."

The other cop had pinned Drake on the grass and cuffed him. Then he dug in Drake's pants to pull out his wallet and check the ID.

"Don't you know who I am?" Drake bellowed from his prone position on the grass. "I'm Drake Mathers, and I'll have your badges for this!" The cop ignored him as he hauled Drake to his feet and stuffed him into the back of the cruiser.

"Get a load of who we just arrested," the officer said as he came up to Connie and the other officer. "That guy is Drake Mathers!"

"Yeah, I already figured that out," the second cop said as he kept a hand on Connie's arm to steady her.

"Are you going to press charges?" the officer asked Connie.

"Do I have to?" she asked.

"You don't have to, but it sure would make things easier for us." Connie nodded that she would.

Soon the EMS arrived. Drake was hauled away in the cruiser and Connie was taken to the hospital. After a brief treatment at the hospital, she was taken to the police station. She pressed charges against Drake by filing a complaint. Then she also told the truth of what happened when Drake and Jesse had their fight. The police were only too glad to drop the charges against Jesse and close that case.

* * * *

Karyn had her first show. It was an afternoon matinee because Myron knew from experience that he didn't dare start anyone out in the big evening shows. It always takes time for a new entertainer to break into the bigger shows. She stood offstage with Myron and Catherine and peeked out to look at the audience.

"You think I'll do all right?" she nervously whispered to Myron as she peeked around the curtains. "There's over 300 people out there, and it's only four o'clock."

"You'll be fine. You just do your songs like you practiced with Karl and they'll love it." She had developed a soft, sultry, almost sexy style that distinguished her rendition from most other singers. She had almost an Eartha Kitt quality. Just then the lights changed and Karl cued Karyn.

"You're on," Myron whispered and gave her a gentle shove on the rump. "Break a leg!"

* * * *

Karyn's debut was only four songs, but it was a resounding success. The audience roared with approval as she finished and took her bow. Myron turned to Catherine.

"She isn't a star yet, but there's no doubt in my mind that she could soon be heading the bill," he whispered to Catherine. Catherine nodded and caught Karyn up in her arms as she bounded off the stage. Karl watched the pert blonde with her spry steps and yearned to get closer to her. *I've made you what you are,* he thought, *and now it's time for some payback.*

* * * *

It was October and Jesse was at Miami University in Oxford, Ohio. As usual, he didn't have much leisure time during the day. He was playing football and his grades were exemplary. Some people were even predicting he would be a Rhodes Scholar. Mike and Willie Bob attended every home game, cheering him on. Jesse had already caught ten touchdown passes, breaking the school record.

In Michigan, Drake had moved into an apartment near work so he could keep more of his time clear for Sandra, but she was getting bored with him. All the while, John slid closer to death.

"You haven't been taking your medicine," the doctor admonished him one morning. "It's difficult for me to help you if you won't take your medications."

"The best help you could give me at this point is to stand back and let me die a natural death," John replied.

"Oh, John, you don't mean that," Anne Marie cried.

"I meant it exactly as I said it," John responded. "There is a time to hold on and a time to let go. For me, it's time to let go." He clenched his eyes shut and stifled another raspy cough.

At that moment, Drake was in the law offices of Edwards and King, starting his divorce from Connie.

"Why are you in such a rush for this divorce?" Mr. King asked after listening to Drake for almost an hour.

"Well, isn't it true that if I'm divorced and suddenly come into a lot of money, I won't have to share it with my wife?"

Drake briefly explained that John planned to leave him one-third of Cox Chemical and that he didn't want to give half of that to Connie when they divorced, adding that if he could keep the entire inheritance, he would control Cox Chemical.

"All right, let's get started," Henry King replied. Before Drake left Mr. King's office that afternoon, the papers had been drafted, assigned to the Honorable Wade C. Keith, Circuit Court Judge, and a bailiff was on his way to the Mathers homestead to serve Connie with the papers. Drake was pleased that the Order to Show Cause prevented Connie from touching any of their assets, bank accounts or the like, until the first hearing in front of the judge in two weeks. Drake left Mr. King's office beaming.

As soon as Connie was served with the papers, she called John.

"I was expecting this," John said. "I'll take it from here." Connie hung up and went to fix herself a cup of coffee, tears forming in her eyes. She had just made a pot of coffee when the telephone rang.

"Hello?"

"Mrs. Mathers?"

"Yes."

"My name is Peter Savoy. Mr. John Malcolm called me about your situation. I would like to see you as soon as possible."

"Mr. Savoy, this really isn't a good time," Connie replied, loudly blowing her nose.

"Mrs. Mathers, I'm a lawyer, and it's important that we talk right away. John has told me your husband has already served you with divorce papers and I need to see you."

"When do you want to see me?" she asked.

"Right now."

A little over an hour later Connie was in Peter Savoy's office. He listened intently to Connie's story while he examined the complaint and *ex parte* order. In another few minutes, Connie and Peter were talking to Mr. Joshua Cohen, a divorce attorney, from Peter's office.

"Mrs. Mathers," he said, "I strongly suggest we allow your husband to complete these divorce proceedings as quickly as possible."

"Why?" she asked.

"I can't tell you exactly, but rest assured, it is in your best interests to do so."

"Does this have something to do with John Malcolm?" Connie asked with a crooked smile.

"Let's just say he is aware of everything that's going on between you and Drake Mathers."

"I'll do whatever you suggest, then, Mr. Savoy," she answered.

* * * *

Over the next couple of weeks, Connie did everything Peter Savoy and Joshua Cohen suggested. Drake was anxious to finish the divorce as soon as possible and conceded to most of the demands Mr. Cohen made. Drake agreed to pay Connie alimony for life, plus four years of college for Karyn. He even agreed to let Connie stay in the marital home. The only real battle was Mr. Cohen's demand for one-half of Drake's current holdings of Cox stock, which Drake finally conceded to. Beyond that, Mr. Cohen didn't ask for much because he wanted to finish the divorce as quickly as possible.

It took only five weeks to finish the divorce. Connie wasn't sure she did the right thing because Drake still kept most of the marital assets.

By late November John began to slip away quickly. Anne Marie had started out using Drake as a toy, but now that John was dying, her intentions changed. She wanted to keep Drake on a permanent basis. She knew she couldn't trust her daughter, and, if she were to marry Drake, their combined Cox stock would control the company. She was sure Drake had serious designs on Sandra and wanted to stop him from seeing her. The Friday after Thanksgiving, as John lay dying upstairs, Anne Marie telephoned Drake in an attempt to bring him into her plan.

"Drake, darling, I've been thinking," she began. "I've been thinking that you and I make a great couple, not to mention the fact that we have great sex together."

"So what's your point, Anne?" Drake asked impatiently.

"Well, you're a smart businessman and you know it would be a good idea to combine our Cox Chemical assets."

"Where are you going with this conversation, Anne?"

"I was thinking that since you're divorced now, and I'll soon be widowed, we should get married."

"Married?" Drake snorted. "*Married?* To you? You gotta be kidding! You're more than ten years older than me! Why would I want to marry you?"

Anne Marie was shocked.

"Drake, you can't mean that," she cried, thinking that he would have jumped at the chance to marry her, in spite of the age difference.

"You bet I mean it," he growled. "The only reason I've stayed with you is because you always threatened to tell John if I stopped. Well, John's not going to be around much longer so you won't be able to hold that over my head any more." Drake didn't add that he wanted Sandra instead as his young new wife.

"You can't mean that!" Anne Marie repeated, anger rising in her voice. "You ungrateful bastard!" she shouted. "You wouldn't be anything if it weren't for John. He made you what you are!"

"Yep! That's right, Love! *John* made me what I am, not *you*!" Drake shot back.

"I'll tell John!" she threatened.

"Go ahead!" Drake bellowed. "But is that the picture you want him to die with? His wife fucking his best friend?"

"You bastard!" she shouted. "You slimy, goddamned *son of a bitch!*"

Drake slammed the telephone on its hook. He was done with Anne Marie Malcolm. He immediately dialed Sandra's number, but got her answering machine. He left a message for her to call him at his apartment as soon as she got in. He rushed out of his office and headed for his apartment. The telephone was ringing as Drake unlocked the door to his apartment. He ran for the telephone, hoping it was Sandra. It was Anne Marie instead.

"Oh, Drake," she moaned between sobs. "John is dead."

Even though he knew it was coming, Drake wasn't emotionally prepared for the news. He knew John had been on the edge of death for weeks now, but still, it was a shock to hear that he was actually gone.

"When did he die?" Drake asked.

"Just about twenty minutes ago," Anne replied, sniffling into a Kleenex. "I've been trying to reach you ever since." Drake tried to collect his thoughts. The moment he'd been waiting for had finally arrived, but even so, he was sad the old man was gone.

"Drake?" Anne said, interrupting his thoughts. "Please come see me. I need you."

"Anne, I don't know —"

"*Please*, Drake. I need you with me now."

"Okay," Drake relented. "I'll be right over."

* * * *

Later, at the Malcolms' house, Anne came to Drake and wrapped her arms around him. She tried to bury her face in Drake's chest but he pushed her away.

"That's enough, Anne," he said.

"I just wanted a hug," she replied, a certain sadness in her voice.

"Well, you won't get any more hugs from me," Drake said as he looked away from her. "No — no more hugs," he repeated. "You can't threaten me with telling John anymore. We're through and that's the way it's gonna be from now on." Anne Marie stared in disbelief.

"You may not want me any more, but you'd better stay away from Sandra!" Anne demanded, but Drake laughed.

"Stay away from Sandra?" Drake asked incredulously. "Less than an hour ago you were trying to get me to join up with you against Sandra. Not only am I going to continue to see Sandra — I'm going to marry her!" he replied, walking out of the room. Anne was speechless with anger.

* * * *

Three days later, Drake, Anne Marie, and Sandra stood in the crowd around John's gravesite. Anne Marie couldn't take her eyes off Drake. Drake slipped over to Sandra's side for the service, but no matter how he tried to talk to her, she wouldn't respond to him, which pleased Anne Marie. After the service, as everyone left the graveside, Drake followed Sandra to her car.

"Sandra, please — I've got to see you," he said.

"Drake, I'm busy this afternoon," she replied casually. She had lost interest in Drake long ago, and after the way Drake had ignored Anne Marie at the funeral, she knew that she had won bragging rights over her mother.

"*Please*," he pleaded. "It's important. Just for a few minutes. I'll follow you to your place."

"No!" she said emphatically. "Not at my place, nor yours."

"But you've *got* to see me! *Please!*" Drake begged.

"Okay, I'll see you. Meet me at the bar next to your office in an hour."

"I'll be there," he promised and hurried toward his Porsche. As he went to his Porsche, it occurred to him that Connie hadn't been at the funeral.

* * * *

Drake had been sitting in the bar for over an hour when Sandra finally walked in. She was still in the plain black dress she wore to the funeral, but the way it clung to her firm young figure, it made her look elegantly sexy. She slid into the seat across from him and leveled her eyes on him.

"What?" she asked caustically, without so much as greeting him.

"How are you?" Drake asked, trying to begin a conversation while at the same time signaling for the waitress. Sandra waved her off.

"I'm fine. What do you want?" she asked without trying to mask her impatience.

"I just want to talk," Drake said, already uncomfortable with Sandra's terse responses. "I want to talk about our future."

"*Our* future? What future?"

"Come on, Sandra," he pleaded like a little boy.

"What do you want?" Sandra repeated, a little more sternly. Drake looked around, then leaned toward Sandra.

"Sandra, I want you to marry me." She stared in shock, and then laughed out loud.

"*Marry you?*" she exclaimed, attracting the attention of everybody within earshot. "You're too old for me! Besides, you aren't half the man you think you are! I just fucked you because it pissed off my mother!" She stood up from the table and walked out of the bar without another word, leaving Drake staring after her in stunned silence.

Chapter 22

On the ship, all of Karyn's performances had been a hit. After every show, Karl made it a point to take her to public areas so passengers could see her and talk to her. He wanted to get her used to dealing with the public. Karyn noticed Karl was touching her more lately, even giving her little pecks on the cheek, but she didn't like his attentions.

* * * *

Three weeks later, Myron was waiting for her as she bounded offstage after one of her shows.

"Karyn, I'd like you to consider headlining your own show. It's just a matinee, but I think you're ready for it."

"Oh, Myron, thanks!" Her excitement was evident as she grabbed his arm. "I won't let you down."

"Don't let me down, either, baby," Karl added when Myron left. Karyn looked at him quizzically but Karl just smiled.

Karl worked with Karyn for the next two weeks preparing her new show. Karyn's mornings were spent practicing with Karl, then she would do her regular shows. The routine was grueling, the hours long, and Karl kept getting more familiar with her. As the days passed, he began putting his arm around her, and soon he was giving her hugs. She liked Karl because he was helping her, but she didn't like the turn their personal relationship was taking. One day Karl tried to kiss her but she pushed him back.

"Karl, please don't," she said with pleading eyes.

"Don't what?" he asked, feeling rejected.

"Please don't try to kiss me or anything like that. Let's keep it strictly professional, okay?"

"Why? Aren't we friends?"

"Yes, and I'd like to stay that way," she replied. He glared at her for a moment then walked away. She watched him go, wondering if she did the right thing. That evening she stopped by Catherine's office.

"Catherine, I think I have a big problem with Karl," she said.

"Tell me about it," Catherine said as she pushed some paperwork aside. Karyn told her all about the rehearsals and how Karl had been slowly becoming more familiar with her.

"Has he ever tried to do anything other than this kiss?" she asked.

"No, but I think he wants more."

"Maybe you've put a stop to it today. Why don't you give it some time to see what happens in the next few days," Catherine offered.

"Did I do the right thing?" Karyn asked.

"You did exactly the right thing," Catherine replied. "If you're not ready for a relationship, no one should force you into something you don't want."

Karyn nodded and left.

* * * *

Karyn debuted in her own show in December and was an immediate hit. However, by this time, Karl wanted more from Karyn than just smiles. Karl had been trying to slowly get closer to Karyn but he was now growing impatient with her. He found himself lying awake one night, trying to figure out a way to get Karyn into bed with him. As he lay there, he grew more frustrated and angry. *She owes me*, he thought. *She owes me plenty and it's payback time!* The next day after the show, Karl caught her arm and ushered her out the back of the lounge instead of letting her talk to the people in the audience.

"Karl, what's going on?" she asked as he tugged on her arm.

"We're getting out of here for a while," he said, almost dragging her down the passageway.

"But shouldn't I be talking to the audience like I always do?"

"No. You and I gotta talk." She pulled her arm free but followed him. Soon they came to his quarters. She didn't like the looks of this.

"Karl, what's going on? Why are we here?" she asked.

"Come on in," he said, holding the door open for her.

"No."

"Karyn, come on," he said again, firmer.

"For what?" she asked, knowing what he was going to say. She knew he had the hots for her, but he was also her mentor and had been working non-stop to help her be a success.

"Just come on into my room and we'll talk about it," he said, grabbing her arm possessively.

"Karl, no. I'm not going into your room. There's no reason to." She turned to leave but he blocked her way.

"Look, Karyn," he said. "I made you what you are. Now it's time for you to repay me what you owe me."

"Repay what?" she retorted angrily. "What the hell are you talking about? And let go of me!"

"No!" he said sharply. "Just get in that room!"

"No! I won't go in there with you!" she protested. "Maybe you helped me with my job, but *I* made me what I am! *I* learned the songs, *I* practiced my delivery, and *I* practiced my arrangements for hours every day! *You* didn't make me. *I* made me with your *help*." She paused and sighed deeply, then continued in a softer voice.

"Karl, I can see we don't feel the same way about each other. I didn't mean for that to happen, but it did. I like you, for sure, and I really appreciate everything you've done for me, but for me to go in that room with you isn't good." She took his hand and held it close to her heart. "Like I said, it's not that I don't like you, because I do. And it's not that I don't appreciate everything you've done for me, but, Karl — we're just friends, not lovers."

Even after her explanation, he still felt cheated and rejected. "You owe me," he muttered.

"Maybe, but I don't owe you my body and my heart," she replied. "I've been used by men before and I know that's too much to pay even for what you've given me."

Karl slammed the door of his room and walked down the passageway.

* * * *

The Monday after John's funeral, Peter Savoy called Connie.

"Connie, it would be in your best interests to be at the reading of John's will," he told her.

"Why should I be there?" she asked. "Drake's the one who is going to inherit the stock and we're divorced now, so there's nothing in it for me."

"Perhaps you should consider this one of John's instructions," Peter replied.

"Okay. I'll be there," she said.

The reading of the will was Thursday, December 7th, in Savoy's office. Drake, Anne Marie, and Sandra were already seated when Connie entered the plush conference room with Peter Savoy. Anne Marie was staring at Drake while Sandra casually filed her fingernails. Drake was sullen and hostile as he watched Sandra. After the way she had rejected him, he couldn't wait to get control of Cox Chemical. He planned to get even with Sandra just as soon as he had control of the company. However, Connie's entrance caught everyone off guard.

"What's *she* doing here?" Drake demanded as he bolted upright from his chair. Anne Marie and Sandra stared at Connie in surprise.

"She's here at my request," Peter replied, not looking at Drake while he arranged some papers at the head of the table.

"She doesn't belong here," Drake countered, pointing at her.

"Mr. Malcolm had specifically requested that she be here before he died," Peter responded.

"Well, *I* don't want her here!" Drake retorted.

"Oh, just shut up and sit down!" Sandra said disdainfully as she went back to filing her fingernails. "Whether she's here or not isn't going to change anything! Let's just get this thing over with!" Drake eyed Sandra but sat as he was told. Peter asked Connie to sit next to him.

"We are gathered here to hear the reading of the last will and testament of John Arthur Malcolm," Peter said as he picked up the papers. Sandra, totally disinterested, didn't look up from her manicure while Drake watched her with hungry eyes. Peter was reading from the will.

"Having learned of my wife's infidelities with other men, along with my daughter's promiscuity with several of the same men..." Peter intoned quietly. Drake went pale, Anne Marie's mouth dropped open, and Sandra had frozen in surprise.

In the will, John noted his wife and daughter's affair in three short, damning sentences. Then John stated that, for these reasons, he left a total of $250,000 each to Anne Marie and Sandra.

"That's *it?*" Sandra shrieked. "That's *all?* Two hundred fifty thousand dollars?" Sandra pounded her fist on the table. "I can't live on a measly two hundred fifty thousand bucks!"

"The rest of my estate shall be left in trust, specifically in the John Arthur Malcolm Trust." Peter Savoy went on, ignoring Sandra's outburst, "for the sole benefit and use of Constance Louise Mathers."

"*That can't be!*" Drake bellowed, his face turning red, and jumped up from his chair. "She's not supposed to get any of John's stock in the company! I am!"

"Mr. Mathers, please sit down," Peter said, but no one heard him. Anne Marie and Sandra were both on their feet, shouting at each other and threatening legal action.

"This is all your fault, you goddamned weasel!" Anne screamed at Drake. He didn't hear her because he was too busy shouting at Peter Savoy. Sandra added to the melee but no one heard her, either. Connie was dumbfounded at what she had just heard.

It quickly became clear that Peter Savoy would get no further in reading the will, so he stood up, gathered all the papers from the table, nodded to Connie and ushered her quickly from the conference room.

Once they were in Peter's office, Connie asked, "Does that mean I've inherited John's estate, including his stock in Cox Chemical?"

"Indeed it does," Peter smiled at her. "I'd say, as of right now, you're probably the richest woman in the state."

"Do you think they can break the will?" she asked, still hearing them shouting in the conference room.

"Not likely," Peter replied. "John was very shrewd and knew what they would try to do. We made sure this will was tightly drafted. He gave both his wife and daughter just enough that they won't challenge it because, if they do, they won't get anything." His smile broadened. "I'd say John has taught the three of them a lesson they'll never forget."

"What will happen to Anne and Sandra?" Connie asked.

"Well, I didn't get it all out at the reading, obviously, but first of all, $250,000 isn't exactly what you'd call a pittance. Second, the will gives Anne Marie thirty days to move out of the mansion before it is to be put up for sale, the proceeds of which are to go to one of John's charities. While Anne Marie can only take her personal belongings, John has also provided for five years of financial support for Anne Marie and Sandra to give them time to find a way to make a living."

"What about Drake?" Connie asked. "Is there anything in there for him?"

"Well, John certainly felt betrayed by Anne and Sandra, but he felt especially betrayed by Drake. Other than to be identified as 'another man' Drake isn't mentioned in the will at all," Peter replied. They could still hear Anne Marie, Sandra, and Drake shouting at each other. After arguing with Anne and Sandra for several minutes, Drake left. Connie and Peter heard the front door slam as he left.

"Time for a phone call," Peter said as he picked up the telephone and dialed.

"Hello, George," Peter said with a grin. "It's all finished here. Drake just left. I'd guess he's on his way to the office. Yes. You know what to do. Thanks." Connie noticed Peter had almost a child-like glee during the short conversation and wondered what else John had arranged.

Just as Peter had guessed, Drake went straight to his office. As he came to the door of his office, George Peoples was waiting for him.

"Not now, George!" Drake said gruffly. "It's not a good time."

"*Right now*, Drake Mathers!" George replied. Drake glared at George, then noticed one of the company lawyers coming toward them.

"George, you've always been a twit and as of right now you're fired!" Drake said through clenched teeth.

"I don't think so, *Drake*," George said with a smirk, emphasizing Drake's name because he had never, ever allowed George to use his first name. The company lawyer came straight to Drake and handed him an envelope. "To use your own words," George said, "As of right now, *you're* fired!"

"You can't do this to me," Drake began to bellow. "I'll have your ass —"

"*I* didn't do this to you," George interrupted. "*John* did. You were terminated as of the moment John died. I'm now the senior executive." Drake was wide-eyed in disbelief. "Oh, it's all there, in the letter," George said, pointing to the envelope. "And there's nothing you can do about it. Shall I call you a cab?"

"A cab?" Drake asked incredulously.

"Yes, to get home. After all, your Porsche is company property. One of your self-provided perks, if you'll recall. You made me use company funds to buy and insure it for you. Well, it belongs to the company now. Give me the keys, please." George held out his hand for the keys, grinning like he'd just broken the bank at the Monte Carlo casino. The dimples in his rotund face accentuated his smile.

Drake couldn't speak. He looked at the lawyer, a man who had been with Cox Chemical for years, although Drake had never bothered to learn his name. The lawyer nodded.

Drake reluctantly dug into his coat pocket for the keys to the Porsche. He slowly pulled his apartment key from the ring. Then he began to pull his office and desk key from the ring.

"Oh, just leave those," George said. "You won't need them. I've already moved into your old office." Drake slowly placed the keys into George's palm. "And in case you're thinking of suing the company, don't bother. You'll find the severance package in there is generous enough to forestall any litigation. And don't bother to use us as a reference, either." George and the lawyer walked away from Drake. Drake knew John had covered all the bases.

* * * *

There was a tap on the door to Catherine's quarters. She roused and looked at the clock. It read 2:30 a.m.

"This better be important," she muttered as she got up and wrapped her bathrobe around her nude body. She opened the door to see a misty-eyed Karyn standing in the passageway.

"Catherine, remember when you said we could talk any time?" Catherine didn't hesitate a second.

"Come on in, sweetie," she said. "What's on your mind?"

"It's Karl," Karyn replied.

"Let me guess," Catherine said as she pulled a pair of diet Pepsis from her little refrigerator. "He tried to get you to go to his room." The cans fizzed softly as she popped the tabs. She handed one to Karyn and motioned for her to sit.

"How did you know?"

"It was only a matter of time," Catherine answered. "Frankly, I'm surprised it took this long." She shook her head knowingly. "I was hoping you'd stopped this thing dead in its tracks when you told him to back off. Looks like it didn't take." She smiled wryly.

"There's more to this story, isn't there?" Karyn asked.

"Well, it's no secret. Karl's a handsome guy, for sure, and has a way with women. He also has a reputation for bedding down all the prettiest girls on the ship." Catherine sighed deeply. "Hell, girl, I even fell for him when I first came aboard."

"You and Karl had a thing for each other?" Karyn looked at her incredulously.

"Well, sort of, but it didn't work out the way Karl wanted it to," Catherine explained. "Jerry Doyle had just landed me this job. I was fresh out of their house and getting my life back together when I met Karl. I'd only been on the ship for two days when he asked me to have a drink with him. I was still hurting and it felt pretty good to have a cool dude like Karl hitting on me. After just a few days, I started to fall for him in a big way, but I was still confused and scared and kept pushing him away if you know what I mean."

"Sorta like what I did," Karyn offered.

"Yeah, exactly like that. Well, he didn't like it and got all steamed up. He's used to getting any girl he wants and he was really pissed that I wouldn't just fall into bed with him. Still, I fantasized about him. I obsessed about him, even had dreams about him, but my feelings were hurt so I called Maggie and talked to her about it. She told me the same thing I told you. If you're not ready for a relationship, no one should force you into it."

"I think he hates me now," Karyn said.

"Oh, he doesn't hate you, but his ego has been bruised. He hasn't said ten words to me since I told him I wouldn't have sex with him."

"Sounds like he's a user."

"That's what Maggie called him, too. Oh, he's charming and manly and all the things a girl loves, but he's that way only so he can get in your pants. Once he's been there a few times, he moves on to find another one, a new conquest." Catherine stopped and smiled at Karyn. "It looks like you saw what was happening and fixed it good before it became a real problem. Lady, you're doing okay!"

They talked a while longer, then Karyn left, feeling much better about how she handled Karl.

Chapter 23

By this time Karyn had completed several cruises on the ship and while Karl hadn't said another word to her since he had walked away from her at his room, he was professional enough to keep the shows going even though he was feeling very rejected by Karyn. She continued to call Jesse or the Doyles once a week, keeping them current on all that was going on in her life.

During the Holiday Cruise in December, Mr. Claude Arnold, the president of United Records, happened to be on board the ship, taking a ten-day vacation with his wife.

"What are we going to do today?" Claude asked his wife, Doreen, as they got dressed in their massive stateroom.

"Well, I was thinking we'd go ashore and pick up some more souvenirs for the grandkids," she said cheerfully. He looked sidelong at his wife and shook his head.

"Honey, I just can't do another day of shop-crawling. We already have a couple thousand dollars worth of junk for the kids. Mind if I beg off?" he pleaded as he glanced at the pile of bags and boxes in the corner of their luxury suite.

"Oh love, I know you don't like shopping," she said understandingly. "And you've been really a good guy to keep me company the last few times." He smiled and nodded. She was right, of course. He loved being with her whenever he could, but his job at United Records kept him on the move most of the time when they were home in New York. They had been married over thirty years and he loved her more today than ever before. "What would you rather do?" she asked.

"Oh, I don't know. I heard that they have a pretty good show in the lounge. I was thinking of taking in the matinee. I can do that while you go shopping." She came over to him and wrapped him in a big hug.

"You just can't stay away from the entertainment industry, can you?" she smiled. "Even if it's a show in a ship's lounge." He grinned back at her and nodded. "Okay," she said. "Let's go see the show."

They got to the lounge early to be sure they would get good seats, although most of the passengers had gone ashore, so the lounge was practically empty. They got the table off to the right nearest the stage. Myron noticed them as he walked through the lounge on his way backstage.

"Hey, you know who is in the audience today?" he asked Karl. "I think that's Claude Arnold from United Records at that table right over there," he said as he pointed them out through the tiny gap in the curtain. Karl peered at the couple but shook his head.

"No. No way," he said. "What would he be doing at a matinee anyway, even if he was on our ship? Why wouldn't he be somewhere on shore?"

"No, I'm pretty sure that's him," Myron countered. "In fact, I know that's him." He continued to peer at Claude and Doreen Arnold through the gap.

"No way, I tell you," Karl said with a shake of his head and walked away. He still held a grudge against Karyn for not sleeping with him and he didn't want anyone like Claude Arnold to see her. Myron continued to watch until Karyn came up behind him.

"What are you watching?" she asked.

"Huh? Oh, nothing," Myron replied as he turned to her. He was afraid that if Karyn had any idea that someone like Claude Arnold was in the audience, she might get stage fright and freeze up. "Just checking the lighting." He walked away without another word.

The show was supposed to start at two o'clock, but the time came and went. Karl wasn't in front of the band although all the musicians were ready and waiting. Karyn and the rest of the entertainers were pacing back and forth offstage as they waited for the music to start. Myron wondered what was going on. Karl had never started a show late before. Myron watched Claude as he and his wife sat almost all alone in the lounge. His heart began to pound.

"Where the hell is Karl?" he asked one of the showgirls.

"Don't know," she said. "I haven't seen him."

"He was supposed to start the show some ten minutes ago," Myron grumbled.

"Myron," Karyn said as she approached him. "What's wrong? Why haven't we started the show?"

"I don't know what the hell's going on," he said angrily. "But I'm going to go find Karl. This isn't good!" Myron saw Claude look at his watch and glance around the almost deserted room.

Claude leaned to Doreen and said, "Maybe there isn't a show because we're in port. I'll go ask." She nodded and he went to find the waitress.

"I don't know what's wrong," the waitress told him. "There's definitely supposed to be a show, but they've never been late before. It's a pretty good show, too. Why don't you wait just another few minutes? I'll go find out what's going on." The waitress went backstage to see what was the matter.

"We don't know where Karl is," Karyn replied. "Myron went to find him."

The waitress nodded and said, "Well, if you don't find him soon, you might as well forget about the show. You won't have an audience. They're all leaving." Karyn looked out into the lounge. It was empty except for two couples. Just then Myron returned.

"I can't find him anyplace," Myron told everyone.

"Myron, we only have four people in the audience. Why don't we cancel this show?" Karyn asked. "It's only four people."

Myron looked back out at the Arnolds and replied, "We're going to do this show if it was only one person," meaning especially for Mr. Claude Arnold of United Records. He knew this could be the chance of a lifetime for Karyn and he wanted her to have it.

"Then why don't you lead the band?" one of the showgirls asked.

"I don't know beans about music," Myron replied sullenly. "I can't read a note. I just organize entertainment; I don't *do* it."

"Myron, you know the show as well as I do," Karyn replied. "We all know the cues from the music. All you have to do is start the band and keep the beat. They'll do the rest."

"Yeah," the rest of the showgirls chorused. "You can do it."

"But Karl was the emcee," Myron balked.

"You can talk to people on the stage," Karyn countered. "I've seen you do it."

Myron thought for a few seconds and looked back at Claude Arnold. The Arnolds were getting up to leave.

"Okay," he said. "I'll do it." He walked out onto the stage and grabbed the microphone.

"Ladies and gentlemen, we apologize for making you wait. But now, it's time for our show!" He locked eyes with Claude Arnold, willing him and Doreen to sit back down. They hesitated for a second then returned to their seats. Myron smiled at Claude and winked.

"And now, here she is, ladies and gentlemen! Always late but worth the wait, *KARYN MATHERS!!*" He jumped off the stage and motioned to the band. They were surprised but immediately responded to Myron's pleading eyes. In seconds the show was going just as it always had. Pretty soon Myron was thinking that this wasn't so hard and began to enjoy himself at the helm of the band.

Claude and Doreen were a little miffed that the show was starting more than twenty minutes late, but within the first two minutes of Karyn's performance, they had forgotten all about the delay. After five minutes Claude leaned to Doreen and whispered in her ear, "That guy was right: she may be late, but she was worth it."

Since there were only four people in the lounge, Karyn was able to make her delivery very personal. While the other couple enjoyed the special touch, the beautiful blonde spellbound Claude. Karyn sensed this and began to sing almost exclusively to him.

That's the way, Myron thought as he mindlessly swung the baton in front of the band. *Sing your heart out to him, Karyn!* Claude and Doreen were visibly enraptured.

The lounge started to fill as people heard the music and came in, but Karyn was now doing the show for the couple at the right side of the stage. This man and his wife seemed to enjoy what she was doing and it made her want to do it more and better. Myron had considered cutting the show short so the evening show wouldn't be late, but decided to let it go the full two hours.

At four-thirty, Karyn left the stage and the lounge lights came up to the usual thunderous applause. The lounge had filled to capacity as people had ambled in to the sound of the music.

When the show was over, most of the people stood to leave. Claude just sat there, riveted in his seat, staring at the empty stage.

"Do I need to wait for a while?" Doreen asked.

"I need to talk to that girl's boss," Claude said simply.

"That's what I thought," Doreen smiled. "I'll meet you back at our suite in an hour." She got up and gave him a quick hug. Claude then raced after Myron.

"Sir, could I talk to you for a minute?" Claude said as he got near Myron.

"Yeah, sure, Mr. Arnold," Myron replied.

"You know who I am?" he asked.

"Not too many people in my business *don't* know who you are," Myron smiled. "And I just bet you want to talk about our singer, don't you?"

"She's great!" Claude said enthusiastically. "Where did you people find her?"

"Well, actually, I found her working in our dining room bussing tables. No one knew she could sing until she did karaoke one night and she won a couple of bottles of champagne. Don't that beat all?"

"How can I meet her?" Claude asked.

"Just wait right here for a minute. She always comes out to meet the audience. In fact, there she is right now. Hey, Karyn! Come here a minute! I want you to meet someone!"

Karyn worked her way over to Myron and Claude through the crowd. Claude watched in awe as she greeted each of the patrons as though she'd known them for years. She made it a point to say a few words to everyone who talked to her, and signed a few autographs on the way. It took her several minutes but she managed to get to Myron and Claude.

"Hi, Myron! You did great! I knew you could do it!"

"Do what?" Claude asked.

"Well, actually, Mr. Arnold, that was the first time I ever directed a band," he admitted sheepishly.

"Yeah. Our regular bandleader sort of disappeared just before the show, so Myron had to fill in. I think he did great, don't you?" She patted Myron on the shoulder. "But what was that wisecrack about 'always late but worth the wait'?"

"Karyn, I'd like you to meet Mr. Claude Arnold," Myron said, ignoring Karyn's comment.

"Pleased to meet you Mr. Arnold," she said, holding out her hand. "I take it that you're a friend of Myron's?"

"Please call me Claude, and well, yes, you could say something like that," Claude replied after a moment's hesitation. "Karyn, tell me — who is your manager?"

"Manager?" she asked, wondering why he would ask that particular question.

"Yes. You know, your agent," Claude replied. She thought about saying that Karl was, but she was incensed that he'd abandoned the show without a word to anyone.

"Why, Myron, here, is my manager," she said with a smile as she tipped her head against Myron's shoulder.

"That's good," he said. "Is there someplace we can go and talk?"

Myron was getting a giddy feeling inside as he said, "Let's go to my office — right now!" The three went straight to Myron's office and, before they even sat down, Claude came straight to the point.

"Karyn, I want you to cut a demo record for me."

"Cut a demo?"

"Karyn," Myron said, "Mr. Arnold is the president of United Records, one of the biggest recording studios in the world." Karyn suddenly felt like she just had to sit down.

"You want me to cut a demo? You mean record a song?" Her wide eyes searched Claude's face.

"Exactly," he said casually. "But I'd like it to be a whole album, if you're up to it." Karyn could barely make a sound.

"That means she'll take it," Myron grinned, remembering Catherine's words. He nodded to Karyn and she nodded back. She was as thrilled as she'd ever been in her life.

* * * *

That evening Karyn called Jesse with the wonderful news.

"He wants me to do an album of 1950s love songs," she exclaimed. "He wants me to do them like Doris Day, whoever she is."

"You don't know who Doris Day is?" Jesse asked, smiling. "She's one of my mom's favorite singers. She's a pretty good actress, too."

"Well, I never heard of her," Karyn said, "But you think she's pretty good?"

"I practically grew up with her. I think Mom had every one of her movies on tape and all of her records. Heck, you can still rent her movies." They talked excitedly for a while longer, and then Karyn had to go. After they hung up, she walked the deck in the Mediterranean evening, thinking.

Karyn knew that Jesse was happy for her. Even if he hadn't said so, she could hear it in his voice. And it seemed to Karyn that their differences were resolved, too. She had grown up considerably and realized she had made some terrible mistakes. She felt terrible about the things she did, but she didn't know how to apologize to Jesse for them. She also wanted to tell him just how much she still loved him, but was afraid he would reject her love because of her past actions. She wanted to tell Jesse about her deepest feelings, so that evening, she wrote him a letter. Her fear of rejection kept her from telling him just how much in love with him she still was, but she knew she had to at least ask forgiveness for what she did to him.

The next morning, she stood in the ship's mailroom holding the thick envelope with express postage on it. The mail clerk smiled as she gave it a quick kiss, closed her eyes, and dropped it into the mailbox.

* * * *

Four days later Jesse received the letter. He trembled with emotion as he read it, knowing he was still very much in love with this girl. He couldn't wait to receive her next call. He didn't go out much because he studied so hard, but now he was afraid even to go out for something to eat in case she would call while he was out. He even ordered pizzas to be delivered to his dorm room just so he could be near the telephone.

It was around 6:30 Saturday evening in Jesse's dorm room. Mike and Willie Bob had come to visit and were devouring the two large combination pizzas Jesse had ordered.

"I don't see why we cain't just go out to a movie or somethin'," Willie said after finishing a bite of pizza. Jesse remembered all the times over the years that his mom had told Willie not to talk with his mouth full, and now, more than three years after her death, it seemed he finally got the message. Jesse studied the remarkable change in his father since he'd stopped drinking a few months back. Not only in his general appearance, but he stood straighter, walked with a new vitality, and had developed a zest for life.

"Dad, I told you, it's real important that I be here when Karyn calls again," Jesse reminded him. "Of all the times I've talked to her, this is probably the most important."

Mike and Willie nodded, and reached for another piece of pizza. Just then, the telephone rang. Jesse stared at it while it rang once, twice, three times. Just before the answering machine turned on, Jesse snatched the handset off the hook.

"Hello?" he said, his heart pounding and little beads of perspiration on his forehead.

"Hi, it's me," Karyn said almost shyly. She didn't know if he'd received the letter, and if he had, how he would take it. Jesse nodded to Willie and Mike, letting them know it was Karyn. They silently rose and stepped out into the hallway to give Jesse some privacy.

"Hi, sweetheart," he said, and then stopped. He didn't know what else to say. He knew he wanted to hear from her again, but hadn't thought one whit about what he'd say to her when she called.

"Jesse? Are you there?" she asked, afraid that he'd hung up on her.

"Yeah, I'm here," he replied. "I — um — got your letter."

"So. Well. Do you want to talk to me any more?" she asked.

"Sure!" he blurted, but still didn't know what else to say, so he said the only thing that was in his mind. "Karyn, I'm so in love with you —"

"You are? Oh, Jesse, I still love you too! So much it hurts!"

Soon they were both crying and talking and sharing all the feelings they had for each other. They had the most intimate conversation they had ever had and finished healing the rift between them. Finally, Karyn paused for a moment.

"Ummm, Jesse? Do you want to be there when I do the recording?" she asked.

"You really want me there?"

"Sure! It's the most important thing that's ever happened to me — except you, of course. I'd really like you to be there with me." Jesse thought for a second.

"Is it okay if Mike and my dad come, too? I know they'd love to see it."

"Sure!" Karyn said excitedly. "I'd love to have them, too! You think they can make it?"

"Just a sec, I'll ask them! They're here, waiting out in the hall! Hey, guys!" he called, excitedly. "Oops! Sorry, sweetheart. I didn't mean to yell in your ear."

"That's okay," she replied, nearly as excited as Jesse. Willie and Mike ambled into the room.

"Hey, Karyn wants us there when she starts to cut her album. Whaddaya think? Can we all make it?"

"When's this gonna happen?" Mike asked.

"Whadda you care?" Willie countered. "You got a meetin' with the President or somethin'? Tell 'er yeah. We'll be there with bells on. We'll all be there fer her," he said with a big grin.

"They say they'll make it, all right," Jesse said, smiling.

Chapter 24

Jesse and Willie had been calling Connie every week to tell her how Karyn was doing. As soon as Jesse hung up with Karyn, he started to dial the telephone.

"Now who ya callin'?" Willie asked.

"Connie!" Jesse replied. "I've gotta tell Connie about this!"

"Uh, Sport — If'n you don't mind, I'd like t' do that." Mike and Jesse studied their dad. His face was expressionless until a slight, sheepish smirk showed at the corner of his mouth. Jesse and Mike both developed big grins.

"Now, it ain't like that," he said defensively. "It's jus' that she's the only woman I ever talk to, an' — well — I sorta enjoy it. An' this news 'bout Karyn'll give us a bunch to talk about. You know what I mean?"

"Yeah, Dad," Mike replied sarcastically.

"We know exactly what you mean," Jesse added, grinning broader than ever.

"Now, I told you it ain't exactly like that!" However, his protestations did no good. Mike and Jesse teased him unmercifully for the rest of the evening.

The following Monday evening, Willie called Connie.

"Connie, I got news that's gonna make you so proud you're gonna bust your buttons!" he said as soon as she answered the telephone.

"Is this about Karyn?" she asked, hoping that it was, but she couldn't imagine what Karyn would be doing that would make her any more proud than she already was. After all, Karyn was doing pretty well in show business.

"Well, would you believe she's gonna go to New York to a recording studio? Now, whaddaya think o' that?"

"New York? To do recording?" Connie couldn't believe her ears.

"Yep. She's gonna be there the second week o' Feb'uary at United Records. Some guy named Arnold arranged fer her t' do an album."

"She's going to record an album?" Connie repeated, the excitement rising in her voice. "You're right, Willie, I could just burst! I'm so proud of her!"

They continued to talk for over an hour about Karyn. Connie had come to enjoy talking with Willie, nearly as much as Willie enjoyed talking with her.

"Oh, Connie," Willie Bob said, interrupting her. "I plumb fergot! We're going to New York to be there when she does her recording. Why don't you come to New York with us?" Connie sighed deeply.

"Oh, Willie," she said and sighed again. "There's nothing I would like better, but I don't think it's a good idea."

"Why not?"

"I don't think she wants to see me."

"Why not?" he repeated.

"Willie, her last words to me were that I'd never defended her from her father, which is true. I always stood back and let him punish her, sometimes for no good reason, as you already know. And to be totally honest about it, she was running away from me, too. I don't think I should go."

"Well, if'n you ask me, an' I know you didn't, but I'm gonna tell you anyway, I think you should be there, maybe even more'n us guys, 'cause you're her mom an' all."

"Then shouldn't we invite Drake? After all, he's her father."

"Well, she invited us, but she didn't invite him, so what's that tell you?" Connie thought about his remarks in silence. "Connie, you know Mike, Jesse, an' me have sorta adopted that girl. She's a member of our fam'ly an' she knows it. We all — that is, Mike an' Jess an' me — an' you, too — we've been right in there for Karyn since this whole thing started. She may not know you've been there for her, but me an' the boys, we know, and heck, you're practically a member of our fam'ly, too. Ain't nuthin' happens 'round here we don't call you right up an' tell you 'bout it."

"I know that, Willie," Connie replied, smiling. She knew she'd been included in everything that happened to the Wallers. She'd felt closer to them than to anybody else in the world since John died. They made it a point to include her in occasional dinners out, and even invited her to go see Jesse play football a couple of times.

"Tell you what, Connie," Willie Bob finally said, attempting to persuade her. "I'll give you a day to think about it, but you might as well know we ain't gonna take 'no' fer an answer."

"How will we get there?" Connie asked.

"Mike'll drive us in his minivan. All I got is my pickup truck and Jess ain't got no car at all. The minivan's the only thing that'll hold more'n two folks."

"I sure hope I'm doing the right thing. I'll go, but you have to let me pay my own way."

"You don't need t' pay fer nuthin' at all. This one's on me," he said with a grin. "I'll even cover your meals an' hotel room, too, if'n that'll help."

Connie thought about how ludicrous that was, to have Willie Bob pay for not only the fuel but her meals and lodging, too. No one except Peter

Savoy knew Connie was the richest woman in Michigan since John had died. She could easily buy a private airplane to fly them all to New York, then buy the hotel they would stay in. But Willie didn't know that, and he was being a gentleman the best way he knew how, and Connie appreciated him for it. She could see why his marriage to Rachel lasted a lifetime.

"I think I have enough to cover the hotel," Connie finally said, deciding the entire trip would be her treat, but she let it pass for the present.

"Well, I didn't know, after your divorce an' all. Sometimes women don't do so good financially after a divorce," Willie conceded. "I know you still live in the big house, but that don't mean you own it or nuthin'. I was jus' bein' careful is all."

"Thank you, Willie," Connie said sincerely. "You don't know how much that means to me. And I'm pleased to be considered a part of your family, too." Indeed, she was very pleased. They were, in fact, the only semblance of a family she had. They were the only people she talked to, and the only ones she ever went out with.

"So you're goin' with us," Willie stated as a fact.

"Yes. I'll go, and I hope I'm doing the right thing when I do."

* * * *

The next day, Willie Bob was shoveling a fresh layer of snowfall from his sidewalk when Mike pulled into the driveway.

"Hey, Dad," he called as he got out of his car.

"Hey, yourself," Willie replied with a smile.

"Did you talk to Connie?" Mike asked as he came over to Willie.

"Yep," he said, not looking up from his work.

"Is she coming?"

"Yep."

"That's good. That's real good."

"Yep," Willie nodded as he tossed the last shovel of snow beside the sidewalk. Mike peered at Willie, knowing something was going on. Willie wasn't in a bad mood. In fact, he hadn't been in a bad mood since he'd stopped drinking, but he was different. Something was clearly on his mind.

"Dad, you're up to something. What is it?"

"Well, Mike, I don't know exactly how t' say it." They started walking toward the house together. "I've been thinking."

"About?" Mike asked, raising his eyebrows.

"I've been thinking about Connie Mathers," he said as he pushed the snow shovel down into the drift next to the porch.

"What about her?" Mike asked as he stomped the snow off his feet, although he suspected he already knew what Willie was thinking. "You asked her out, didn't you?"

"Well, not exactly. Mike, do you think she'd really like to go out with me?"

"Don't know. Guess you'll have to ask her." He watched Willie's face screw up.

"Mike, I ain't asked no woman fer a date in over twenty years. I don't know how it's done nowadays." He opened the door of the house and went in with Mike following.

"It's the same as it's always been, Dad," Mike said as he unzipped his Carhartt jacket. "You just call her and ask her if she wants to go."

"It ain't that easy," Willie Bob said, unzipping his own jacket. "I ain't been around no women since your mom died. You don't think your mom would mind, do you? I mean, it's just goin' to dinner is all. It ain't like we're gittin' married or nuthin'. We're just good friends is all."

"Dad, Mom wouldn't want you holed up here in this house for the rest of your life, that's for sure. And for sure, I know she'd want you to be happy." He handed Willie his jacket and Willie hung it in the closet next to his own. "As I recall, the vows were, 'until death do us part' and Mom died over three years ago. Dad, it's over."

"But I feel like I'm betrayin' your mom," Willie said. Mike could see Willie's eyes were becoming misty. "But at the same time, I feel like I need to git on with m' life, you know?"

"And that's exactly what Mom would've wanted you to do." They went into the kitchen where a pot of hot coffee was waiting. "Before she died, Mom told me to take care of you," Mike continued as he poured a cup of the thick, black brew. "Right now, I take that to mean to give you the best advice I can. I think you should call Connie right away and ask her out. You're not betraying Mom — not at all. I honestly believe she would have wanted you to get on with your life." He handed the cup to Willie Bob.

"Yeah, I suppose you're right," Willie agreed. "It's just that some things is harder than others."

"So what's so hard about picking up a phone and dialing a number that I know you've already memorized?" Willie stared at Mike, thinking for a minute.

"Okay, git outta the kitchen. I need some privacy fer this." He snatched the telephone handset from the cradle. Mike grinned and sauntered down into the basement rec room and turned on the television.

"Connie — it's me, Willie," he began. She could hear his voice was subdued and tentative.

"Willie, what's wrong?" she asked immediately.

"Um, nuthin'," he replied, but his voice couldn't mask his nervousness. "I was jus' wonderin'..."

"Yes?" Connie encouraged.

"Well, I was jus' thinkin' maybe — maybe you an' me, we could — well —" Right away, Connie knew what was on Willie's mind.

"Yes." Connie said.

"I don't know how t' say this. I'm sorta outta practice."

"Willie, I said 'yes'. Yes, I'll go out with you. I think it will do us both good."

"How'd you know what I was gonna ask?"

"Because I've thought about asking you, but I didn't know how, either. I've been out of the dating game even longer than you. I was thinking that if I'm going to get back into circulation, it would probably be best if I start with a friend that I knew pretty well. That describes you, don't you think? But I didn't know how you felt about Rachel."

"Maybe that's something we kin talk about," Willie offered. "If'n you don't mind," he added.

"I think that would be fine. Sharing what's in someone's heart is what makes the best relationships, don't you think?"

"Well, I don't know 'bout that," Willie said. "That sounds like a girl thing t' me, but I do know it's good to talk about what's on your mind from time t' time."

"It's all the same thing — just different words," Connie said. "So when do you want to go?"

* * * *

On the ship, Karyn was as excited as she could be. Her bookings were going well and her confidence was high. She had just hung up from talking on the telephone with Claude Arnold when she burst into Catherine's office.

"Catherine, Claude has booked three weeks for us to work on the album! Can you imagine that? Three weeks in New York!" Catherine just smiled at her. "So, can you get the time off and come with me?"

Smiling, Catherine waved a sheet of paper.

"They granted your vacation time! That's great! You'll get to meet Jesse! I just know you'll like him."

"Girl, I wouldn't miss this for all the gold in Fort Knox," Catherine replied. "We need to start planning. So what's the first thing you want to do when we hit the Big Apple?"

"Catherine, the only thing I know how to do in New York is shop. That's all my mom and I ever did there.'

"Karyn, there's a zillion things for us to do there. They've got shows and museums. We can go ice skating in Rockefeller Center, not to mention that they have the best restaurants in the world. We can go to Greenwich Village and all sorts of places."

"I don't know how much time I'll have," Karyn warned. "But I just know we'll have a blast when I'm not recording. Do you have your tickets?"

"E-tickets. Waiting at the airline. I'll be sitting right next to you."

"Great!" Karyn bounded out of Catherine's office.

* * * *

The telephone rang in Drake's apartment. He'd had little to do since he'd been ushered out of the Cox Chemical headquarters on December 7th. There wasn't a lot of demand for fired CEOs in the business world, so he found himself in forced retirement. The drastic cut in income wasn't as bad as not being at the helm of a large corporation. His ego wasn't just damaged, it was crushed. The telephone rang a second time before he reached for it.

"Hello?" He was hoping it was one of the headhunters, a professional placement service, calling to tell him he had an interview.

"Drake? It's Anne Marie," she said.

"Anne. Hello," he said sullenly as he slouched onto the couch. He didn't particularly want to hear from Anne, but no one else had called him. He hadn't spoken to anyone except the bartender for two weeks. "Why are you calling me?"

"Just to talk. I haven't talked to anyone in a long time."

"Yeah. I bet. So what do you want to talk about?"

"Drake, have you thought any more about us?"

"Not really. Why?" he asked.

"Are you sure you and I can't maybe get together?"

"You mean like in your marriage proposal?" he asked.

"Yes."

"I don't think so, Anne. We're not what anyone would call the perfect couple. I've had a few weeks to think about everything that happened and I know that most of it is my own fault."

"Are you planning to contest the will?" Anne Marie asked.

"What's to contest? I'm not a blood relative. I have no reasonable claim to any of John's estate. What about you?"

"No. I checked with a lawyer. He said I might win a little something, but for the most part, the will is ironclad. Besides, I guess I got what I deserved. I'd better find a way to support myself in the next couple of years, shouldn't I?"

"Anne, you'll do all right," Drake said.

They talked a few more minutes, then hung up. Drake sat on the couch in the nearly dark apartment, thinking. It was obvious from the telephone call that Anne still wanted him. But he wasn't sure what he wanted. What was it he wanted more than anything else in the world?

As he thought about it, he realized that more than anything else, he wanted to be the pilot of Cox Chemical and make the company bigger and more glorious than ever. Second to that, he also wanted to get even with George Peoples and Sandra. George had insulted him and Sandra had rejected him. The only way he could accomplish those goals would be to get control of Cox. The only way he could get control of Cox was to — remarry Connie. He reached for the telephone.

"Hello, Connie. It's me, Drake."

"Hello, Drake," she replied, wondering why he would be calling her.

"Can we get together, maybe, for dinner or something?"

"Why?"

"I think we should talk. We haven't talked very much, you know."

"Yes, Drake, that's true. We haven't discussed much of anything for the past fifteen years."

"Why do you suppose that is?" he asked, pleased that she would at least carry on a conversation with him.

"Well, probably because you are used to talking and not listening," she replied, "and that's not a discussion."

"Yeah, well, maybe you're right," he condescended, although he didn't really believe that. He felt he was the height of awareness in all matters. "So can we meet for dinner?"

"I don't know, Drake. This may not be good for either of us."

"What's not good about it?" he asked. "We meet for dinner, we talk a little, and then you go home. What can happen?"

"What happened the last time we went out together?" she countered, remembering their last visit with John.

"I don't know. What?" he asked, not connecting with her question.

"You hit me, that's what," she replied, not angrily, but firmly.

"Oh, yeah, *that*. Well, it won't happen this time," he said. "I promise."

"It seems to me that twenty five years ago you promised to be faithful to me, too."

"Connie, this isn't doing us any good. Can we meet for dinner or not?" He had hoped to begin charming her right away, but it wasn't happening with this telephone call.

"When and where?"

"How about I come by and pick you up Saturday at six?"

"Saturday's not good," she said. "And don't come to pick me up. I'll meet you at the restaurant."

"Why not Saturday?"

"If you must know, I have a date," she said. Drake was shocked.

"You have a date?"

"Yes."

"You can't have a date — you're my wife," he said incredulously, still thinking of her as he had for the last twenty-plus years.

"Unless I'm mistaken, you were the one who sued me for divorce. I'm nobody's wife and I can go out with whomever I wish."

"Who are you going with?" he asked.

"Frankly, I don't see that it's any of your business. Drake, I'm tired and I think we'd better cut this short."

"But won't you go out with me?" he asked.

"I don't think it's a good idea."

"Please? How about brunch on Sunday?" Connie thought for a moment.

"Okay. Brunch on Sunday. Where?"

"Giullio's at the Hyatt in Dearborn. Okay?"

"Giullio's? Okay. Eleven?"

"That's fine with me," he said. "I'll see you there."

Connie hung up, wondering if she'd done the right thing, to plan meeting Drake for brunch, or for anything else. She was going to meet the Wallers at Willie's house at one-thirty Sunday afternoon, and they planned to leave for New York at two. She knew the schedule would be tight, but she should be able to handle it okay.

Chapter 25

It was Friday morning and Karyn was waiting in the hotel room for Claude Arnold to pick her up and take her to the United recording studio. He called her hotel room from his cell phone.

"Karyn we're just pulling into the hotel right now. I'll meet you in the lobby."

"Okay," she said excitedly. "I'll be right down!" She grabbed her coat and shouted to Catherine. "Claude's meeting us in the lobby! Let's go!"

"I'm a-coming," Catherine said stubbornly as she struggled to finish buttoning her blouse. "Damn!" she said. "I'm so nervous I can't even dress myself! I'm in worse shape than you and I'm supposed to be the steady one around here." Karyn laughed as she held the door, waiting for Catherine.

They made their way to the lobby where Claude was waiting.

"Normally, I'd send a driver to pick you up, but I wanted us to be together," he said. "Is this your first time in New York?"

"Oh, no. I've been here several times, but I haven't seen very much of it. Catherine and I were hoping to do some sightseeing while we're here."

"Well, that won't happen right away," he replied. "You're going to be a busy young lady for the next couple of weeks, but we'll try to schedule some time off after that for you guys." He turned to Catherine. "And you must be Catherine," he said, offering his hand.

"Yes, sir," she replied, giving his hand a firm shake. "This is too cool! I can't believe we're here to cut an album!"

"And that's just what we're going to do," Claude replied. "Come along, ladies." He led them out the lobby doors to the white limousine parked out front.

"This is for us?" Catherine asked in disbelief. She was expecting to be riding in one of the many yellow taxis in New York.

"I thought it would be a nice touch for the first time," Claude replied. "It's just this once, but who knows? If Karyn's records take off, she could be riding in one of these to just to go grocery shopping!"

"If I had one of these, I'd be paying someone else to do my grocery shopping," Catherine said as she slid into the plush interior of the stretch limo. "And I'd be paying them to do my cooking and cleaning and laundry, too," she added as she looked over the luxurious interior. Karyn and Claude slid into the ample seats and chatted happily on the way to the studio.

At the studio, Karyn had the expected jitters and a queasy tummy but Claude had a calming effect on her. She was excited and asked a lot of questions. Claude introduced her to everyone there, whose names Karyn promptly forgot, except for the chief engineer. His name was Tom and it was obvious that he knew exactly what he was doing. He was a no-nonsense man who had done this job for over twenty years for some of the biggest names in the industry.

"Normally, there would be a producer, too," Claude explained, "But for this album, Tom will double as the producer. I'll be the executive producer for this album myself.

"Now, whatever Tom says, goes," Claude was telling them. "This is his domain, and that includes even me in the recording studio."

"Yeah. You sure don't want to get on his bad side," one of the aides laughed. "I saw him throw Mr. Arnold himself out of here a few years ago." Claude laughed, too, remembering that incident.

"We were recording a charity special and I was talking too much," Claude explained. "After he had to tell me to shut up for the third time, he told me I had to leave."

"But you're the boss," Karyn said.

"Not in here," Claude replied. "In here, it's Tom's world. He rules with an iron fist. And that's the way it needs to be. This studio will be used almost sixty hours this week alone. If someone real disciplined isn't in charge that can go to eighty hours in a hurry. That means there will be people in here at midnight and somebody won't get their cuts done without paying exorbitant overtime charges. That's bad for everyone."

"But he threw you out," Karyn repeated.

"Tom has no sense of humor whatsoever," the aide added. "But he's one of the best." Karyn's jitters just got worse.

She stayed close to Claude as he showed her around the studio, pointing things out and letting her get a feel for the place. After about forty-five minutes she told Claude, "By the way, I have three friends coming to watch the session. I guess I should have asked if that's okay before I asked them," she said.

"Oh, we can handle three. They can sit in the booth with Tom and his crew," Claude smiled. "One of them wouldn't be this Jesse I've heard so much about?" he asked. Karyn's blush answered Claude's question for him.

* * * *

By five o'clock Saturday evening, Connie was a bundle of nerves. She'd checked her hair at least three times and had removed and reapplied her makeup twice, just to be sure it was perfect. Finally, she sat on he bed, thinking to herself, *What is wrong with me? Why am I trying so hard? Willie has seen me at my worst, and he didn't care. It's like I was going on my first date all over again.*

Of course — that's *exactly* what it was. She was having her first date in twenty-five years. The doorbell chimed, indicating that Willie Bob had arrived. She took one last look at herself in the mirror and opened the door to see a handsome man in a Carhartt jacket standing in the freshly falling snow. Willie Bob nodded his greeting as he spoke.

"Evenin', ma'am," he said politely. "Are you as nervous as I am?"

"Yes," Connie laughed. "I've been a nervous wreck all day. No wonder dating is for kids. We older folks can barely take it. Won't you come in while I get my coat?"

Willie stepped into the foyer. He surveyed the area, remembering the hostile entry he'd made the last time and feeling a little foolish about it. Connie draped her coat over her arm and remembered the last time he stood there, taking note of how different he looked now. They'd been together for a number of dinners but always with his two boys. This was the first time they would be together alone and she wanted it to be perfect.

Willie was an absolute gentleman as he first helped her with her coat, then held the door open for her as she stepped into a red Chrysler LeBaron that he had rented just for this occasion.

"I didn't want to put you in that rasty ol' truck o' mine," he said as he eased himself into the driver's seat.

They went to a local Mexican restaurant, where they talked about the kids and laughed about their days of dating as teenagers. Willie told jokes and stories about his childhood in the hills of West Virginia. She thoroughly enjoyed the dinner and, at the last minute, decided not to go to the movie. Instead, they went to the local mall and just walked around, looking at the displays and talking.

The mall closed at ten o'clock and they walked out to the car. The Michigan snow was falling again in wispy flakes that bounced and drifted off the Chrysler's hood. Their conversation fell into a lull, but after a few moments of silence, Willie put his gloved hand on hers. She looked into his eyes and fell into his arms.

In seconds, they were embroiled in a deep, longing kiss that warmed

Connie all the way down to her boots. She felt a flush of energy start at her heart and flow out to her arms, which only made her pull Willie closer.

He felt her strength as she pulled him closer, and responded in kind. He crushed her body to his so powerfully that she could barely breathe. She pulled back from him for just a moment, just to catch a breath of air, and then kissed him again. Only this time, instead of a long kiss, it was two, then three quick kisses. She cradled his face in her mittened hands and kissed it all over, again and again. He pulled her close again and kissed her with all the feeling he had inside.

Willie was the first to unzip his Carhartt, and then Connie unbuttoned her own long coat. That helped for a little while, allowing them to get a little closer, but, after another few minutes, even that wasn't enough for Connie. Connie pulled her mittens off, tossing them aside. She ran her hands on Willie's torso, feeling the lean, tight muscles underneath the fabric of his shirt. Willie sighed and leaned back to let her caress him. She rubbed harder and harder, kneading his hard body. Their heavy breathing had completely fogged the windows as Willie shut the engine off.

She continued to work her fingers over him as he closed his eyes and let himself be drawn into the wonderful web she was spinning. Then she stopped and he opened his eyes. She sat there, her breath coming in puffy clouds of steam. She leaned back, her coat wide open, as he scooted over to her, sliding his arm around her shoulder, but not pulling her close this time. He guided his hand down between her breasts, looking down at her nipples standing erect even under the bra, blouse, and sweater. That's when he realized he had a huge erection.

He worked her blouse up and out of the way and then undid her bra. He cupped her bare breasts in his hands and began gently stroking them with his tongue. In another few minutes his warm kisses alternating with the cold air on her nipples made her squirm. As she writhed, she moaned softly. Then she grabbed Willie's head and thrust her breast into his hot, panting mouth.

He sucked both of her nipples and then blew on them. She moaned louder as Willie did this over and over, slowly driving her wild. She let out a shriek and buried his face against her boobs, wiggling back and forth, as she had her first orgasm in years.

Suddenly, there was a sharp rapping on the window. They both jumped with a start, Connie instantly struggling to re-dress herself.

"Hey, you kids in there," the security man yelled. "Take it home! You can't be doing that shit here!"

"He thinks we're kids!" Connie muttered with a sheepish grin as she arranged her bra. Willie chuckled and started the car. He scraped a small opening in the frozen mist on the window to peer out at the security man. The man was already climbing back into his SUV.

"It's been a long time since that happened," he said, his eyes twinkling. "Not since I was a kid in West Virginia." Connie giggled as she finished and sat upright in the seat.

"Maybe we should go home like he said?" she asked as a suggestion.

"Maybe we should just go home," Willie replied. "You to yours and me to mine."

Connie understood what he was saying. He was saying he wanted her very badly, but he wasn't emotionally ready to go that far, at least not yet. At Connie's house, Willie saw her to the door.

"You can come in if you want," she offered.

"Naw, I'd better git on home. It's almost eleven-thirty."

Connie smiled at him and said, "Are we turning into old fogies that have to be home by midnight?"

"I'd prefer to think we're like Cinderella," Willie replied. "If'n we ain't home by midnight, ever'thin' turns back into pun'kins."

"Yes, that's a better comparison. Cinderella it is, then," she smiled. "I had a wonderful time."

"Me, too," Willie replied. "Me, too." He turned and stepped off the porch.

"Willie?" she called after him. He stopped and turned to see her blow him a kiss. She was still dreamy an hour later as she slid into her bed. For the first time in a long time, she missed having a man next to her.

* * * *

The next day she met Drake for brunch. She was still thinking of Willie and the wonderful, dreamy, sexy evening they'd had the night before. She entered the restaurant and saw Drake was already at a table. She noted the pallor on his face and how much he seemed to have aged. Even in his tailored English suit, he wasn't as handsome as William Robert Waller.

"Hello," she said as she came up to the table. "Have you been waiting long?"

"Just got here. I ordered a gin and tonic for you."

"Thanks," she said as he took her coat and motioned for her to sit. He had always ordered a gin and tonic for her, and the truth of the matter was that she really didn't like gin at all. She preferred fruity German wines, like Piesporter.

Drake took her coat as he always had, but stopped to stare at Connie for a moment. He couldn't help but notice she'd lost weight and now she looked pretty good.

"So what do you want to talk about?" she asked as she took her seat.

"Well, I was hoping we could come to a meeting of the minds. You know, sort of an understanding."

"About what?"

Just then the drinks arrived and the waitress asked what they would have to eat.

"I'll have the eggs and pancakes," Drake said, "And she'll have —"

"I can order for myself," Connie interrupted. She remembered that Drake had almost always ordered for her, too, but now she realized it was simply a control technique. "I'll have one egg, poached, whole wheat toast, and a glass of orange juice."

Drake was disturbed by her new attitude, but didn't argue.

"Connie, I'll get to the point. I'd like to get back together with you."

"You mean to get remarried?"

"Yes. What would that take?" he asked, like it was a business deal.

"A lot more than one breakfast," she said with a smirk. "There's been a lot of damage done between us, Drake. Besides, I'm not sure that's what I want now."

"Why not? Because now you're rich and you don't need me? Now you think you can have any man you want?"

"Drake, that's your logic, not mine. I admit the money makes it easier because now I could marry a poor man if I wanted since we wouldn't be limited by his income." Her message was lost on Drake.

"Look, it's just logical that we get back together," he said. "We shared a lot of years and memories, not to mention we have a daughter out there somewhere that needs us."

"I know exactly where she is and, to be honest, she doesn't need us at all. She's doing fine on her own."

"Doing what? Singing? She never sang in her life! She's never had any talents! She needs to go to college and find a real man with a real career to take care of her."

"She had a real man and you tried to drive him off," Connie replied casually.

"That kid was a hillbilly with no future."

"That kid is in college on a football scholarship and making straight As."

"That kid's not making a dime yet, and there's no telling if he'll ever make anything."

"Drake, we're not here to talk about Jesse. We're here to talk about us. Honestly, I don't think we have a future between us."

"Well, *I* do, and I want you to let me prove it to you."

"It's always about what *you* want, isn't it? It always has to be Drake's way or the highway."

"What do you want from me?" he demanded angrily.

"The same as I've always wanted — to be a part of your life, not just an appointment."

"You're talking nonsense," Drake muttered.

"I suppose I am," Connie said. "Especially to you. I don't think you can understand a word I'm saying, can you?"

"I understand you want a fairy tale life," he said, "But that's not real. No one has a life like that!" Connie thought about last night with Willie Bob and knew that was exactly what he and Rachel had.

"Oh, I can think of a few people who do. But what you say is all that needs to be said. I rest my case." With that Connie pushed back her chair, stood up and picked up her coat.

"What? Where are you going?" he demanded.

"Drake, with all that you've done to me and Karyn in the last ten years, I should hate you, but I don't. In fact, I sort of pity you. You don't have a clue to what you're doing to yourself, but I'm doing okay on my own now." Drake looked up at her blankly.

"I can see this little meeting isn't going anywhere," she said. "Maybe the wounds are still too fresh, but now I've got a chance at life and I'm going to take it. Good-bye, Drake."

Chapter 26

In New York, Karyn learned that cutting an album was a lot more complicated than she had imagined. There were rehearsals, equipment checks and sound checks, not to mention the background musicians doing their thing. Jesse had called her and said that they would leave Sunday afternoon and would be in New York around midnight. That would get him to the studio Monday morning. She was so anxious she could barely stand it. It was like she was five years old again, waiting for Christmas to arrive.

On Monday morning she arrived at the studio at eight o'clock, halfway expecting Jesse to already be there. She was disappointed that he wasn't.

"Hey, it's early," Tom said. "If he didn't get into town until midnight, that means he wouldn't have made it to bed until after one or so. Let the guy get some sleep, will you?"

"Yeah. You're right," Karyn conceded. "He'll show up later."

They practiced all day in the studio. Claude dropped in twice to see how Karyn was doing.

"She's a natural for this gig," Tom said to Claude as he adjusted the huge Mackie mixer. "She doesn't think she's better than everybody else and she listens to what you tell her. And you only have to tell her something once, too."

Claude nodded as he watched Karyn though the soundproof window. Karyn was working hard but constantly kept an eye toward the door, hoping to see Jesse come in. Then, during a break, Karyn came into the mixing room to see Claude and Catherine.

"I sure wish Jesse would get here," she said forlornly. "I hope he's okay."

* * * *

At that moment, Connie was standing in the rain outside Champion Ford, a dealership in Scranton, Pennsylvania. She and Mike had ridden in the tow truck that had dragged Mike's minivan off Interstate 80. The engine had stopped smoking but the awful smell was still there. Just then Jesse and Willie Bob arrived in a taxi.

"How bad is it?" Jesse asked as he climbed out of the cab.

"I don't know, but Mike's in there now, talking to the service manager."

"I don't think he's gonna save it," Willie said. "It's burnt up somethin' awful."

"But there was no warning," Jesse said. "No lights, no noises, no signs whatsoever."

"That happens when you're on the freeway," Willie replied. "The engine's smokin' but you cain't see it 'cause it's blowin' out the back, an' in this rain, Mike couldn't see it in the mirror. Then the cool rain'll keep it running longer than it should."

"How long you figure we'd been running with the blown radiator hose?" Jesse asked as they walked into the dealership.

"Ten, twenty miles, maybe," Willie replied. They met Mike as he was coming out of the service area.

"Well, it's pretty much toasted," Mike told them. "The technician gave it a good once-over and says the same thing you said, Dad. It's locked solid and there's no way to fix it short of a new engine. God, I'm sorry, gang. I should've been watching closer."

"It's not your fault," Willie said. "When a hose goes, it goes. That's it. Kablooie and it's gone!"

"But the warning lights didn't even come on," Mike complained.

"That's why they call 'em 'idiot lights'," Willie replied.

"So, what do we do now?" Mike asked. There's no way we can get an engine in there for at least three days. Besides, they say it'll cost more to fix it than what it's worth."

"We can rent a car," Jesse offered.

"Or we can buy one," Connie said.

"Buy one?" Willie asked.

"This is a dealership, isn't it? From what I'm hearing, the van is essentially done for. See what they'll give you for trade-in and get a price on a new car." Connie waved at the long line of new vehicles glistening in the cold rain.

"Connie, I can't afford a new car right now."

"Maybe if we all pitch in we can come up with the down payment," Jesse offered.

"I'll take care of it," Connie said. She strolled onto the showroom floor and hailed a salesman. The men followed her, stunned.

"What kind of car do you like?" she asked Mike as the salesman approached.

"Connie, you can't do this," he said.

"Just watch me," she replied. "Tell me what you want or I'll pick out something myself, but you might not like it," she grinned.

"Connie, you can't —" Mike repeated desperately. He couldn't believe what she was doing.

Willie grabbed her arm and said, "Connie, this don't make no sense!"

"Willie, I need to make a confession. I haven't been completely honest with you." He eyed her cautiously.

"I probably should've told you right at the beginning, but I own Cox Chemical."

"You mean the whole thing?"

"I'm the majority shareholder, at least eighty percent."

"What about ol' man Malcolm's wife an' daughter?"

"I didn't tell you whom Drake was seeing."

"I didn't think it was any o' my business."

In the next few minutes, Connie told Willie Bob all about Drake's affairs with Anne Marie and Sandra, and how John had given all his stock holdings to Connie to teach them a lesson.

"Don't that beat anything I've ever heard!" Willie said with a whistle and a shake of his head. "I guess I was bein' pretty lame when I offered t' pay your way here."

"Willie Bob Waller, that was the sweetest, most gracious thing anyone has ever done for me in my life. You were making sure I would reunite with my daughter. No one else has ever done such an important thing for me." She held his hand as she spoke. "I've come to realize Drake didn't have a clue what real love was. He always thought it was giving me things, big extravagant things that *he* could show off. He never gave me any part of himself.

"You, on the other hand, have always been concerned about me, how I feel, and the quality of my life. Willie, you have more real, honest love in your little finger than most people have in their whole bodies!"

Fifteen minutes later, Connie had sealed the deal, authorizing payment electronically from her bank. An hour later, they were on the road again, with Mike driving a brand new yellow Ford Escape sport utility vehicle that he absolutely loved. Jesse sat up front next to Mike. Connie and Willie sat in the back. It was very quiet in the car as they drove. Finally, Willie spoke up.

"Connie, I don't feel good 'bout this at all."

"What? That I bought a new truck?"

"That you bought it fer Mike." Connie sighed and looked at the man sitting next to her. Even with the stubble of a beard on his chin, he was a handsome man. The crowfoot wrinkles at his eyes gave him a certain look of maturity that appealed to her.

"Willie, I understand that you don't want charity. No one does, but we were supposed to be in New York last night, and no one else here had the money to get us a new SUV."

"But you bought it fer Mike."

"It doesn't make sense for me to buy it for myself, now does it? I already own a car and Mike needed one."

"You paid cash fer it."

"Oh, I see what the problem is. It's the money, isn't it?" Willie's silence answered her question. She leaned closer to him in the back seat of the new Ford Escape.

"Willie, darling, I can afford this truck. And you, Mike, and Jesse have all been the best friends I've had ever since Karyn ran away — maybe the best friends I've ever had. Plus, I think an awful lot of you and this is something nice I can do for all of you. Please let me do it. It's to show you all how much I love you." Mike and Jesse were trying to ignore what was going on in the back seat, but they were listening to every word.

"It jus' don't seem right," Willie muttered.

"Tell me how it's so bad, then," she challenged.

"Maybe it ain't so bad, but it ain't the way things is done — leastways not where I come from."

"Do I detect some male pride peeking through?" she asked as she reached into the placket of his jacket. Her fingers weaseled their way between the buttons of his shirt and she impishly tugged at the hair on his chest. Mike and Jesse kept their eyes forward on the road, but their smirks were growing broader by the second.

"Stop that!" he said, but he couldn't help but smile as he pushed her hand away, embarrassed that Mike and Jesse were sitting up front and could see what she was doing. "Maybe I'm bein' old fashioned," he admitted. She leaned her head on his shoulder and started to stroke the hair on his chest again.

"Hey, you two!" Mike called back to them. "Knock it off! You've got impressionable youngsters up here!" Mike and Jesse laughed out loud. Connie grinned and sat back upright and Willie turned beet red.

When they stopped for fuel, Connie and Willie Bob drifted away to talk while Mike and Jesse fussed over the new truck. Off to the side, Connie and Willie Bob watched the kids.

"They certainly love that truck," Connie said, smiling as she slid her hand into Willie's.

"Yeah, they're doin' all right," Willie agreed.

"Willie, I've been meaning to talk to you about the other night."

"I guess I weren't too much of a gentleman, was I?" he said, wrinkling his nose.

"You were fine," Connie countered. "We both wanted it. At least I know I did."

"Yep," Willie said with a snort. "I guess you know I wanted it, too." He smiled sheepishly at her.

She grinned. "It's probably a good thing that cop came by when he did, or else we'd have some explaining to do to the kids!" They laughed together for a moment, then gazed at one another. After several moments, Willie sighed.

"It's jus' not right, is it?" Willie asked. "Between you an' me, that is."

"No, I don't think it is," Connie confirmed.

"You thinkin' o' goin' back t' Drake?" he asked.

"No. He wanted to get back together just last Saturday, but I walked away from him. I don't think he's good for me." She took a deep breath. "Willie, it's not that I don't like you because I do. I love you and your boys as though you were my own family and maybe that's the problem. Maybe we're too close. You're more like a brother to me than a boyfriend." Willie could see her eyes growing moist as she talked and patted his hand. Then she smiled and said, "But what you did to me in that car nearly drove me wild!"

Willie smiled back and said, "I think I know what you mean. We can be close, even love each other, but we ain't what you would exactly call a perfect match, are we?"

"No, I don't think we are," Connie replied sincerely.

"I didn't think so either," he confessed. His stomach was filled with butterflies. He wanted to pick her up and carry her away like he did with Rachel twenty years ago, but he knew it would be the wrong thing to do. He knew their backgrounds were far too different, their lives too far apart to find a common ground suitable for a long-term relationship. Still, there was electricity between them that was powerful and addictive. He had to let go of her hand and look away for a moment, just to get his bearings.

"You're a good woman," Willie finally said. "You deserve a good man, one a whole lot better'n me."

"You're a fine man, Willie," Connie countered. "There are many women who would die to have a man like you." He smiled at her and nodded. Just then, the boys waved at them to hurry up and get back in the truck. Willie stretched and walked toward the truck. Connie watched for a few seconds before she followed, knowing she would never feel his firm body again.

* * * *

They rode in silence for about fifteen minutes until Connie spoke up.

"Guys, I'd like your opinion on something. Now that you know I have control of Cox Chemical, I have to make a decision. I need to decide what I'm going to do with it.

"I have three options," she began. "I can try to find another executive that's open for a move, or I can hire Drake back. But frankly, I wouldn't trust Drake back in charge. He has openly vowed revenge against Sandra Malcolm and me. The third option is that I can take over the company myself." As she finished, she said, "I just don't know what to do. I've never run anything in my life, let alone a big company! I'm scared to death!"

"Fear's good," Willie replied. "It keeps you from doing something stupid. So why don't you want to run the company?"

"Willie, I can't. I don't know how."

"Did you know how to raise kids when Karyn was born?"

"No, of course not," she smiled.

"Well, I'd say raisin' a kid's a lot more important than runnin' a company, an' prob'ly tougher, too," Willie Bob said. "An' judgin' from how she's doin', I'd say you did a pretty durn good job."

"Oh, Willie, I made my mistakes," she said. "There are a lot of things I'd do differently if I could go back."

"An' you'll make mistakes when you start runnin' Cox, but you'll learn from them just like you did with Karyn and you won't make them again." He looked at her sincerely. "Connie, I ain't an educated man. I don't know much 'bout nuthin'. But I know you're a smart lady. I know you can do anything you set your mind t' do. That includes learnin' how t' run a big company like Cox."

"Willie, I don't know where to begin."

"I recall somethin' my high school history teacher said 'bout Franklin Roosevelt. He said ol' FDR weren't too brilliant at anythin' in particular, but he knew how t' find the people that were, and he got them t' do all the hard work o' runnin' the gover'ment. I figure you kin do the same. Find the people around you that're good at their jobs and let 'em do it. Then all you gotta do is make the big decisions."

"Willie, what if I destroy the company?"

"That ain't likely. Heck, a lot o' big corporations go through times o' bad leadership and they survive. But I don't think you'll be a bad leader. You're a real smart lady an' you'll learn fast. Cox is a big place and there has to be a lot of good people there. You just need some time to find them and get them going in the right direction."

* * * *

At the studio, it was close to four o'clock when they were ready to cut the first song. Karyn was in the sound booth, headphones on, and the director was cueing the musicians when the door to the mixing room opened and Jesse walked in, followed by Mike and Willie Bob.

"Jesse!" Karyn shrieked with joy, as she threw off the headset and ran from the studio right into Jesse's arms. Mr. Arnold and the surprised studio crew soon began to smile as Karyn hugged Jesse, then showered him with kisses.

"I think she sorta likes him," Claude confided to Tom, hoping to keep him from becoming too aggravated at having his schedule interrupted while Karyn continued to hug Jesse.

"Looks like it," Tom replied. He shrugged his shoulders and got on the PA to tell everyone to take a twenty-minute break.

Karyn hugged Willie and Mike, also, then began to introduce everyone.

"This is Jesse, everybody," she chimed. "I knew you'd make it," she said to him. "I just knew you would!"

"And this is his dad, Willie, and his brother, Mike," she said, her voice bubbling over with enthusiasm. She noticed Catherine eyeing Mike. "Mike's about the best friend anybody could have," she told Catherine. Catherine smiled at Mike and shook his hand.

"I've heard a lot about you and Jesse," she said.

"I've heard about you, too," he replied. "Seems like you're a pretty good friend, too, based on what Karyn tells us." They immediately liked what they saw in each other.

"I try," she nodded. Soon they had drifted away from the clutch of people and were talking by themselves, huddled close together.

Connie was standing by the door. As Karyn continued the introductions, Connie glanced at Willie and noticed him eyeing her intently from across the room. He nodded his head, as if to say, "Be patient."

Karyn continued the introductions until she noticed a slim, attractive lady standing just inside the studio door. Karyn looked closer, but at last she recognized her mother. She slowly approached her mother in silence and began to smile.

Her mother had lost so much weight that Karyn had barely recognized her. *What has happened to Mom?* she wondered. Connie's cheekbones were high, proud and elegant like a magazine model. Her neck was long and serene, enhanced by the sharp outline of her collarbones.

"Mom! You're so thin! What happened?"

Connie stepped forward and gathered her daughter up in her arms.

"I just lost some weight is all," she said as she nuzzled her cheek against Karyn's hair. "I just lost some weight. I'm okay, really." Karyn stepped back to study her mother again.

"Mom, you look good. You look really good!" she said, noticing the designer blouse and slacks that showed off her new shape.

"You think so?" she asked. No one had told her she looked good in a long, long time.

"Yeah! You're a real fox!" she said, bringing laughter from the crowd around them. The crowd began to break up as Connie and Karyn talked.

A few moments later Karyn turned to Jesse and said, "Jesse, I have something to tell you. I've made up my mind. I want to go to college like you."

"Where? Miami?" he asked hopefully.

"Yes. They have a great music school there. I've already checked and I can start there next fall. I want to get a Bachelor of Arts in music." Jesse grinned and gave her a big hug.

Mike and Catherine slipped out to get a cup of coffee with the rest of the crew. Twenty minutes later everyone was back in the studio, milling about and chatting. Willie Bob stood up and stretched.

"Well, Tom," he drawled. "I ain't never been in a recordin' studio b'fore. How 'bout you show me how it's done."

Everyone nodded and went to their places.

"Let's go through it once more, just to be sure we've got it right," Tom said into the PA. "Then we'll do a real cut." He cued the musicians and soon Karyn started to sing.

"She's good, ain't she?" Willie Bob said as they watched her singing. Connie nodded proudly, then glanced at Willie.

"Do I detect some pride showing on your face?" she asked him.

"Well," he blushed, "She's a lot like a daughter t' me. I got a right t' be proud o' her." They both smiled as Karyn put her heart into the first song.

"That's close enough!" Tom said. "Let's do it for real. This'll be the first cut of the first song of the album entitled *Paper Moon.* Let's make it good, people!" Everything got very quiet and Tom cued the musicians.

Connie, Willie Bob and his boys, Catherine, and Claude all stood in the mixing room proudly watching as Karyn recorded her first song, *It's Only a Paper Moon.*

Epilogue

Karyn's album was an immediate hit and went platinum. She continued to record albums and do occasional live performances while she attended Miami University in Oxford, Ohio. She married Jesse after graduation.

Connie Mathers took control of Cox Chemical and although Cox stock lost value for a year, it ultimately rebounded and began to set one new high after another. She married Peter Savoy two years later.

Drake Mathers continued to try to re-establish a relationship with Connie until she announced her engagement to Peter Savoy. Then he went to work for a small manufacturing firm in Northern Indiana. He began to send Karyn occasional birthday and Christmas cards, but made no attempts to see her. He did see two of her concerts, however.

Jesse Waller played football at Miami University, made Parade All-American and graduated Magna Cum Laude. After graduation, he went to work for Connie Mathers at Cox Chemical.

Mike and Catherine's relationship blossomed. Within a year, Catherine landed the manager's position of a top-notch Michigan restaurant, which allowed her to be closer to Mike. They began to plan their wedding as soon as she started her new job.

Fourteen months after John Malcolm's death, Anne Marie Malcolm accepted a marriage proposal from a Hollywood producer. Sandra Malcolm moved to Paris, France, where she had a live-in relationship with a fashion designer.

And Willie Bob Waller returned home a better man. He never remarried, but kept a close friendship with Connie and her new husband, Peter Savoy. With Peter's help, Willie started a pension plan that would see him well into his senior years.